A Lost Friend In Pennsylvania

**An Undead-Earth Novel
Book 3**

M.P. Esham

Undead-Earth Series:

Contents

Chapter 1

We were snaking our way through the mountains in the old green Buick Haeslig had gifted us when escaping Delaware, working our way up the mountain along the highway. "Stop," Justine said to me. "I think I know this place." I pulled over, and we climbed out of the Buick. "I've been here. I know where I am!" she said, full of astonishment and excitement as she looked at the jagged cut in the mountains in front of us.

We were on the curve of a mountain road. Behind us there was a steep drop to a valley far below. In front of us was a crevasse that split the face of the rock, disappearing into the mountain. I looked at the cut in the rock face, not sure what Justine was looking at. She ran across the highway, actually looking both ways as she did, which made me chuckle. There weren't likely to be any other cars on the road these days.

I reached into the car to grab my machete, strapping it to my leg. When I looked back, Justine was gone. I darted across the highway, the machete in my hand. Justine stepped out of the cut in the mountain laughing, almost skipping. She saw me and put her hands together while giving me a toothy smile. "You have to see this," she said, her deep-brown eyes sparkling with excitement.

She grabbed my hand and led me into the cut. High, steep walls rose up around me as she pulled me into the crevasse. From the road it looked like a jagged cut down the side of the mountain, but walking through it I realized that the path twisted and turned, leading us through to the other side. Justine pulled me along until we were standing at the top of a rocky trail leading down into a secluded valley.

We walked down the gentle slope leading to the valley floor, hand in hand. Justine was practically skipping. We stopped as we reached the bottom of the trail, just about to step into the shade of the trees. "This is real," she said, looking all around. I nodded, wondering what she was thinking as we moved down the trail.

"Where are we heading?" I asked after we'd walked for half an hour.

"There was a dirt-bike track," she said distractedly, not really answering my question.

"You're OK, right?" I asked. She was freaking me out with the faraway sound in her voice.

"Yes, I promise," she said, turning to look me in the eyes. "I'm just trying to remember." I shut up and kept walking.

Sometime in the midmorning, the game trail merged with a path of hard-packed earth built up into a berm that was easily eight feet across. "See, see, see? A dirt-bike track," she said, jumping up and down with excitement. I couldn't keep the smile from my own lips as we walked onto the hard, compacted berm. "What?" she asked, seeing that I was more amused than I should be.

"Nothing," I said, still smiling a little.

"It's a memory from when I was a little kid," she said defensively. "Tell me," she demanded, pushing my shoulder.

"You'll figure it out," I assured her and kept walking, refusing to give her an answer. A little while later, we passed over a small stream that passed under us through an archway of massive stone blocks. I raised my eyebrow, but she just huffed and walked a little faster. Near midday we walked into the remnants of an old town in the middle of the valley.

A water tower stood off the path to our right, its huge, old timbers leaning away from us, barely holding it upright. "I'm an idiot," Justine said with a groan. "This is an old railway bed."

"You were a kid," I reminded her. "And I had a huge advantage. I've hiked on beds like this before on the Appalachian Trail."

"You could have just told me what it was," she chided me.

"That wouldn't have been much fun," I said, looking out over the remnants of the town.

"When do you think the people left?" Justine asked. The town consisted mostly of stone foundations around depressions in the ground. The tilting water tower was the most upright artifact around us.

"A long time ago," I said, staring at what was left of the water tower. I wondered how much longer the timbers would hold out and how long after that before nature erased any evidence that the town had existed at all. There were already trees growing up from the center of some of the foundations that were easily four or five decades old.

"I remember a four-wheeler and how much I liked to take rides," Justine said in a hushed voice. "We would always zoom by the town here. I remember being told it was haunted." There was a smile in her voice as she said it, but she was still keeping her voice down. We moved on quietly, trying not to disturb the bones of the old town.

I wanted to ask her if she remembered who the "we" was, but I could almost feel the energy coming off of her. She was remembering things, and I didn't want to interrupt whatever flood of thoughts and recollections were coming back to her. I wondered what we were walking toward, wondered how accurate her childhood memories were. She'd always told me the happiest memories of her childhood were from the cabin in the Poconos. I didn't want to taint that by asking questions I knew she didn't have answers for, at least not yet.

So I bit my tongue and lost myself in my own memories as we walked, looking over at her every now and then and remembering how it had all started. I'd been in bad shape when I got home from the Marines. To appease my father, I'd agreed to go see the counselor who worked out of the local church. I could remember walking into the waiting room and seeing Justine dressed in baggy, dark clothing and thinking that her parents must love the Goth look. I hadn't realized then that she was the counselor's stepdaughter.

We'd started to talk, each of us sharing a bit of our pain, and something strange happened. I found I actually wanted to talk to her. It was a strange feeling for me. I'd always been very comfortable being alone; it was a side effect of growing up with a congenital eye disorder. As a child, my basement membrane corneal dystrophy left me in pain and blinded for days on end. When I was six, right around the time my mother passed away, my father got me into a gene-therapy trial that gave my corneas the strength they needed to not fall apart at the lightest touch. The light sensitivity that came with the disorder never left me, but I was allowed to wear sunglasses in school. And my night vision was superb. The psychological impacts of growing up fairly isolated and mostly in the dark were harder to quantify.

On the one hand, I always figured that after my eyes were "fixed," my ability to operate in near-pitch black had given me a huge advantage as a Marine scout. Even more importantly, my childhood had taught me to function as a singular entity. I never needed to have other people around me to function normally—at least, not until I met Justine.

I looked over, wanting to tell her how much she meant to me, and was surprised to see her emotions seesawing back and forth as she scanned the woods, trying to remember. She'd always told me the time she'd spent at the cabin was one of the only happy memories of her childhood. Right after leaving the cabin and being adopted by Sam and his wife, Justine's brother had disappeared. Years later we'd found her brother's initials in a file of digital photos of other children that Sam, her stepfather, had murdered.

Which was why a growing knot of tension was building between my shoulders and in the middle of my gut. Justine had fond memories of swimming and riding four-wheelers, but whoever had been out in the woods with her had eventually handed her over to Sam. She caught me staring at her and met my eyes, her face shifting rapidly between concern and uncertain happiness. I pushed away my own feelings of unease and smiled back as naturally as I could. If bad memories were at the end of the valley, then I'd help her deal with them as best as I could.

We were a half hour down the trail from the town when Justine stopped, looking at a massive tree a short distance off the berm. "I remember this," she said, climbing down the dirt slope in a series of half steps, half jumps.

"It's a tree," I mumbled to myself as I followed. She paused a few feet from the tree trunk and then stepped up on one of the gnarled roots surrounding the base of the tree. She moved lightly, stepping from root to root as she circled around the tree, gradually getting closer to its trunk. I followed her, coming up behind her just as she came to a stop on the far side of the tree. She reached out, putting a finger on the bark tentatively. She was hyperventilating.

Her finger gently traced the initials "JM & TM" that were carved into the tree. Justine's last name had been McWatters before Sam had adopted her and her brother as a kid. She traced the letters, looking at me with tears in her eyes, some lost memory of her brother coming back to her. In some distant past, she'd stood exactly where she did now, looking at those initials when her brother was still alive—before Sam had used him like he'd used so many other young men and women.

I put my hands on the back of Justine's neck and rubbed the tension from her muscles. "You were here," I said to her, trying to sound positive. She leaned back against me, nodding in agreement. She held my hand as we walked back up to the berm.

"What do you remember about the cabin?" I asked, trying to keep my voice from betraying the anxiety I was feeling. Part of me had secretly hoped that we weren't in the same valley she'd been in as a child, but the tree and the initials had put an end to that.

"Pancakes," she blurted out, as if the thought had just hit her. "I remember having pancakes and looking at the lake." She stopped to think. "It's all a jumble, though," she admitted. "I remember being so happy that there was always food. I don't remember anything from before the cabin as a real memory. I just remember being hungry a lot, and scared. It's all very blurry." I rubbed her back, feeling as helpless as she did lost.

After finding the tree, Justine was a horse with the bit in her mouth. We followed the railroad bed for another hour or so, and then Justine stopped, looking off into the trees at the mountains that rose up at the far end of the valley. "It's this way," she said without hesitating. The berm curved slowly to the right, but Justine kept moving straight ahead.

I barely got to say, "OK," before she was moving again. I rushed to catch up, watching the sun and the mountains, building a map in my head. "You remember anything else?" I asked her as the sky started to darken. I had my machete, and she was—well—she was Justine, but we didn't have any heavy firepower with us. We'd barely gotten out of Dover alive.

"I remember swimming, and," she struggled to put it into words, "and strange feelings of being safe. It's all fuzzy, but I know it's not something bad," she declared. I was slightly less convinced. Sam had adopted Justine and her brother as small children, but he'd adopted them from someone, and Sam had been a very bad man. The closer we came to the end of the valley, the more anxious I became. I found my hand resting on the hilt of my machete as we walked, the gradually darkening sky matching my mood perfectly. The uncertainty of what might be at the end of the trail felt like a rock in my stomach. Justine was running full tilt toward a memory from her childhood that was just a hazy outline, and I just wasn't sure if it was going to be a good memory or a bad one once we found it.

The night continued to darken around us as we made our way along a game trail, gradually climbing. The trees thinned as we followed the trail up the slope, the ground beneath us turning to stone as the mountains grew around us. It was full dark by the time we made it to the far end of the valley. We were standing on a flat section of terrain atop the rise we'd just climbed, looking forward at the mountains that closed in from either side, forming a narrow path that ended somewhere out of sight in front of us.

Justine stopped suddenly, her head swiveling in the dark until her chin fell to her chest and stayed there. "Are you OK?" I asked, afraid something was happening. Flashbacks from Delaware rushed through me. She'd had a few bad moments when we were in the first state. If she tried to run on me like she did then, she would have a whole valley to get lost in.

"Look down," she said, her voice a whisper but completely hers.

We were standing on poured concrete. It was covered in leaves and windblown dirt, but reflective paint was still partially visible here and there on the surface of the slab. I walked around, clearing random bits with my boot, looking at the landing lights set into the pad. I looked down in shock; we were standing on a helipad.

Why had someone built it in the middle of nowhere? But the answer struck me as soon as I thought it: being in the middle of nowhere was the reason.

"The path," Justine said, pointing to the deeper line of black leading up into the mountain in front of us. It was almost invisible in the darkness. "Let's go," she said, grabbing my sleeve. I could feel her excitement through her touch. She was almost vibrating.

"We need to take it slow—we don't know what's up there," I said as our hands changed positions, and I found myself holding onto her sleeve, holding her back. Justine tried to pull me forward, tugging me almost off balance. I refused to give way, pulling her back to me. She slammed into my chest; I'd been expecting her to resist, and when she didn't, well, she didn't. I opened my mouth to say something but found her lips on mine, kissing me gently.

"You're worried," she said when our lips separated.

"Only for you," I said.

"You want to wait until daylight?" she asked, not sounding happy about it at all.

I looked up into the darkness between the two stone faces where the mountains came together, unable to see anything ahead of us. "Yes, I think I would."

She paused for a long while before she spoke. "OK, we wait," she said, kissing me again.

We moved off the helipad and followed the rock face back into the underbrush until we found a small overhang. We climbed into the space and settled in. It wasn't long before we were huddling against the cool air of a late-summer night. I locked my arms around her chest, holding on to her as she talked.

Seeing the tree with her initials had brought back a flood of memories and feelings. She talked nonstop as we huddled in the dark. Bits and pieces of her early childhood had started to come back to her. Sometimes her voice was too quiet for me to hear, but she wasn't really talking to me so much as she was making the memories real by speaking them out loud. She remembered rides through the woods on an ATV, and swimming. She remembered feeling safe and content. There was a man who lived in the cabin. She couldn't remember his name, just that she and her brother had called him Uncle, even though she knew he wasn't any direct relation. He'd been the one to carve the initials, because she wanted him to.

I fell asleep sometime during the night, my hands locked together around Justine's torso. I'm not sure if she slept, but as soon as the sun rose above the mountains and the first rays of light started to filter into the valley, she was ready to go, pulling me to my feet. "The sun's up; get off your ass," she whined. I was only half awake and ended up smacking my head on the overhang as I climbed out from under the ledge.

"The sun's barely up," I complained, rubbing my skull. The helipad was still shrouded in shadows. Justine was already trying to walk away. "Whoa," I said, pulling her back. "I'm taking point."

"Lead the way," she said, waving me forward with an impatient flourish of an arm.

I moved to the mouth of the path, looking up at the narrow passage that was still cloaked in shadows. I moved slowly, scanning the way ahead and putting my feet down carefully, taking care not to step on loose rocks. Justine was on my boot heels, walking so close behind me I could feel and hear her breathing. We crept up the path as the walls on either side of us closed to within four feet of each other. Farther up there was a thick tangle of vines and thornbushes growing out of the side of the rock face, almost obstructing the path forward. I crept up to the tangle of vegetation, being careful not to disturb it. I hugged the rough stone to my right, lowering my head until I could see through a gap in the brush in front of me.

The path directly in front of me opened up onto a level expanse of ground roughly twenty or so feet across before ending in a sheer rock wall. I could feel Justine's impatience behind me; she was having a hard time standing still as I scanned the way ahead, trying to make sense of the shadows and limited light in the gorge.

I put my hand behind me, groping until she took it in hers. I squeezed it slowly, trying to will patience into her as I crouched, watching as the sun slowly rose and pushed back the shadows. It took a moment for my eyes to adjust to the growing light. The gorge didn't end in a sheer rock face forty feet in front of us; it was blocked by a wall made of massive pieces of cut stone that stretched from one side of the gorge to the other. It looked like a section of an old-world castle had been dropped directly in our path. In the middle of the wall, a wooden door stood partially open. The door was bound with wide strips of rusting steel.

I froze in place as the sun hit something higher up in the gorge, above the section of castle wall, and reflected the morning sun in a sparkling flash. I backed away slowly, giving Justine time to move first. The reflected burst of sunlight looked like the glare off the end of a pair of binoculars, or a scope. I forced Justine far enough down the path that we could put a jutting section of rock between ourselves and anything that might be able to see us from above.

"There's a wall and something shining higher up in the gorge. It could be binoculars or a scope," I said, holding on to one of her shoulders to keep her still.

"I promise I'm not going anywhere," she said, trying to shrug my hand off. I pulled back slowly, watching her as she hugged the jutting stone and peeked around it so she could see the flare of reflected light up above us.

"It's not a scope; I never saw any weapons here when I was a kid," she said, sounding very sure of herself.

"You don't remember anyone hunting? A rifle maybe?" I asked, trying to sound reasonable and maybe jog a memory at the same time.

"I don't remember ever seeing any guns," she said, shaking her head in mild frustration as I took my own turn looking back up at the glare.

"The sun is still coming up; let's just sit tight and see what we can see when there's better light."

"You worry too much," she said, clearly unhappy, but she leaned back against the wall to wait.

We took turns checking on the path ahead. Justine

laughed at me on her third turn, pulling me forward to point up at the source of the reflected light above us. Someone had built a cabin in the cut between the mountains several stories above us. A glass safety railing formed the forward edge of the deck around the structure.

"The cabin," she said, staring at the house above us.

"Better safe than sorry," I said, moving just as carefully back up to the thicket of thorns.

I watched the cabin for any signs of life for a minute, and then moved after Justine poked me in the back for the third time. I drew my machete and slipped around the thornbush so I could sprint across the open ground to get to the wall next to the heavy wooden door. Justine followed close behind me, stopping on the opposite side of the door. She looked at me and I gave her the "go" nod. She slipped her fingers around the edge of the door and pulled it open with a quick, sharp pull. Metal squealed as rusted hinges moved, the sound dying as quickly as it had started.

I slipped inside the moment the thick door opened enough to let me by and moved along the inside wall, looking around me. The wall had been built to cut the open ground in the gorge roughly in half, leaving a decent-sized courtyard on the far side. The majority of the courtyard was unused space, but a small toolshed sat in one corner, and workbenches lined the wall to our right. The gorge continued in front of me with a set of wooden stairs built into the cut, leading up to the cabin.

Justine strolled into the courtyard, staring at everything around her. "It doesn't feel like anyone has been here for a while," she said, staring at the general state of the courtyard. "I rode that as a kid," Justine said, pointing to a four-wheeler half covered by a tarp in front of one of the workbenches. Another sat in pieces, parts of it strewn across a tarp laid out on the courtyard floor.

"Come on," she said, grabbing my hand and dragging me to the stairs. I stopped at the first riser, looking up. "This was always a happy place," Justine reminded me, utterly convinced no bad waited for us at the top of the stairs. I let her tug me up the first step and then kept a hold of her hand to keep her with me, restraining her from running up to the cabin without me. "I remember this," she said as we reached the top of the stairs and stepped onto the deck. The house was small and perfectly square, and was surrounded by a deck that went all the way around the structure. The front and back of the deck each had glass railings, while the left and right sides were formed from rough-hewn rock that rose up into the mountains around us. I turned around, momentarily frozen as my eyes swept across the valley. The view was amazing. The whole valley stretched out in front of the house. "It gets better," Justine said, turning me around.

"OK," I said, pulling my eyes away from the view and refocusing on the cabin. I could see through the structure from where I was standing. The front and back of the cabin had been built from sets of sliding-glass doors, giving us a mostly unobstructed view through the house. There was a couch, a table, and a kitchen, but otherwise the inside looked empty. Justine took my hand and pulled me around the deck to the rear of the house.

"The water never really warms up," she said, leaning over the railing to look at the expanse of sparkling blue water beneath us. My breath caught in my chest as I looked down at the secluded lake. A set of wooden stairs off to the side led down to a small, pebbly beach beneath us. A wooden sunbathing chair sat off to one side of the beach next to a small circular table. Someone had left towels draped over the chair.

Whoever had built the cabin had picked the place very carefully. It was beautiful and secluded, and had the attributes of a fortress—only one way in, and with a lake surrounded by mountains at its back. I was watching the sun dance across the deep-blue water when I heard Justine pull in a breath.

"What's that?" she asked, pointing to the chair.

I took a second look, wincing. "I don't think those are towels," I said, realizing I'd already noticed what she was looking at. "You're sure nothing is up here?"

She sniffed at the air and shook her head. "Nothing up here," she confirmed. We took the stairs down to the beach, our eyes locked on the chair until we were halfway down. I relaxed a little as my boots crunched onto the rocky beach. Whoever the fellow was, he wasn't a threat to anyone anymore. His body was thin and partially mummified from exposure, and the back of his head was missing. He was wearing what looked to be pajamas and an oversized robe, and his finger was still in the trigger guard of the small semiautomatic resting on his chest. Blood had dribbled out of his nose after he put the weapon in his mouth and pulled the trigger, giving his thick mustache a matted and unkempt look.

I picked up the gun carefully, sliding it free of the man's finger before pulling the slide back. There was a round in the chamber. I stuck the gun in my waistband for later. I'd have to clean it and make sure it was still functional before I'd trust it with my life, but even so, having a firearm, any firearm, made me feel a bit better.

Justine moved to the foot of the corpse, looking at it intensely. "Dietrich," she blurted out, seemingly just as surprised as I at the outburst. Her eyebrows wrinkled and furrowed over her deep-chestnut eyes as she thought. "His name was Dietrich," she said with more conviction after thinking about it for a moment.

"You remember him?"

"Bits and pieces just hit me; it's him, though. I remember his mustache." She sounded sad as she said it, her eyes glazing over as she looked at the remains of the man with a look of confused grief on her face.

"Come up to the deck; I want to check the rest of the house out," I said gently, putting my hand out for her. She took it, but it was slow and lazy movement. I didn't exactly pull her up the steps, but if I hadn't being holding her hand, I think she would have just stood where she was. I led her over to the closest sliding-glass door, looking at the interior of the house.

It looked clear. There really wasn't anywhere to hide, or at least that was what I thought at first. The floor plan was a simple square dominated by the kitchen island. A table sat on the near side of the kitchen, and several pieces of furniture were arrayed about to sit on. It wasn't until I pulled open the door and went inside that I realized everything wasn't what it appeared.

The couch to the right of the sliding-glass door hid a stairwell leading down. From outside it looked like the couch was placed a few feet from the wall, but once inside I realized the gap behind the furniture was a stairwell dropping into the mountain beneath the cabin. Justine startled me as she brushed up against my side, grabbing the fabric of my shirt. "I lived here; I can remember running up those steps in the morning to get breakfast." Her voice was thick with emotion. I looked down at the stairs leading into a pit of black, and held my tongue.

"Hold tight," I begged her, going behind the kitchen island and opening drawers. I found what I was looking for on the third try. Every kitchen had a junk drawer. This one had some tape, several screwdrivers, and two LED flashlights. I checked them both, confirming they still had some life in them. I put one in my pocket and moved back to the stairwell, cutting in front of Justine as I lit the way ahead with the flashlight. The stairs descended at least forty feet down, ending in a short hallway I could barely see.

The descent felt odd, claustrophobic, and the air felt musty and old as we descended. As we climbed down into the mountain, a short hallway came into view at the bottom of the stairs, gradually revealing an oval blast door set into a concrete wall. I glanced at Justine as we walked up to it, expecting her to comment, but she was already nudging me forward, apparently unfazed. There was a large numbered dial on the outside of the door, but it wasn't locked, it wasn't even closed all the way. I grabbed metal handle of the blast door and pulled.

The smell of stale and damp air flowed out of the underground as I swept my flashlight along the hallway on the far side of the door. Two doors sat evenly spaced on each side of the hallway, and another blast door faced us at the far end. I stepped into the underground with the flashlight in one hand and my machete poised to strike in the other.

"I…" Justine started to say, then paused. I looked behind me to make sure she was OK, only to have her dart around my back. She was past me and slipping through the first door on my right before the first curses could escape my lips. I charged into the room, sweeping the flashlight around, but the room held no threats. When I turned to Justine, she was standing at the end of a child-sized bed, staring down at it. As I watched she turned and plopped onto the mattress, kicking up a puff of dust. She didn't care; she was looking around the room, lost in memory.

I left Justine sitting on the bed and went to the closet, sliding the door open to look inside. The closet was fairly empty save for a few board games and a set of spare sheets. I turned around, scanning the room. The walls were flanked with bookshelves and multicolored, plastic cabinets adorned with stickers. The pastel-colored walls were dotted here and there with what looked to be hand-painted ponies.

The room was frozen in time, eternally belonging to a little girl.

I went over to Justine, standing next to her until she looked up at me. "You good?" I asked gently. She nodded numbly. "You stay here," I said mostly to myself, pulling the second flashlight out of my pocket and turning it on for her. I set it on the bookcase to bathe the room in dim light. I know she probably didn't need the light, but the thought of her sitting there in the dark creeped me out.

"Yeah, I'm just going to sit here for a while," she said to me, running her hand over the pastel sheet covering the bed. "Yell if you need me," she added from far away as I walked to the door.

The room across the hall was similar but nondescript, an empty bedroom with no hint as to who if anyone had ever slept there. The bookcase was empty, and the only thing in the closet was a spare pillow without a pillowcase on it. I went back out into the hallway and moved on to the second set of doors, going into the one on my left first. It was clearly the master suite. It was bigger than the other bedrooms, deeper and wider, and filled with more belongings.

I entered the room and paused, sweeping it with the flashlight to make sure nothing was waiting in the dark for me before walking around, looking at what was left of Dietrich's personal belongings. All the furniture appeared to have been made by the same craftsman. Everything was built from darkly stained hardwoods and bore the same beveled edges with the occasional scrollwork here and there. I went to his dresser, examining the scattered collection of expensive-looking lighters and pipes.

I lingered a bit longer at the desk. There were several documents in another language that I thought was German, but what really caught my eye was the Polaroid image in a polished silver picture frame. The little girl in the picture bore a striking resemblance to Justine. It was the only picture in the bedroom.

I ran a finger over the top of the hardwood desk as I walked away. A thin layer of dust covered everything, but even so, it was easy to see the quality of the items in the room. I'd never heard of Lange & Sohne, but the watch sitting on the end of the desk bearing the name looked like it cost a small fortune. I went over to the closet and slid the door open. It was filled with sturdy and functional clothing. I wanted to root through the rest of the stuff in the bedroom more closely but forced myself to go back into the hallway to the door across the way. There would be time to figure out who Dietrich was once the living quarters were cleared.

The final door led into a large bathroom that looked like it had been taken out of an expensive European hotel. A door just inside the entry hid a toilet and a bidet, opposite that was a stand-alone shower big enough for two. Farther in were a set of double sinks in front of a massive mirror, and then a large garden tub. I left the bathroom and turned to the second blast door.

It was identical to the one at the entry to the living quarters. I took the flashlight between my teeth and put my hand on the lever to the blast door. It wouldn't move; it was locked. I touched the numbered chrome dial sitting at chest height and gave it a spin. It clicked away as it spun and gradually came to a stop. The door was still locked.

I knocked gently and paused, sincerely hoping that nothing would respond. I counted to ten in my head and was relieved when nothing knocked back. I patted the steel door and went back down the hall to check on Justine, slipping my machete into its sheath.

She was kneeling on the floor, going through a plastic box full of art supplies next to a child-sized easel. "I used to sit here and draw," she said, pulling a pack of colored pencils out of the box. I didn't know what to say. I stood there, looking at her and the room, not sure what in the world any of it meant. Who was Dietrich, and why did he have a house hidden in the mountains in Pennsylvania? Why had he brought Justine and her brother here as children? Why had he taken his own life?

I collapsed on the bed, not sure what to say or do as Justine sat on the floor, pulling things off the bookcase one at a time to look at them before putting them in a growing pile around her. I watched her, faintly anxious as she pored over what I could only guess were memories from her childhood. I'm not sure how long I lay there, wanting to say something and afraid to disturb her at the same time. Eventually my stomach started to rumble loudly, reminding me I hadn't eaten in almost a day.

Justine's head popped up from the children's book she was paging through, and she looked at the mess she'd made around her before turning to me sheepishly. She climbed to her feet, careful not to topple any of the items stacked up around her, and stepped over to the bed, putting a hand out to help me up. "Let's go see what's in the cupboards," she said, giving me a smile that melted away the anxiety that had settled in me.

"Is more of it coming back?" I asked as we climbed the stairs.

"Not really, more like memories of emotions. I know this was a happy place. I remember swimming in the lake with my brother and feeling safe and content. They're half memories and half feelings," she said as I followed her up the stairs.

I made my way behind the island, opening cabinets as I went, whistling appreciatively. The cupboards were fully stocked. Our friend outside hadn't eaten a bullet because he was hungry. I peeked inside the fridge carefully, opening it only far enough to confirm that the inside smelled horrible before moving back to the cabinets. I pulled down two cans of soup and turned the knob on the gas stove absentmindedly as my eyes scanned the countertop, looking for a can opener. The fact that the burner ticked, ticked, and then whooshed into a ring of blue flames took me by surprise. I'd never been so happy to see a stove light. I made a mess as I tore the kitchen apart to find a can opener and a pot. I was afraid if I turned the burner off or took too long, the miracle would end and I wouldn't get to eat hot soup.

It wasn't until I walked over to the table on the other side of the island with a bowl of soup in either hand that I noticed Justine flipping through the pages of a leather-bound book. "It was just sitting here," she said, closing the cover and resting a hand on top of it. I put our soup on the table and sat. "It's his journal," she said, opening the front cover and showing me the text written in careful script on the inside. The text stated in precise handwriting, "Property of Dietrich Heilbronner." She fanned the pages with a finger, and then shut it carefully, pushing it to the side so she could pull her soup closer to her.

"You're not going to read it?" I asked, picking up my spoon to take the first mouthful.

She didn't answer me right away. "I remember him. He was nice to me. I'm not sure I want to know what's in...here," she said, putting one finger on top of the journal. She looked around the cabin. "This isn't normal."

I looked around and couldn't disagree with her. Most cabins in the woods didn't have twenty-foot walls guarding their entrances, or a helipad. And that wasn't even touching on the blast doors guarding the downstairs. The place must have been built as a nuclear-bomb shelter.

We ate our meal in relative quiet after that, enjoying the warmth of the soup as it soaked through our bodies. "I think it's your turn to clean up," I said, moving from the table to one of the low, soft couches behind us.

"Thanks," she said sarcastically, taking our bowls to the sink and looking around the kitchen. I'd managed to open pretty much every drawer and cabinet in my search for cooking utensils. She tried the faucet, but it didn't even rattle. She settled for wiping the bowls and pots out with a dishtowel as I let myself sink into the couch, my eyes half-lidded. When she was finished, she came over and sat down next to me, settling against my side.

I'd only intended to rest for a moment, but the combination of Justine's closeness and the warm food in my belly filled me with a sleepy haze. I found my eyes drifting shut, my muscles uncoiling as days of weariness pulled me under. I was sure there was something else I should be doing, but we were as safe as we had been in weeks and had a pantry full of food to eat.

Sometime later Justine woke me up as she shifted away from me. I opened my eyes, looking at her as she tried to get off the couch without disturbing me. "Where are you going?" I asked sleepily.

"I couldn't stop thinking about him sitting down by the lake. I need to bury him."

"OK," I said, rubbing the sleep out of my eyes as I worked my way to a sitting position. "You look around for a shovel or something while I get him wrapped up," I said, pushing off my knees with my hands as I worked my way to my feet.

"I'm not squeamish," she reminded me as if I'd mildly insulted her.

"I know, but he's kinda like family to you. I don't want getting him out of that chair to be your last memory of him," I said.

"Thank you," she said in understanding, her hand trailing across my chest as I moved away from her to run back down the stairs to get a sheet.

She waited for me out on the deck, and we went down to the beach together. I wrapped him in the sheet as gently as I could and lifted his body, working his stiffened form onto my shoulder. We made our way back up to the cabin and then down into the courtyard. Justine found a shovel in the work shed behind the half-disassembled four-wheelers, and we made our way through the wall. We walked a short ways into the valley until Justine picked a quiet place in the trees.

I laid Dietrich's body down and took the shovel from Justine. We took turns; one of us would dig while the other would backtrack up the trail to haul chunks of stone and rock. It was late afternoon by the time we buried Dietrich and finished stacking stones on top of his grave. Justine said a few quiet words when we were done, thanking him for the kindness he'd shown two orphaned children. Shadows were already creeping across the valley floor as we made our way back up the trail to the cabin.

I shut the heavy gate behind us and slid the locking bolt in place. It made wonder what Dietrich had hoped to protect himself against. I doubted the high wall would stop a gray, but it would definitely be effective against thralls.

We ate another meal of canned goods by the light of a candle Justine found in the kitchen and drank cold, clean water we hauled up in a pot from the lake. "We should try and find the propane tank, figure out how much is left," Justine said, slurping noodles off her chin as she spoke.

"You want to stay for a while?"

"There's food, and there's plenty of water," she said, hiking her thumb toward the lake.

"OK," I said, agreeing halfheartedly. Part of me wanted to let my guard down and enjoy the feeling of safety the high wall and the locked door beneath us provided, while another part of me kept whispering that we'd be safer out in the woods where no one expected us to be.

Justine tried to talk me into sleeping in the bunker below the cabin when we were ready to turn in for the night, but I didn't like the idea of trapping ourselves underground with no way out. Justine laughed at me and tried to coax me into it, but I stretched out on the couch and shut my eyes, telling her to wake me up when it was my turn to take watch. Sometime during the night, Justine went into the bunker and brought some sheets and a pillow up. I got to use them after my second shift, sleeping through till morning.

The sun woke me with little stabs of pain. Even through my eyelids, the light was enough to make me pull the pillow from under my head and shield my face with it, groaning at the lost opportunity to sleep in. I tried to settle back to sleep, but Justine was moving around the kitchen, and the smell of food cooking was enough to get me to lift my upper body and squint at her through the morning light.

"You hungry, babe?" she asked, smiling from ear to ear. I distinctly heard the sound of meat sizzling as she turned back to her frying pans.

"Is that bacon?" I asked, putting on my sunglasses against the light.

"Crispy or chewy?"

"Crispy."

"Crispy it is, and I got you a present," she bubbled.

The bacon was enough to get me off the couch by itself, but there was something else sitting on the end of the island, hidden under two dishtowels. My hand froze, about to pull away the towels when my eyes locked on the light over the hood of the range. "The power is on," I said dumbly.

"I'll explain everything, but after you open your present," she whined excitedly, pointing with her spatula.

I pulled the dishtowels away to reveal a finely crafted weapon covered in a matte-black finish. I picked up the German-made UMP40 and hit the clip release before working the bolt to make sure there were no rounds in the chamber. A piece of paper lay under several spare magazines and a box of .40 S&W ammo. There were two lines written on it. The first said, "I love you." The second said, "I was wrong about there not being any weapons here," with a smiley face next to it. I grinned as I read it, deciding not to point out the pistol we'd already found on Dietrich's body.

"I want to ask you where you got this," I said, touching the weapon. "But it doesn't matter at the moment." I exchanged the weapon for the piece of paper and walked around the island so I could grab her and pull her close. "Tell me I'm not dreaming," I said into her neck, squeezing her hard as I breathed in the smell of her, lifting her off her feet and spinning her around as I hugged her. Those three little words had me flying.

"I love you," she said, her lips kissing my cheek until I turned to meet them. My hand rose up along the back of her robe until I reached her hair. It was damp. And she smelled like soap.

"What's going on?" I asked her, trying to talk around her

mouth as she kissed my lower lip.

"I'll explain everything after we eat," she told me, squealing as she realized our eggs were on the verge of burning. I tried to hold on to her, but she twisted away, leaving me to stand there puzzled and stunned.

"What's going on?"

"Your breakfast is getting cold," she said. Then she refused to talk to me until I sat at the table and picked up my fork. After that she distracted me with real bacon and scrambled eggs. When I finished eating, I pushed my plate away and pulled the UMP in front of me, running a finger along the body of the gun. The surface of the weapon was still slick with gun oil, as if it had been in storage until that morning.

"I feel bad; I still haven't replaced the shotgun like I promised," I said, picking up the weapon to put it to my shoulder and aim across the room.

"There are other ways you could make it up to me," she said slyly, looking at me with sultry eyes. Her hips swayed under the robe as she walked the dirty plates back to the sink.

"And how is that?" I asked, feeling a lump form in my throat.

"You could get a shower and scrub down with some soap," she said, smiling and wrinkling her nose at me as she turned and looked at me, her hand on the faucet behind her. "You should really get cleaned up," she said, pulling the lever up. Water immediately poured from the fixture. She laughed and shut the water off, taking a few steps toward the stairs. For just a moment she was outlined against the sliding glass doors, the sun shining through the light fabric of her robe, revealing her legs.

I put the gun down, looking at her with hunger. She raised her eyebrows and dashed for the stairs. I thought I had her at the top of the staircase but only managed to run a hand across her back. I took the stairs as fast as I could as she laughed, always just a step ahead of me. She let me catch her just inside the blast door, spinning her back against the wall so I could press myself close, stealing a kiss. "Such a hunter," she said throatily, kissing me between words. "But you still smell." She pushed me back with a hand on my chest, smiling as she said it. I made an unintelligible sound as she pushed me away. "Shower first," she said sternly, pointing with her other hand down the hall. She was having a hard time not smiling as I struggled to control myself.

It wasn't until that moment that I realized we were standing in a well-lit hallway. What had seemed dark and gloomy yesterday was now bright and fresh. The lights were on, but it was more than that; the ventilation system was also running, circulating fresh air.

Justine closed her fingers around the fabric of my shirt, pulling me down the hall to the bathroom. She pushed me in and mouthed one word to me: "Hurry." Every question I had about how she'd turned the power back on left my head. All I wanted to be was in her arms. I rushed to the shower and turned the water on, stripping as quickly as I could. Stepping into the hot shower took my breath away. I stood there, luxuriating in the warmth as the water ran off me in shades of brown.

I turned the temperature up as high as I could take it and scrubbed myself clean. We'd been diligent about our personal hygiene when we were stuck in Dover, but our bag of sun-warmed water couldn't hold a candle to an actual hot shower. The combination of soap and an endless stream of heated water carried away dirt I was so used to seeing on me that I'd actually thought it was part of my skin.

As amazing as the shower was, it was also torture. Justine was just outside the door, and that was where I wanted to be. I scrubbed furiously until the water ran clean, then shut off the spigot and toweled dry as quickly as I could, almost slipping on the tiles in my rush to get back to her. I looked at the pile of clothes on the floor, but there was no way I was putting them on until they'd been doused in bleach and washed. I settled for wrapping a towel around my waist and walked out into the hallway. Soft music spilled out of the open doorway to the master bedroom.

I'd been a Marine scout when I was in the service, an elite member of a small team used to being on the leading edge of the fight. I'd spilled blood on four continents, earning myself multiple battlefield citations—two silver stars, three bronze stars, and two purple hearts—and yet I was filled with anxiety as I thought about what was going to happen when I walked into the bedroom.

The last time we'd started to get intimate had not turned out so good. She'd lost control when she got excited, and not in a good way. Long story short, she ended up running, and I followed her. It turned into one hell of a night.

Since then we'd both been cautious, afraid to push too far, too fast. And then, after the battle in Dover had removed certain complications, we'd been on the move. It's hard to feel frisky when you're dirty, tired, and fleeing cross-country in a beat-up, old Buick.

My fear and anxiety evaporated as I stepped into the bedroom doorway. Justine was lying on the bed, her robe untied and lying partially open to reveal a swath of pale skin from her neck down to her waist. I climbed onto the bed and put a hand on the side of her face, kissing her slowly as her fingers splayed out across the back of my skull. Her touch sent electricity shooting through me.

My hand traced its way down her neck, then over the thin fabric of her robe, caressing a small breast, her nipple a hard marble under my gently rubbing fingertips. She bent her head back, moaning as I kissed her neck, sliding my hands over her breasts and along her flanks.

She grabbed the towel around my waist, pulling my full weight down on top of her with a sudden yank. Our lips joined in a hungry kiss as our hips ground together. I could feel the heat of her groin as I pressed my body against hers, the only thing between us the soft fabric of her robe. I slid one hand inside the garment and worked the cloth over her right shoulder, freeing one pert breast. I bent my head and put little kisses onto her areola as my hand slid the robe off her other shoulder. Justine gasped as I pulled at her nipple with gentle kisses. I slid down her body, planting little kisses as I went.

"What are you doing?" she gasped as I continued to work myself lower in the bed, kissing the flatness of her belly as I descended. She tried to protest, but it turned into a gentle moan as my tongue parted her slowly and gently.

She was sweet and soft, a flower that slowly bloomed as I ran my tongue along its petals. I made a slow, lazy circle with my tongue as her fingers caressed the back of my head; then I shifted to a gentle but steady rhythm. Her fingers tightened on the back of my skull as her hips began to move gently with the strokes of my tongue. I could feel the heat building in her like a furnace. The pale skin of her belly flushed rose red as she started to breathe heavily, her thighs clamping around my ears as her hands balled up the covers, panting as she cried out, one hand slapping the mattress as waves of pleasure rippled through her.

I continued to kiss her gently until she was pushing my head away, panting as she pulled me back up, her mouth meeting mine in a wet and sloppy kiss. Her legs wrapped around my waist, pulling her body up to meet mine.

"I love you," I told her between kisses.

"I love you," she breathed into my ear. "And I need you," she panted, "right now."

Heat enveloped me as our bodies joined in a slow press. I moved steadily but carefully, afraid to hurt her. She sucked in a breath as our hips closed on each other, and I froze, afraid I was hurting her. "No, keep going," she said into my neck, her fingers raking across my back. My hips touched the inside of her thighs, pressing tight against her as she shivered in pain and pleasure. I moved my hips in a slow and steady rhythm, pulling my upper body away just far enough to look at her. She had her eyes closed, her mouth open as she cried out lightly with each thrust. A deep blush started just above her small breasts and moved in a slow wave up her neck.

Seeing and hearing her start to climax again carried me over the top. Our bodies slid together on a film of sweat as I picked up the tempo, unable to hold out any longer. I cried out as I came, holding onto Justine tightly, feeling her pulsing around me as both our climaxes slowly faded. She winced as I withdrew, but her expression was replaced with a lazy smile as I slid next to her and wrapped an arm around her, telling her I loved her.

My fingers traced the little white lines crisscrossing her arms as she fell asleep. It took me back to the first time I'd seen them in my old bedroom in Jersey. She'd been so afraid, so ashamed of them. It was hard to believe how far we'd both come since that day. Justine's breathing slowly turned into a quiet snore as I lay there watching her. I'm not sure how long I lay there before the pressure in my bladder forced me to get up. I untangled myself as carefully as I could and went to the closet. I found a decent terry-cloth robe and slipped it on. It was tight across the chest, but it would do. Dietrich had been a good bit smaller across the shoulders than me.

I left Justine snoring quietly as I walked back out into the main hall, heading to the bathroom. Once I'd relieved myself, I stepped out into the hallway and stood there, looking at the blast door just a few feet away on my right. I stepped up to the door and put my hand on the lever, pushing it down. It moved easily, clicking as it hit its full range of motion. The door was heavy, but it opened easily and without a sound. It opened into a cavernous space full of steel shelving units packed with boxes, cans, and other supplies. I stepped inside, looking at the workbench to my left and the armory on the wall in front of it where various rifles and handguns were on display.

"Oh, Dietrich, what were you into?" I asked myself as I walked down the aisles between the shelves. The storeroom had everything from freeze-dried food to glow sticks and spare sets of arctic and woodland fatigues. There was enough gear to arm and equip a small tactical squad. At the other end of the room, another heavy blast door stood open. The hum of equipment drew me to the door. The room on the other side was filled with control panels and equipment.

I walked into the room and down the path lined with various systems, looking at the panels as they flickered and flashed various statuses. There was mechanical and air-handling equipment, along with a panel that showed ranks of batteries with a readout of the health of the solar panels feeding them. We hadn't seen any panels, but I figured they must be hidden somewhere in the mountains around the lake. A master control panel occupied one large section of the wall at the far end of the room. The panel was broken down into a series of squares, all of them glowing faintly green.

I scratched my head as I looked at the equipment, not sure which part of it all was making me the most uneasy. Where was I? What was this place? Who made a bunker at the end of a dead-end valley and then blew his own head off?

I walked back down the hall, taking another look at the equipment. Anywhere there was a set of knobs or switches, there was a set of laminated cards hanging from a length of fine chain. Someone had spent a good deal of effort to make the installation idiot proof. I picked up a set of cards near the water filtration system.

The first laminated card had a graphic of the control panel. A circle had been placed over a square, green "On" button with the instructions written at the bottom of the card to press the button to turn on the water filtration unit. I flipped through the cards, stopping here and there. Each card was broken down into a very simple step and outcome statement.

Another blast door sat at the far end of the room, slightly different from the ones in the rest of the complex. A steel slider with a bulky knob sat in rails at head height. I pulled the slider back and looked through the mildly distorting safety glass. The room on the other side had two massive pistons on either side of a short hallway angling up into the ceiling.

"It's a ramp leading out to the helipad," Justine whispered at my side. I yelped involuntarily as I jumped, my heart catching in my throat.

"I'm going to make you wear a bell if you do that again," I told her, putting a hand on my chest. My heart was thudding under my fingers.

"That might be fun to see you try," she purred, putting her arms around me so she could rest her head on my chest and listen to my heart.

"How did you get the door open?" I asked her.

"I couldn't sleep last night. I was reading the journal, at least the parts that aren't in German. Dietrich always liked puzzles and games. I found a Sudoku puzzle on the last page of his journal. He'd written a series of compass points under it. The numbers located at the compass points unlocked the door once I filled out the puzzle."

"Seriously?" I asked, pulling her away so I could look at her face, not sure if she was telling me the truth or making fun of me.

"I don't remember everything, but little things are coming back. I remember being at the lake with Timothy and playing board games with Dietrich; I was never allowed down here though. I guess he figured if you had the journal and could puzzle it out, you deserved to get in."

"Did they bring you here in a helicopter? Was there anyone else here with you?"

"I can't remember being brought here. My first memory of being here is of the deck and lake," she said after thinking about it for a moment. "I can vaguely remember hearing helicopters, but they only came at night. I never actually saw one. I don't think I really knew what they were. I just remember I didn't like the sound; it seemed out of place here."

"Did he write anything about...?" and I paused, not sure how to say what I meant. I settled on "Everything that happened."

"No, nothing about any of that. There are a few notes about other children, and he wrote that he learned a lesson, and I am quoting here. 'They all have the same stunned silence when they arrive. It is so easy to grow fond of them, but I have learned my lesson, for there lies heartache.' I stopped reading after that," she said, her voice thick with emotion. I hugged her tighter and stroked the back of her head.

"Do you want me to look at it?" I asked softly.

"No, not yet," she stumbled, looking for words. "Maybe—once I remember more."

"Let me read it; there doesn't have to be anything bad in there," I told her, pulling her chin up to put a kiss on her lips.

"Oh really?" she asked around my lips.

I pulled back far enough to look into the depths of her chestnut-brown eyes. "You have nothing but happy memories of this place. Dietrich is dead. Why risk ruining it?" I said, rubbing my hands on her sides.

"You're right," she said, perking up. "We have food, water, a beautiful view," she said, a mischievous grin forming on her face as she pulled away from me, her hips swaying under the robe.

We barely made it back to the bedroom.

Y

Chapter 2

Two weeks passed in sweet bliss. We swam in the ice-cold lake, ate hot food, and took long showers together. We didn't talk about anything except the here and now, pretending the rest of the world didn't exist. Even the bit of target practice we had down by the lake was mostly for fun. Justine had picked one of the Walther pistols from the armory on the wall and decided it was time to shoot some tin cans. It was a wonderful vacation from reality while it lasted.

It ended too soon.

We were sitting on the deck eating dinner as the sun set. I was in the middle of saying something when Justine froze, telling me to be quiet with a finger to her lips. The sound of a far-off shotgun blast echoed through the valley a moment later. We jumped out of our chairs at the same time, almost tripping over each other as we rushed to get into the house at the same time. We quickly dressed and strapped on our gear.

My heart was heavy as we descended the wooden steps and passed through the curtain wall out into the valley. It was the first time we'd left the safety of the cabin since burying Dietrich. For just a few days, the rest of the world had seemed far away, but the sound of the shotgun in the distance had changed all that. I sighed heavily as I pushed the melancholy aside and concentrated on the ground in front of me. The last of the day's light was rapidly fading, the shadows dancing across our path, growing as we ran until we were fully surrounded by the darkness. Two more shotgun blasts echoed through the valley close together just as we made it to the deserted town.

"You think you can keep up?" Justine asked, a hint of excitement in her voice.

"Your legs are shorter than mine," I said, trying not to pant as I spoke. "Pour it on, babe." She did her best to run me into the ground, pushing me to get to the entrance of the valley as rapidly as we could. I was in the best shape of my life, but she made me feel like I was back in my first week of basic.

I was soaked in sweat and winded when Justine slowed, her footsteps growing more paced as we heard the faint noise of animals fighting in the distance. "We're close," Justine whispered. I would have said something smart in reply but didn't have the breath to waste. We were almost to the far end of the valley; we had to be close. Whoever had done the shooting must have fled off the road, but they'd only just made it into the trees before their progress was stopped. We crept forward through the darkness as the sounds of hungry animals grew louder.

It sounded like a pack of dogs snarling and fighting, which made me think of the mutt we'd saved back in Dover. I had no idea if Dog or our friend WC had made it out of the city alive after we'd been separated. I wanted to think they had, but dogs evoked a violent response in thralls and grays, and WC was a nice kid, but I'm not sure he had the skills to survive on his own.

I forced the thoughts away as the scene in front of us resolved beneath the moonlight. We were on the border of the tree line, looking up the path at a stunted oak tree struggling to survive in the rocky soil. Four men were growling and pushing, fighting each other to be the closest to the prize dangling from the tree. Sitting astride a low branch was another man, his legs hanging to either side as his upper body lay against the thickness of the branch. The thralls were fighting and pushing as they grabbed at the man's dangling legs, jerking his upper body from side to side as they pulled on one leg and then the other.

I stepped to the left and whistled at the thralls as I pulled the UMP to my shoulder, watching as they spun around, their heads moving in exaggerated motions as they searched for the source of the noise. I took several more steps to my right as I whistled, pulling the thralls away from the tree. I didn't want a through and through to hit the man on the branch in the event he was still alive. "Right," I called out lightly. The thralls were moving in our general direction, searching for the source of the noise.

"Left," Justine called back. Two of the thralls were

charging, running with an odd, loping stride as the others shambled behind as fast as they could. Justine and I fired at the same time, two rapid shots apiece that lit up the night and filled the valley with the echoes of gunfire. She took down the two on the left, while I took the two on the right.

I kept one hand on my UMP and reached into my pocket with the other, snapping a glow stick in my fist before throwing it out in front of us. Dull-green light bathed the ground, revealing the four thralls we'd just drilled. I walked over to the two closest bodies, keeping them covered as I approached. Justine walked up more casually, her pistol already in the holster on her hip. "Fresh," she said, walking past the first set of dead thralls to the second, "and not so fresh." The two stragglers were partially decomposed with bits of their flesh missing here and there, but the two runners looked as if they could have been alive not too long ago. I picked up the glow stick and carried it to the tree, holding it up in front of me as I looked at the man sitting astride the low branch.

"He's still breathing," I said with surprise, looking at the man's legs. His pants were in shreds, and one of his legs was almost torn off at the knee. Blood ran in a stream from his mangled legs to pool on the ground beneath him.

"He'll turn soon," Justine said, her hand resting on the pistol at her hip.

I reached up and shook the man's shoulder gently, "Where did you come from?" He didn't respond. I shook him more firmly and held the glow stick up to his face. His eyelids squinted up and his mouth opened in a moan. "Where did you come from?" I repeated more loudly.

"Kill me," the man mumbled, his lips barely moving.

"What happened to you?" I asked, shaking him again.

"We thought we were safe," the man said, stirring himself. "We had a small camp with twelve people," he said, breathing out in a long sigh. I grabbed his chin and shook his head until his eyes opened to slits. "They came in three days ago, or maybe four," he said. He was almost gone. "Biters and something worse attacked the camp. I came back from hunting and heard them screaming. They were torturing my wife. She didn't know what they wanted," he said, exhaling his last breath with a long rattle.

I stepped back as he died, wishing we'd gotten there a little sooner or that he'd had just a bit more life left in him. Justine drew her pistol as the man's hand started to twitch and move about, feeling around the branch. She raised the weapon just as the thrall lifted its head, putting a bullet into its skull to give the man his final death. I waited a moment for the body to stop twitching and then grabbed the man by his belt and the fabric of his shirt, pulling him sideways out of the tree. I laid him on the ground and patted him down, checking his pockets. Other than a decently made folding belt knife, he didn't have anything on him.

"How far you think he could have walked in three or four days?" Justine wondered as I clipped the knife to my own belt.

"No way to tell—could have been ten miles or fifty."

"Let's hope for fifty," Justine said.

"Yeah, but let's sit tight for the night," I said. "I want to make sure there aren't any more thralls or a gray following this guy."

"I didn't bring a blanket," Justine said jokingly.

"Wow, a few days in a comfy bed and you've gone soft." I got punched for saying it. "We'll have to plan on bringing some more gear out this way, maybe make a camp at this end of the valley?"

"Let's find someplace to pitch a tent then," Justine said in halfhearted agreement.

We left the bodies where they were and hiked north for ten minutes until we were at the foot of the mountains. We camped out beneath the stars, taking turns keeping watch until the sun came up. It was an uneventful night. At first light we dragged the bodies back out onto the highway and pushed them over the guardrail to fall out of sight below. In the process we found what was left of the man's shotgun shattered next to a thrall he'd brained with it after running out of shells.

We made the trip back to the cabin quietly, moving through the woods as we scanned the ground and the forest around us. We'd only found five thralls in total, but that didn't mean they were the only bad things that had slipped into the valley. We kept our eyes and ears open but didn't see any signs of other undead as we made our way back to the cabin.

We barred the heavy door on the outer wall and climbed the stairs up to the deck, glad to be home. In just a handful of days, the cabin had become something familiar, warm. We collapsed on the couches as soon as we were inside, exhausted. I lay with my head on the back of the couch, the softness of the cushions pulling me into a near slumber. Justine sighed heavily next to me, her hand reaching out until it found mine. We were both tired, but the fatigue we were feeling went beyond physical exhaustion. We'd spent two weeks ignoring the world around us, and now that was over. The incident at the far end of the valley had brought the real world crashing back down around us. It left us both feeling a little depressed.

"If I don't get up, I'm going to sleep here," I said.

"I'll stand first watch," Justine replied without opening her eyes or moving anything but her mouth.

"Tempting," I grunted, forcing myself to a sitting position, "but I promised myself I wouldn't go to sleep grubby and grimy again if I didn't have to. You care if I get the first shower?" I asked.

"Go for it," she said, waving from her wrist as I forced myself off the couch, never taking her arm off the cushions.

The shower helped. I came out of the bathroom feeling like I could make it all the way to the bedroom. I was planning on going straight to sleep, but the door to the storeroom was open and I could hear Justine moving around inside. I poked my head through the door to find Justine going through boxes in the racks of supplies. I leaned on the doorframe as she stood on her tiptoes to look in a box before pulling it off the shelf, apparently having found something she was looking for.

"Thought you were tired," I said, holding back a yawn.

She shrugged as she put the box on the workbench to my left. "I started to think how lucky we got hearing that shotgun, and then I couldn't just lie there; I had to get up," she said, pulling a thick red tube the size of a stick of dynamite out of the box and tossing it to me. I caught it reflexively, turning it around so I could read the label.

"Which one of us is the well-trained soldier and which one is the teenage girl?" I asked. She hated it when I called her a teenager. Her eyes narrowed as she stepped in front of me and pulled the flare out of my hand, setting it on the workbench next to the other supplies she'd already collected.

"Teenage girl?" she said, stepping close to me. "I like to think of myself as a mature young lady." She slid her hand between us, grabbing me gently in a very sensitive location. She slowly increased the pressure as she tilted her head ever so slightly, her eyes never leaving mine.

"I thought you were a tired young lady," I said, swallowing hard. She was causing me to have a physical reaction and was applying just enough pressure that I wasn't sure if I was in pleasure or pain.

"Sweaty and dirty, too," she said, moving her hips against me.

"You know that's not going to stop me, right?" I said as I grabbed her and spun her around, sitting her butt on the workbench.

"I was kinda hoping it wouldn't," she said hungrily as she wrapped her legs around my waist. I picked her up and walked her into the bathroom, not stopping until I had her back against the tiled wall of the shower. I turned the water on, struggling not to freeze or burn us as I got the temperature right with one hand. Justine managed to get her shirt over her head, but I had to put her down so she could get her pants off.

At some point we made it into the bedroom.

"Harder," she breathed, her hips rising up to meet me as beads of sweat rose on her skin.

I could see the blush slowly rise from the top of her belly as she got close. She saw the smile touch my lips and grinned back, pulling me down so my chest slid across hers on a sheen of sweat. "I'm going to cum," she said into my ear, her arms and legs tightening around me. I could feel her muscles start to convulse, her mouth sucking at my neck.

Her hands flattened against my back, her fingers

splayed back so her nails wouldn't hurt me. "It's OK, I love you," I said to her as we both rose to the edge, just about to slip over into the abyss.

"I'm scared," she half groaned, half mumbled, her voice an octave deeper than normal. Her tongue slid across my neck, licking the sweat off me and leaving a cool streak that sent a chill down my spine. "I want..." she started to say, and stopped, burying her head in my neck.

"It's OK," I said, pushing into her in a last long stroke, holding there as our hips met and touched. I could feel myself pulsing inside of her as she clenched around me. "Do it, I'm yours," I said, nudging her with my head, putting her cool mouth back onto my neck as I strained to merge my hips with hers.

I climaxed just as her incisors slid smoothly into the side of my neck.

A long moan passed across my lips as she locked her legs around my waist, holding me in place. I gasped as she pulled softly at my neck, slowly increasing the pressure as warmth flooded down my spine, working its way down my legs until my toes tingled. I tried to keep my full weight off of her, but my ability to control my own muscles was rapidly fading. She rolled me over easily, switching her position from bottom to top as she pulled her teeth out of my neck. Her fingers traced electric lines across my skin as she caressed my jawline, gently licking clean the punctures on the side of my neck. I tried to tell her I loved her again, but my lips wouldn't form the words through the sweet euphoria of her kiss.

I fell asleep with my head resting on her naked chest, completely at peace. I drifted off with her humming to me and stroking my cheek.

Chapter 3

I woke up happy and content. Sometime in the night we'd moved about, but Justine was lying there with me, curled up against me under the covers. I stroked her side and kissed the back of her head. "I was so afraid for so long," she said, her voice choking with unexpected emotion.

"You're all I ever wanted," I whispered in her ear.

"I love you," she said back, hugging my arm around her waist. We lay there for a while, enjoying the warmth and the closeness.

Eventually I stretched and forced myself to get out of bed to use the bathroom. When I came back, Justine was still there, curled up under the covers. "We should get moving," I said, pulling on a pair of pants.

"I thought about getting out of bed, but it's chilly this morning," she admitted.

"I'm sure walking to the other side of the valley will warm you up," I said, sitting on the edge of the bed so I could slap her butt through the covers. When I was finished dressing, Justine was still hiding under the blankets. I put my foot on the bed and shook it.

"You're mean," she grumbled as she rolled out of bed and got to her feet.

"This was your idea," I reminded her as I went to get my gear together.

Inside the hour we were hiking through the valley loaded down with backpacks full of supplies. "I really hate the morning," Justine complained as we hiked. I kept my mouth shut. It was the safest thing to do when she was being grumpy. By midday we were at the far end of the valley. We dropped our packs near where we'd camped out a day before and then made our way out to the highway before turning around.

We walked the path into the valley, studying the way the ground opened up in front of us. There was no way we could string trip wires everywhere, but there were several likely paths for anyone making his or her way into the valley from the highway. We used fishing line and flares Justine had found in the storeroom to rig simple trip wires. The sun was getting low in the west when we finished up.

We returned to where we'd left the rest of our gear, and I set up a small tent as Justine built a fire ring and got a little campfire going. We sat by the fire, listening to it burn as the stars came out overhead. We took turns, one sleeping while the other sat by the fire. It wasn't the best way to keep watch, but the nights were starting to get cold, and the trip wires would give us some early warning.

On the trip back to the cabin the next day, we hugged the mountains making up the northern edge of the valley. It meant spending an extra night out in the woods, but it was an enjoyable side trip. We scared up a few deer and felt like we were walking on virgin ground.

"Think you could hit a deer with that?" Justine asked after we startled our second group of deer and they went bounding off into the woods.

"Not really the weapon of choice. If we were hunting deer, I'd want to shoot from farther out before we spooked them. Less chance of a messy kill that way."

"Fresh deer steaks," Justine said tantalizingly.

"I saw a few hunting rifles in the storeroom," I said, enjoying the thought of some fresh meat just as much as she was. "If we were hunting, I think we could have had two of them already."

"I get to shoot, too," she said, looking at me challengingly.

"Of course," I said with a genuine smile, nodding my head. She was a special girl.

A week passed in relative calm and peace. I spent the daylight hours trying in vain to get one of the two four-wheelers running. All the bits appeared to be there, but somewhere in the teardown, parts from each of them had been intermingled; and while they were both from the same manufacturer, one was a 420-cc engine while the other was 475. It made all the parts look just about right, but nothing wanted to fit together quite right. Justine sat on the deck while I worked, paging through Dietrich's journal.

When the sun set, we'd take turns cooking dinner.

Afterward we played board games and cards or sometimes just sat and talked about what she'd discovered in the journal that day. It was a struggle not to grab the book and read it myself at times. Justine seemed perfectly content to spend a day studying a few pages at a time. In the course of four days, I learned that Dietrich had made a fortune designing industrial equipment and that he seemed to have been some sort of naturalist. Justine said he could take up a whole page writing about a bird or a family of squirrels.

On the seventh day, she came down to the courtyard and told me to give it up; she wanted to go hunting. I cleaned the grease from my hands with a rag, nodding my head. She seemed off, a little angry and sad. I asked her if she was OK, but she just said she wanted to get out under the trees for a while. I followed her up to the cabin and then down into the living quarters and into the storeroom.

Dietrich was a real nationalist when it came to his weapons. Besides the UMP there was a collection of Walther semiautomatics we'd already raided, four variants of the G36, and two Blaser long rifles. Both the R8 and R93 were chambered for .30-06, but the R8 was in a shorter barrel configuration and had a lower powered scope; so I picked the R93. I carefully disassembled the weapon and inspected each part, laying the pieces out on the workbench. At some point Justine wandered off and then came back eating a granola bar, leaning against the end of the workbench as she watched me clean and reassemble the weapon.

"You know where everything goes? I don't see a manual."

I laughed at her. "Guns are like women; they're all a bit different, but they all have the same basic anatomy," I said, not looking up from the parts in my hands. I braced myself just in time, knowing the punch was coming. "But," I continued as she crossed her arms and glared, "when you find a truly exceptional example, you tend to hold onto it forever." I finished the assembly and pulled the bolt back, turning around to present her the cleaned and reassembled rifle.

"It's still not a shotgun," she reminded me, taking the

weapon and feeling its weight. It looked oversized in her hands, but she held it naturally, looking completely at ease with the weapon.

"You're never going to let me live down losing that gun, are you? It wasn't as if we were being chased by grays and thralls and the building was on fire at the time—or anything like that."

"Nope," she said with an exaggerated motion of her lips. "So now we go hunting?"

"No, now we go shoot some targets and teach you the basics." She gave me a look from under raised eyebrows. "Hunting deer isn't shooting thralls at twenty feet. This will be a lot more challenging." She nodded grudgingly, not quite believing me.

We packed our gear and walked out into the valley until we had a long straight section of the berm in front of us. "One can every hundred meters," I said, passing her the sack with the four empties.

"You know, you switch between standard and metric a lot," she said, raising an eyebrow at me as I pulled a beach towel from my bag to lie on the dirt.

"Sorry, whenever it's guns I always go to metric. Now move your ass," I said, watching her as she sprinted down the berm, putting out cans at roughly hundred-meter increments. When she was back, I flipped out the bipod and laid the rifle down so the butt rested on the end of the beach towel.

Justine lay down and settled herself behind the rifle, closing one eye as she sighted through the scope. I stood watching the first target with binoculars as she worked the bolt, chambering the first round. "Stay relaxed, sight your target, and fire on your exhale," I said quietly. "Oh, and the recoil is going to be a bi—" The last word was drowned out by the crack of the rifle.

"Oh fuck," Justine giggled, setting the rifle down to roll onto her back, holding her shoulder as she laughed. "That kicks like a mule."

I smiled at her from under the binoculars. The first can had been obliterated. "Make sure you snug it up tight before you fire. If it's loose it'll hurt worse," I warned her. She was still giggling as she rolled back onto her belly and shouldered the rifle again. Another rifle shot cracked through the air, and the second can flew into the woods downrange, spinning out of sight into the trees.

She missed her third target, but not by much. The round punched up a puff of dirt three feet in front of the can. "This is where it gets fun," I said, explaining to her that if I dropped a bullet at the same time she fired it parallel to the ground, they would both hit the dirt at the same time, just much farther apart. I walked her through using the elevation settings on the scope to account for bullet drop, and within two rounds she had it. She hit the third and fourth targets in a row without needing any further input from the trained marksman, and thoroughly enjoyed it. She was grinning from ear to ear between shots. She asked me about the windage knob, and I explained its basic functionality; but given the calmness of the day, she didn't really have to worry about it.

"You're a natural," I said, kissing her lips as she stood up and slung the rifle over her shoulder.

"Now we get to hunt?" she asked, a smile lighting up her face.

We spent the rest of the day stalking our way north, looking for signs of deer. We went home that night empty-handed, but it was still a good day. It was as if the deer could sense we were no longer just harmless hikers. We spent a week trailing a group of deer, tracking them back and forth across the valley. I might have found it frustrating at another point in my life, but with Justine next to me everything seemed perfectly OK.

A week after our first target practice, we started the day early and were sitting in a natural hunting blind of fallen logs and some brush when we heard the faint pop and hiss of a flare going off. The sun was at the perfect height to blind the flare's travel back to the ground as it fell, but there was no mistaking the sound, even from a distance.

"Maybe it was a deer that tripped it," Justine suggested hopefully, slinging the rifle over her shoulder.

"Yeah," I said, standing up and nodding my head. "Let's go and see if you're right."

"Either way I get to shoot something," she said happily as we started for the mouth of the valley, completely unfazed by the turn of the day. I was less enthusiastic, I had really been looking forward to some deer steaks.

We found the three thralls in a loose group, shambling about the game trail leading to the berm. They moved with the lazy movements so common to their kind during the daylight hours. Thralls liked to rest and hide from the sun if they weren't disturbed or commanded by a gray. We watched them from two hundred meters down the trail as their forward progress slowed, the shade of the trees overhead lulling them into a stupor.

Justine slipped the rifle off her shoulder and braced her arm on a tree, using it to stabilize the weapon as she sighted in. She was happy; she was still getting to shoot something. "One hundred eighty meters?" she whispered.

"Send it when you're ready," I agreed, watching through the binoculars. Her first round struck the male thrall in the neck, dropping him instantly. The female next to him went to rigid attention, her head turning from side to side, scanning the woods. She had probably been a pretty woman before she was turned. Her bright-red hair fell past her shoulders, and she had the tall, lean body of a distance runner.

Justine's second shot struck a low tree branch before it hit the red head, deflecting the round low and into the thrall's chest. The woman stumbled and almost went down, her arms windmilling as she caught her balance. Justine worked the bolt, chambering a new round as the redhead lifted her head and locked on us. She took several steps, building to an awkward run. Justine's third shot hit high and to the right, taking the upper corner off the woman's head. It was enough to bring the thrall down.

The third and final thrall had broken into a run. I watched as she charged, sprinting at us with a snarl on her lips. "Do you want me to do it?" I asked gently, pulling my UMP to my shoulder. The third thrall was wearing jeans and a SpongeBob sweatshirt and was maybe twelve or thirteen years old. Bright-red hair was pulled back in a braid that whipped around her head as she ran.

"It's different when they're on top of you and you don't have a choice," Justine said thoughtfully, holding her shot.

"It's not a person anymore."

"I know," she said, pausing just a moment longer before she pulled the trigger. The third thrall dropped to the ground and rolled to a stop.

We stayed where we were, scanning the trail ahead for a good ten minutes, waiting to see if anything came to investigate the sound of the rifle shots. It only took us thirty steps to reach the little thrall. She'd been fast, and Justine had given her time to run. I rolled her over gently, trying not to look at the gory hole punched through her head. I patted her down softly, concentrating on the details as my hands moved quickly over her clothing. It made the job easier to focus on each small part versus seeing the whole. The girl's skin was still intact, and her fingernails were neatly trimmed except for the pinky on her right hand, which was bitten off. Her clothes were a little worn but clean. I found a bulge in one sweatshirt pocket and pulled out a baggy full of what had to be wild blackberries. The berries were small and tough, the last of the season, I suspected, but they weren't rotten yet. I squished one between my fingertips, letting its reddish-black juice drip to the ground.

"These are too fresh," I said as we walked to the second corpse, looking at the woman. She had the same red hair as the little girl.

"She was bitten," Justine said, holding up a limp arm, showing me where the woman's clothing had been torn away and a chunk of meat had been torn out of her forearm.

"They had to be relatively close by," I said. Thralls on the move tended to try to walk through things before they went around them. It usually left their skin and clothing in poor shape.

"Maybe they heard the rifle shots and were drawn in," Justine thought out loud as we walked to the male.

"Look at him," I said, lifting the man's shirt to reveal a small gut. "He was well fed, and they're all clean. They thought they were safe. It wasn't just some random thrall that bit them and turned them." My voice got louder as I spoke. Justine nodded, knowing the anger in my voice wasn't directed at her.

"I guess we're still going hunting then," she said flatly, no longer excited. If there was a gray or a herd of thralls so close to our valley, we were going to have to find them and put an end to them.

We carried the bodies out to the highway one by one and dropped them over the side of the guardrail to fall out of sight into the trees below, neither of us saying much. The trip back to the cabin was equally quiet, each of us thinking our own private thoughts. We took turns getting cleaned up, and then both of us ended up in the storeroom. I spread out a map of the surrounding area, looking at the mountainous terrain and the way the highway snaked through the ranges. Justine set aside two packs and then organized other gear we'd need if we were going to be away from the cabin for any extended period of time. I was still studying the map when she finished, finally settling on one of the two most likely places the thralls could have come from. Justine looked from me to the map, her eyebrows raised.

"We start here," I said, putting the tip of my pencil on a speck of a town not six miles from the mouth of the valley. It was my best guess as to where the three thralls had come from. There was another town half the distance away, but it was on the other side of a stream, and the map showed no bridge for ten miles in either direction. None of the bodies had showed any signs of wading through a stream.

We were a sad pair when we set out the next day. Justine snipped at me when I helped her adjust her pack straps, and I felt like I could feel the seams on my socks with every step. She groused for thirty minutes about leaving the long rifle behind, but I didn't take the bait. We'd already talked about it the night before. In the types of fights we were likely to find, the rifle wouldn't be much good. So she had a Walther on one hip and a large hunting knife on the other while I had the UMP on a bungee sling and a Walther P99 under each armpit as well as the folding belt knife I'd taken off the man in the tree.

We made it to the highway shortly after lunch and held our steady pace, continuing on down the road. Once we were out of the valley, the sun seemed twice at strong, making sweat and irritating my eyes at the same time. I unbuttoned my fatigue shirt, wishing I'd been able to get at least one of the four-wheelers running as we followed the highway higher into the mountains. Here and there we saw abandoned vehicles, but we didn't see thralls or any huge clots of traffic like we had closer to the cities.

"How you doing?" Justine asked when we passed the road sign telling us we were just a mile from our destination. I gave her a thumbs-up and kept walking, not wasting breath on replying. The last two miles had been all uphill. My thighs were burning from the long, slow climb.

The ground mercifully leveled off just a bit as we approached the exit ramp to the town. We stopped just off the highway, looking at the road in front of us. Two police cruisers were pulled bumper to bumper across the off ramp at the edge of town.

"No smoke, no movement I can see," I said, waving my hand at anyone who might be hiding in the town as I held the binoculars to my face with one hand.

We walked to the police cruisers, keeping an eye on the town for any sign of movement. The cars were coated in a thick layer of dust. They'd been sitting there for a while. I peered inside each of them as we passed, half hoping to find a shotgun to give Justine as a present, but the cars had already been cleaned out.

Once we were in the town, there were signs of violence everywhere we looked. Every building had broken windows or kicked-in doors, and there were shotgun shells and brass casings lying around here and there. But as clear as the evidence of violence was, it was also just a bit washed out, covered in a thin coating of dust and grime. Whatever had gone down in town had happened weeks or months ago.

We were halfway down the main strip when we saw a large construction dumpster sitting off a side street. A pickup was backed up to it, its bed still half full of cut logs. The paint on the outside of the dumpster was blistered, and the metal along its edge was blackened with soot. We moved to the pickup carefully, scanning the buildings around us. Justine jumped into the pickup bed and peered into the dumpster before jumping down.

"Someone did some cleaning up," she said, nodding for me to take a look.

I stepped on the bottom edge of the dumpster and pulled myself up enough to get a look inside. The interior of the dumpster was blackened and still reeked of smoke and burned meat, even weeks after the fire had burned out. The bottom of the dumpster had a foot of soot and ash in it that only partially covered the remnants of multiple sets of bones. The survivors must have tried to clean the thralls out after the initial outbreak, burning the bodies to dispose of them. I climbed down and gripped the UMP.

People had clearly survived the initial attack.

We were almost through the town when we found the first body on the street. The man looked to be in his late twenties and was lying at the end of a wide smear of blood trailing around the corner. He was facedown and naked except for a band of duct tape around his waist that held his arms at his sides. Blood covered his body, and his flesh bore too many wounds to count. It looked like someone had worked him over with a box cutter before deciding to really hurt him. The fleshy parts along the top of his thighs all the way up to his buttocks had been cleanly cut away, exposing the muscle beneath.

"What happened to him?" Justine asked quietly. Grays and thralls bit and tore, but if the man in front of us had been bitten, he would have turned. His wounds had all been at the end of a blade.

"I'm not sure," I said, looking at the blood trail, amazed he'd made it as far as he had. "They cut his Achilles," I said, pointing to the deep cuts just above each of his heels. "Maybe they left him for dead, and after they left he tried to get away but couldn't get his hands free." I shivered as I said it. The man had pushed himself along the macadam until he'd bled to death.

"Who does this to another person?" Justine asked, shaking her head in disbelief.

I knelt, looking at the man's left upper arm, not telling her I'd seen men do worse in the name of drugs, money, and religion. Men were capable of horrible things when given an excuse. Even so, there were things worse than man walking the earth. "I don't think it was people," I said, looking at the piercing wounds around the man's bicep. It looked like a clawed hand had grabbed him, putting neat holes through his flesh in a distinct pattern. Justine crouched next to me, watching as I put my hand near his upper arm, hovering over his dead flesh. If I'd had claws tipping my fingers, the piercing wounds would have lined up perfectly.

"It doesn't quite fit," Justine said, looking the man over from head to toe. There were cuts and blood everywhere but no visible bites. "A gray might play with his food, but he's still going to eat at the end, and there's a lot of blood here. Even if the gray left him, there must have been thralls about."

"I guess we follow the trail and see if we can figure out what is going on," I said, creeping up to the corner and slipping around it low, my UMP on my shoulder. I froze on one knee, my eyes shifting between targets. The street was littered with bodies. And there were thralls about; they just hadn't finished eating what was already on their plates yet.

"Wow," Justine said from above me as she leaned around the corner.

"Cover me," I whispered, letting the UMP fall to my chest as I drew my machete. A gun made some jobs easier, but sometimes quiet was best. The body of the machete was a flat, matte black, but the edge, even nicked and gauged, gleamed with sharpness as I padded to the closest thrall. I killed it with a strike to the back of its neck before it knew I was there. The other thralls on the street picked their heads up from their gruesome feasting and focused on me, standing. Thralls always wanted fresh meat.

I rushed to the next to two thralls and cut them down with vicious swings of my blade, stepping over their bodies to meet the next small wave of undead. Justine followed behind me, her pistol in her hands, covering my back. I cut down one, then another, aiming for their necks or heads. They weren't grouped too tightly, which made for easier going as I cut through them.

I hacked and slashed until Justine and I stood alone on

the street, surrounded by fallen bodies.

"All freshies," Justine said, her voice a tad deeper than normal.

"You good?" I asked, peering over my dark sunglasses to look at the mercury swirling in her eyes, almost obscuring her beautiful brown irises.

"Just got the juices flowing I guess," she said, shaking her head and shoulders briskly. When she looked back at me her eyes were own again, and I was grinning at her. "Don't even think about it," she said, shaking her head as she looked at the bodies strewn about our feet.

"What?" I asked innocently, turning away from her so she couldn't see my guilty smile. The brief moment of distraction lasted only until I started stepping over bodies to get to the curb, Justine right on my heels. It's hard to feel frisky when stepping over dead people.

"More duct tape," Justine said, scanning the bodies that had been feasted upon. Several of them had their hands duct-taped together or to their sides like the poor fellow around the corner.

"Some of the thralls, too," I pointed out with the machete. Something bad had happened here, and recently; the thralls were all fresh. They couldn't have been more than a week old. The question was, why had some of the survivors been bound and then tortured?

"A gray comes in, tortures a bunch of people, and then feeds from the rest?" Justine said, summarizing the scene in front of us the best she could.

"Sounds about right; maybe they had something he wanted," I said thoughtfully, looking for something out of the ordinary. The building at the end of the street caught my eye. Its windows and the main door had been boarded over with plywood.

We approached it carefully, watching the dark square where the door had once stood. The main entry had been sheeted over with plywood and strengthened with several cross members of lumber. It hadn't helped the survivors any. The door had been ripped off its hinges and was lying on the lawn. I clicked on my flashlight and peeked inside before pulling back. "Don't," I said to Justine, shaking my head. "It's bad."

I tried unsuccessfully to keep the image from burning itself into my memory. The front room had been full of cots and sleeping bags, and a massacre had taken place inside. A solid-looking man with graying hair was duct taped to a cot leaning against the old mail counter. Half his chest was skinned, and several objects I didn't care to look at too closely pierced his flesh in odd locations. All his fingers had been bitten off. They might have been on the floor with the bits of other bodies' parts strewn about, but there were too many pieces to be sure. Some of the parts were very small. Justine ignored me as I switched off my light and pulled back, peeking inside anyway.

"Someone needs to die," she growled, her voice falling several octaves. When she withdrew her head from the building, there was no hint of brown left in her eyes. There was nothing but deep swirls of slate, and her lips were pushed out as if she were wearing a mouth guard. It wasn't until she spoke again that her elongated teeth were revealed. "Think this was a brute?" she asked, gritting her teeth and forcing the change back.

"Maybe," I said, looking at the undamaged overhang above our heads. "But I don't think so. A brute would have damaged the ceiling I think." Brutes were massive creatures, easily half again as tall as any man, and much stronger. They were the gray's shock troops, used when destruction and carnage were more important than anything else.

I circled the outside edge of the post office, walking through the tall grass to where the rear parking lot was fenced off. The mail trucks were all missing, but the survivors had turned the fenced-in space into an extension of their living quarters. A pavilion had been strung up to shield four picnic tables from the elements, and just beyond that a long firebox had been built of bricks and topped off with grating. A long stack of cordwood sat at the rear of the fenced-in parking area, and close by was a blackberry bush growing through the fence. Nearby there was a makeshift playground with a plastic playhouse, a sandbox, and a small slide. A tricycle sat sad and alone in the middle of the yard next to a bright-pink jacket.

"This looks familiar to me," I said as we walked away from the post office. Justine raised her eyebrows at me. "Not the specifics, the mechanism," I explained as images of Somalia came back to me. We'd been called in to rescue a diplomat who'd thought his local connections and friendships would protect him. Our team had gotten there too late. The Somalis had tortured him, believing he had money and guns secreted away in the house. They'd tortured his family and his staff in front of him before putting a bullet into each of his knees. He'd bled out long before we reached his house.

"The door gets torn down," I said, nodding behind me as we walked back to the highway. "The gray finds the man he thinks is in charge. Starts asking him questions; he doesn't talk. They start killing people in front of him, trying to break him. When he dies, they still don't have what they're looking for, so things get ugly for anyone who's left." I passed the first body on the road. "But they don't know the answer to the question, so they die, one after another." We passed body after body, turning the corner.

"Why do you think they didn't know what the gray wanted?" Justine asked. We were both looking at the man with the backs of his thighs and buttocks missing.

"Regular people don't take this type of torture and not break. No, I don't think whoever did this got what they came for. This feels angry; these people were punished for not being able to give up something they didn't have." I wasn't sure, of course; I was making an educated guess, but the words felt right when I said them. It clicked, and I'd learned a long time ago to trust my hunches. I pulled the map out of my breast pocket and unfolded it.

"Where to next?" Justine asked, slipping her pistol into its holster with a whisper of metal on ballistic nylon.

I looked at the map for a moment before answering. "If they got back on the highway and continued past our valley to the north, they would have to go thirty miles to reach the next town; but if they cut across this county road, there's another town not eight miles from here and then another stretch of major expressway."

"Eight miles is closer than thirty," Justine said with a sigh. We backtracked through the town and found the county road, setting out for the next dot on the map.

I managed to only look back once as we walked farther away from the mountains that hid our valley.

Chapter 4

We walked all day after leaving the post office, stopping only briefly to eat and adjust our packs and gear. We made it to the city limits just as the sun was setting, pausing to look at the municipality in the distance. "From here it almost looks normal, like the power's just out," Justine said as we started moving again.

It was full dark by the time we were halfway there. And the clouds that had hinted at rain during the later afternoon were still overhead, hiding the moon and the stars. The only thing I could see was a single splash of light somewhere in the heart of the blacked-out city where a fire burned, casting dancing light against the side of a multistory building. "I'm pretty much blind," I whispered to Justine as we walked. I had exceptional night vision, but pitch black is still pitch black. Justine took the lead, taking my hand and putting it on her shoulder to guide me.

I knew when we were getting closer to the city streets; the traffic was heavier and Justine was forced to twist and turn to find a clear path for us to walk through. The dancing fire I'd seen from farther off had disappeared, hidden by other structures as we closed the distance. "Curb," Justine whispered a moment before I felt her shoulder lift as she stepped onto the sidewalk. "Building on the right, lots of thralls one street over," she warned in a quiet hiss. I knew the building was there; my shoulder occasionally rubbed against it as we walked. I tried not to think about the thralls. Knowing they were there and not being able to see them set my nerves on end. "Curb," she whispered as we hit the end of the block, and then again as we stepped up onto the next.

I kept quiet, one hand on her shoulder and the other on the body of the UMP to keep it from bumping against my chest and making any noise as we walked. I could hear things moving around us, could smell the rot and decay of thralls as we crept by them in the dark. A strange sense of the familiar overcame me as I walked through the pitch black, my eyes closed.

When I was a child, before my corneas had been

repaired, I'd lived in darkness for days at a time. It was strange to think they were the fondest memories of my mother, the smell of her, the feel of her holding me, rocking away the pain in the dark. She'd passed when I was very young, before they'd found a treatment for corneal basement membrane dystrophy. I had pictures of her but no memories of what she looked like locked in my own head, by my own eyes. The memories of her touch and smell in the darkness were all I had of her. My fingers must have tightened around Justine's shoulder involuntarily. "It's OK, I got you babe," she said and patted my hand.

I smiled in the dark, knowing she was telling me the absolute truth.

At first the noise was faint, barely heard. It was easy to think you were imagining it. But as we closed the distance, the sounds of gunshots grew more distinct. First we heard the shotguns as distinct sounds, and then more slowly small-arms fire and the screams of people became clear. We turned a corner trying to follow the source of the noise, only to find the fire we'd seen from farther away flickering in the distance, giving me a reason to open my eyes. At first the light was a small flame in the dark, but as we closed on it, the cloud cover overhead broke up, and the town around us slowly took shape for me.

Two-story buildings lined the streets on either side of us, and the windows that weren't broken advertised pizza, ice cream, a hardware store, all the normal things a small town needed. We were halfway down the block when we saw the first thrall body lying dead on the ground. "It's older, rotten," Justine said as we passed it. Near the corner were three or four more dead thralls, and the ground was littered with brass casings. Someone had been caught out in the open, but it looked like they had escaped, at least from the corner.

We hugged the deeper darkness close to the buildings on our right as we moved forward, creeping to the end of the block. We reached the corner and stopped. In front of us was a large field with soccer nets at either end, and in front of that, a middle school. A fort of sorts had been built in front of the school out of cargo containers stacked two high and three long on each side, backing up to the front of the school. An opening just large enough for a vehicle to drive through sat in the center of the cargo containers and was closed off with a cyclone gate. Not far away, thirty feet in front of the gate, a jeep was burning. Bodies were shambling forward, outlined against the burning vehicle as they filed toward the horde already pressing against the cyclone fence. The sound of multiple fists beating on the metal siding of the cargo containers filled the air as the thralls hammered away.

We pulled back from the corner and found the stairs leading to the apartment over the storefront, climbing them as quietly as we could. The front door was kicked in, but a quick sweep revealed nothing except for a ransacked apartment. We crouched on either side of the window looking out over the field, watching the horde of thralls surrounding the stacked cargo containers.

Two men climbed into view, taking positions on either corner at the front of the containers, firing pump-action shotguns into the thralls in front of the fence, trying to take the pressure off the gate. The thralls continued to press in from behind, their numbers easily fifteen to twenty deep around the front of the containers.

"That fence is going to give soon," Justine said from across the window.

"Soon," I agreed unhappily. There were a couple hundred thralls we could see out there, and who knew what else was out of sight? We had a few pistols and my UMP— there wasn't much we could do about what was going down in front of us, and we both knew it.

The first burst from the automatic caught me off guard. I jumped and pulled my head back from the window. I looked over to see that Justine had been similarly caught off guard. We grinned at each other for just a moment before looking out again. Someone had taken position on the other side of the fence; we couldn't see him, but we could see the damage he was doing as rounds tore through the thralls, felling them in ranks. I guessed it was a M249 from the sound of it. The thralls in front of the gate were slaughtered as the light machine gun opened up in evenly spaced bursts.

"Why didn't he pull that out sooner?" Justine asked between two bursts. The gunman had rapidly cleared an opening in front of the gate, allowing us to see him as long tendrils of flame leaped from the front of the weapon and thralls were torn apart in front of him.

"That's why," I said as someone else came into view carrying ammunition. In the space it took for the man to open the cover and set a new belt of ammunition, the thralls were pouring through what was left of the gate. The thralls made it a few steps into the compound before the man had the weapon back to his shoulder, clearing the ground they'd taken in a matter of seconds. The two men with the shotguns continued to fire down from above all the while, unloading as fast as they could pump their weapons.

I'm not sure if I saw the gray pull down the first man or imagined it after the shotgun went silent. One moment he was standing and shooting, and then he was a bump on the top of the cargo container. The man on the other cargo container kept firing right up until he was pitched off the edge into the waiting hands of the thralls below. I watched the mass of bodies moving about where he'd fallen, wincing as his shotgun went off one last time.

"They breached," Justine said, calling my attention back to the gunman with his M249. He had the weapon on his shoulder, leaning forward into the recoil as he fired. He never saw the thralls streaming up behind him from somewhere out of sight. He continued to shoot right up until hands gripped him from behind, and even then I'm not sure he realized what was happening until the first teeth sank into his shoulder. I slipped down to hide behind the wall as the man held the trigger to the M249, firing a long wild burst as he was pulled to the ground. It was unlikely the wall would have helped much if a round had come our way, but it was instinct.

I raised my head back to the window just in time to hear a few more shots, and then a small pack of people broke free of the side of the school, running from a fire exit as fast as they could. I watched them disappear down a side street off to our left as thralls poured out of the fire exit behind them a few moments later, following the survivors.

"The gray will be hunting them," Justine said eagerly.

"And we'll be hunting him," I said. Killing the gray would put an end to whatever craziness was going on, and then we could go home.

Justine led the way, backtracking down one block and then cutting west, moving in the same direction the survivors had fled. We passed through a residential neighborhood at a fast jog, moving as quickly and quietly as we could without attracting attention. The neighborhood was infested with thralls. They milled about front yards and driveways, waiting for something to trigger them into action. We left them behind, running low, using the cars in the street to give us what cover was available.

We made it out of the residential area and were just making our way into an industrial park when a shotgun blast lit up the loading dock of a warehouse off to our right. We darted across the street, making our way to the front office of the warehouse as a horde of thralls flooded around the loading docks and more small-arms fire popped off from inside the building. We climbed through a shattered plate-glass window into the front office, making our way through the cubicles to the door leading into the warehouse.

"We bolt if they take any shots at us," I said, waiting until Justine nodded her head in agreement before I opened the door. Huge racks filled the warehouse, stacked with pallets and crates of goods waiting to be shipped. Flashlight beams cut across the darkness from a few aisles away, cutting wildly through the building as people ran. We moved to the end of the aisle the survivors were on, hiding behind pallets as we watched them moving toward us. Thralls were already inside, entering the other end of the building through the loading docks. Some of the survivors had climbed into the racks and were pushing pallets down into the aisles to slow the undead, trying to give their friends time to escape.

"I hate this part," I said as I pulled my flashlight out of my pocket and flipped it on and off down the aisle, keeping my body behind the pallet as I did.

A woman screamed, and more pallets came crashing

down, but someone flashed me back. "Come on," I yelled, risking a quick look around the corner as I turned my flashlight on and let it light the space just in front of my feet. Several people were rushing toward us, their flashlights swaying and bobbing as they ran. "Move, move, move," I yelled, letting them see me but keeping half my body hidden behind the pallet in case I had to duck back. I really didn't want to die from a panicked shot from a scared survivor.

A teenage girl was the first one to reach me, her hands trembling as her flashlight flickered weakly, just about out of juice. "How many?" I demanded, darting glances over her shoulder.

"Not sure," she mumbled as another small group of people reached us.

"How many?" I repeated urgently. Someone tried to ask who we were, but I talked over him. "We need to move; they're going to be coming down the street any moment. How many?" Two more people, a man and a woman, showed up as I spoke.

"Regi and John are the last ones down there; they're in the pallets," one of the newcomers said. I looked down the aisle just in time to see two men climbing down off the racks before running in our direction.

"They're moving up the other aisles," Justine said, returning from a few racks away.

"Go, follow her," I said to the small gaggle of people, pushing shoulders to get them moving. Justine gave me a look, clearly not happy with my choice to hang back. "I'm right behind you, babe," I assured her. She led the survivors away as I yelled for Regi and John to haul ass. They were halfway to me when the gray darted across the aisle, taking one of them by the back of the neck and pulling him into the darkness and out of sight in a blur of motion. The other man screamed, putting his shotgun over his shoulder and firing into the darkness behind him.

"That thing got Regi," he said, looking behind him as he reached me. He jumped back when he realized I wasn't one of his friends. "Who the fuck are you?" His eyes were large with fear.

"I'm the one saving your ass—now go," I said, pointing him toward the door into the front office with my flashlight.

Justine already had her group of survivors crossing the street when we made it into the front office. "Follow them," I said, turning my flashlight off with a click. He gave me a brief puzzled look and then ran, leaving me standing in the dark. I slipped down behind a cubicle and watched the door to the warehouse.

The gray was used to being the hunter, not the hunted. He slammed the door open and charged into the front office, never thinking something might be waiting for him in dark. Even so, he was alert and fast. I think my first rounds hit him, but he moved so quickly it was hard to tell whether the short scream that came from his lips was from surprise or pain. A jet of fire reached out from the UMP as I swung the weapon in an arc, firing blindly into the cubicles the gray had just fled behind. Bits of wood and cloth filled the air as my rounds chewed through the office before my bolt locked open. As I slid a new clip into the weapon, the plate-glass window directly to my right shattered.

I darted to the window, trying to find the gray, but he had vanished. I cursed, looking down the street at the thralls coming my way. If I was lucky, I'd wounded him, but I didn't have any time to look for a blood trail; the horde was already halfway down the exterior of the warehouse. I jumped from the window and ran across the street, hoping Justine had kept the survivors moving. All the gunfire had pulled every thrall in the city in our direction.

I caught up to the man with the shotgun at the end of the block, yelling at him not to shoot me when he heard my footsteps and started to turn toward me.

"Sorry," he said shakily when I came even with him.

At the next street, we caught sight of Justine's group off to our left and turned to follow them. As we ran by side streets, I could see thralls everywhere, closing on us as we ran. If they broke onto the street before we caught up with Justine's group, we'd be trapped. "We need to go faster," I urged, not sure if the man could see what was coming for us in every alley and side street. He had his flashlight pointed at the ground in front of his feet.

"O—K," he said in two breaths.

We cut the distance between us down to a half block in the space of a few adrenaline-filled minutes, but it was just as much because we were hauling ass as because Justine's larger group was starting to slow down. We caught up to them at the edge of the city, joining them as they crossed a small field to get to a steep hill leading up to the highway.

"Up the hill," Justine growled, waiting for me at the base of the slope as the survivors scrambled, climbing as fast as they could manage. Thralls were pouring out of the city, plumes of bodies shambling from every street in view toward us. The closest were only a hundred feet away. "You get him?" she asked as she surveyed the wall of undead closing on us.

"No," I said, shaking my head in self-disgust.

"Get on the highway and run for it?" Justine asked.

"If it were just the two of us, I'd say yes, but some of them look like they're almost in shock. I think we either lose the thralls quick, or we're going to be hurting by sunup. It looked like there was a large tract of forest west of the town, just past the highway. I think it's our best chance."

Justine looked up at the survivors struggling to climb the hill and sighed, knowing I was right. I put a hand on her shoulder and squeezed it as I made my way up the steep hill, not looking forward to taking a group of tired and shocked survivors into the woods any more than she was. The shotgun blast from the top of the hill took me off guard. My feet kicked up dirt as I dug in, climbing as fast as I could. I passed by the stragglers as I charged up the hill, Justine hard on my heels.

"No," I said, grabbing the end of John's shotgun and pointing it down as he raised it to take the head off the closest thrall. The group of survivors was huddled behind him, and one of the girls was searching her pockets, trying to find rounds for the open revolver in her other hand. "Don't waste your shells," I said, shoving the barrel of the weapon away as I let go. My machete rasped as I pulled it out of its sheath and took the old, decayed thrall's head off.

Thralls were scattered across the highway around us,

and a thicker horde of them were already shoulder to shoulder as they climbed the on ramp to the highway a quarter mile away. A pack of fresher, quicker-moving thralls was already sprinting toward us from the ramp. The gray must have gotten them moving the moment he saw us running.

"Get them into the woods," I said to Justine, slipping my machete into her hand.

"Don't be a hero," she said to me, her eyes bright and intense in the night.

"Just a little target practice, babe," I said with a smile, bringing the UMP to my shoulder.

"Stay together and behind me," Justine barked to the survivors, leading them into the scattered thralls with a grunt as she took one's head clean off with my machete.

I walked more slowly, following her trail as I sighted on the pack of fresh thralls rapidly closing the distance between us. I fired every third step or so, picking off the fastest thralls first, sending them spilling to the ground. I only wounded some of them, but as long as they weren't able to run full tilt anymore, I didn't care. I really had only one job as I walked and fired, to keep the fast knot of thralls from getting to Justine and the survivors. When the last of the fast movers fell, I let the UMP fall and ran, catching up to Justine where she was waiting for in the trees.

"You should have kept them moving," I said quietly.

"Was afraid the gray was going to show himself and I wouldn't get to have any fun," she said with a complete lack of any "fun" in her voice as she slipped the grip of the machete into my hand. She'd been thoughtful enough to already wipe it down.

"I'll take point," she said with a sigh.

"I got the rear," I said to her back as she walked away.

"Are you guys from the Tobyhanna base? We heard there were army holdouts there," John said, scanning my fatigues and the UMP with his flashlight. Everyone in the group had turned to hear my answer.

"No, we were just passing through," I said, shaking my head. "We're here because of dumb luck," I added, the words ringing in my ears as false. Whatever was going on, it didn't feel like luck.

"No more talking," Justine said, taking control. "Single file, every other person gets to use a flashlight; we might be walking all night." She was a natural leader.

Justine led us off into the woods at a fast walk as I looked behind me at the highway one last time. The thralls covered the road all the way back to the on ramp, and some of them were already making into the trees farther down the highway. At first the survivors did well, staying in a tight line as they burned off the last of their adrenaline. Within a half hour, I was playing traffic cop, calling out now and then as people started to get too far out of line. It was easy to do in the woods. You went around one tree to the right, then the next, and pretty soon you were heading off at an angle away from everyone else, too tired to realize you were leading yourself and possibly the people behind you away from the main group.

Our fast walk quickly became a slow plodding as the survivors started to stumble and show signs of shock and exhaustion. Whatever ground we'd gained was rapidly lost, and even the sound of the thralls moving through the woods did little to make the group move faster. Justine tried to increase the pace, and I tried to prod them along from behind, but they were running on empty.

The sound of thralls moving through the trees was hard to describe. It was almost like a loud static as they marched through everything that wasn't immovable, breaking and grinding away everything in their path. We pushed on for another fifteen or twenty minutes before Justine called a halt at the edge of a shallow stream, walking along the line, speaking quietly to each person as she passed them. As she moved from person to person, flashlights clicked off. "Put your hand on their shoulder and shut your fucking light off," Justine growled at the woman two bodies in front of me, leaning forward to get into her face. Justine was petite, but she did menacing very well.

"Who are you?" the woman asked.

"I'm the one risking my life to save yours," Justine said, driving a finger into the woman's chest. The woman flicked the light off and whimpered when the last light behind her flicked off.

"You're not leaving us, are you?" a voice asked in the dark as Justine pulled me a few steps away from the group.

"We aren't going to leave you; just sit tight," Justine said as if she were talking to an unruly five-year-old.

I knew what Justine was thinking and how much she hated to do it. "It's OK. You take them downstream; I'll buy us the time we need," I said to her, a shiver going through me as she put a hand on my chest. "Just be careful, OK?"

"The same right back at you," she said, lifting onto her toes to kiss me before turning and walking back up the line, giving quiet instructions. "Keep your feet in the water, don't splash, and anyone who turns on a flashlight is going to be left behind."

I backtracked through the woods, moving closer to the leading edge of thralls tracking us through the dark. I stopped next to a solid pine, resting a shoulder against it. I could hear thralls, and they were close, but my ability to make their forms out in the dark beneath the tree cover was fairly limited. I reached into the pocket on my thigh and pulled out a glow stick, bending it quickly to break the capsule inside before throwing it into the dark in front of me.

The woods were full of thralls.

The glowing green light revealed the closest undead only twenty feet from me. I raised my UMP and started to take down thralls. I aimed, shot, and moved to the next silhouette, not seeing the targets in front of me, not letting their faces register. They weren't men and woman anymore; they weren't kids. They were thralls. I emptied my clip and reloaded, listening as the sounds in the woods shifted. The light and the sound of the gunfire were pulling every thrall toward me.

I fell back a hundred paces and stopped behind another tree, planning on repeating my little performance a second time. I had my hand in my pocket, reaching for another glow stick, when I saw it. I was watching thralls move through the trees in front of me, their bodies blocking off the light of the first glow stick as they moved. And then everything froze; every thrall stopped moving and the woods went eerily quiet. A moment later the glow stick lifted into the air. I couldn't see who picked it up, just the movement of the light as it rose off the ground.

I let go of the glow stick in my pocket and breathed out quietly, abandoning my position as I fled slowly, putting my feet down carefully in the quiet. As soon as the thralls started to move and the woods were full of the sounds of their passage, I started to run. I'd bought Justine at least thirty minutes for a head start, and that was if the thralls got right back on her trail and not mine. So I figured it was more like an hour. If it had been a clear night and I'd known the terrain better, I might have tried to take the gray on. But fighting him while he had a horde at his back and I could barely see wasn't a toss of the dice I was willing to take.

I ran at a diagonal away from Justine's, heading for a full twenty minutes after the sound of the thralls moving through the woods was lost in the distance. Then I stopped and drank some water from my canteen before moving off to intercept her. An hour later I was soaked through with sweat, but I'd found the stream. I waded in up to my calves, letting my teeth chatter as the ice-cold water sucked the heat out of me. My teeth were chattering when I heard Justine's group moving through the water a half hour later. I caught up to within fifty feet and called out to Justine. At least two of the survivors yelped in surprise.

"Took you long enough, Daniel," Justine called to me as she turned and met me halfway. We met in the middle and hugged. "Next time you get to baby-sit," she whispered.

"You see any thralls?" I asked as we walked up to the miserable-looking group standing in the stream.

"No, not since you drew them off. We were heading to a campground. John said it was the bug-out location if they had to run. He said there's food and some supplies there."

"Anyone left back at their camp who knew about it?" I asked.

"John said only three of them knew about it, and he saw the other two get killed."

"Any other ideas?" I asked as we walked back to the main group.

"Not really," she said. "They're almost done as it is. If the camp isn't as close as John remembers, we're going to be sleeping on the ground soon."

We walked another half mile in the stream before John croaked something. It took a second try for him to point out what might have been a trail leading down to the stream off to our right. He was pretty sure it was the trail from the campsite. Everyone was tired, cold, and miserable but happy to climb out of the water. Even following the trail, we almost missed the campground in the dark. It was just a clearing in the woods with a small oblong building in the middle of it. One end of the small building was an outhouse, while the other was a supply closet locked shut with a padlock. A fire ring sat a short distance away, circled by sections of cut logs to act as benches. None of the survivors had the key to the padlock on the door, but it was easy enough to kick in. The inside was packed with camping gear and several cases of canned food.

By the time I was done handing out sleeping bags, everyone except for Justine was already passed out on the ground. I handed her two more bags and grabbed a few cans of food from a shelf. We sat down against the side of the building, our shoulders touching.

"What's for dinner?" Justine asked as I turned the cans, trying to figure out what the labels said. It's hard to read in the dark.

"Raviolis or Beans 'n' Weenies."

"Raviolis," she said. I had to agree with her; cold Beans 'n' Weenies did not sound appetizing.

"Who are you two?" one of the sleeping bags close to us said. John pulled the top of the bag down just enough so we could see his face.

"I'm Daniel and this is Justine. Our group got scattered back in Middletown weeks ago," I said, picking a town I'd seen on the map out of memory. "We've been working our way along the highway since then, but those things are everywhere. You're John, right?"

"Yes, I used to be John W, but the other John didn't make it out of the school."

"I'm sorry," I said. "What happened back there?"

"I'm not really sure. It hasn't been that bad since the initial outbreak. For the last several months, we thought we were safe. We stayed quiet and hidden at night. Up until yesterday the walkers never pushed on us like that. Even with the warning, we almost didn't get locked up in time."

"What warning?" I asked.

"The guy and the girl," he said, nodding behind him. "They came in early this morning; they'd been running hard. They said they were from the next town over; they were lucky to get out before it was overrun. Maybe they're running out of food?" he asked, trying to put some sort of order to something he didn't understand.

"Maybe," I said.

"I thought we were going to make it; we held them all day, and then the thralls started streaming through the far side of the school. Not sure how they got in. We had the doors and windows barricaded, and there were rolling gates to cordon off the gym and the school auditorium. They shouldn't have been able to get in, not without us hearing them."

"I'm sorry," I said. I was guessing the group had never seen a gray. It sounded like they had no idea what they were really up against.

"I didn't get a chance to say thanks earlier," he said, swallowing. "I really appreciate you not walking away and leaving us there."

"Not our style," I said, pulling the lid off the first can of ravioli. I was going to offer him some food, but by the time I got the second can open he was already asleep.

We ate our food, and then I told Justine I'd take first watch. She didn't argue; she was curled up and asleep in her sleeping bag in minutes. I sat with my back to the wall, listening as Justine added her gentle snoring to the sounds of the night. I was tired and reasonably comfortable, which meant I had to fight to stay awake. When I woke Justine to take her turn at watch, I climbed into her sleeping bag and fell asleep in less than a minute. The bag was warm and still smelled like her.

Chapter 5

It was predawn when Justine woke me with a gentle shake. "How many of them were there?" she asked, her voice a quiet hiss of urgency. I groaned, not really understanding what she was saying until she repeated herself. "How many of them were there?"

"Twelve, an even dozen," I said, rubbing the sleep from my eyes as I sat up. I counted sleeping bags on the ground with my finger. There were only nine. I got my feet under me, the sleeping bag falling around my knees as I raised the UMP, suddenly much more awake.

"I went to the bathroom on the other side of the building," Justine said, angry with herself. "It took me a minute to realize something was different when I got back."

"John," I said, shaking the sleeping bag closest to me with my foot. The man stirred but didn't wake. I shook him harder.

"No," Justine barked, grabbing me and pulling me away just as John's hand shot out from the sleeping bag, trying to grab my ankle. He looked up at us, his eyes shot through with blood, his lips pulled back in a snarl. There was a dark wound on his neck that had soaked down one shoulder, staining his clothes black in the near dark.

I moved instinctively, trying to get way, only to find my feet tangled in my sleeping bag. I cursed as I fell hard on my ass, kicking with my legs as John got a hold of the bag. He pulled it to his chest by the handful, biting and snarling as he tore into the empty material before realizing my feet were no longer in it. He threw the bag to the side, reaching for my feet as I pulled my legs hastily back, taking a poorly aimed shot between my knees. The bullet grazed the side of John's head but didn't slow his hands as they slapped into the ground in front of me. He was trying to crawl closer, but his own sleeping bag was still around his body, hampering him.

Justine reached down and took my free hand, pulling me to my feet as I fired again. The second round hit John in the middle of his back as one of his hands landed on my boot. I made the third shot while standing, the tip of the UMP almost touching his head. The shot cracked, and then John collapsed back to the ground.

People all around us had surged to their feet at the sound of the first shot. There was a brief moment where everyone stood there among the sleeping bags, and then one of the men near the edge of the group grabbed a woman in a bear hug and bit down into her shoulder. People screamed as friend turned on friend. It was chaos.

I popped a glow stick and threw it among the sleeping bags as Justine chanted curses to herself and stepped up behind the closest thrall, who was a good bit taller than her. She took a little hop and wrapped her arm around its neck, jerking her upper body hard as her feet came back to the ground, only to let the thrall fall free in a single smooth motion, its neck snapped. She was pissed. I scanned the mess of intermixed bodies in front of me and let go of the UMP with a sigh, drawing my machete.

I took the closest thrall down with a shot to the neck that buried my machete in the man's spine, binding the blade momentarily in bone. I yanked the blade free as the thrall fell and found myself standing face to face with a young man, his eyes wide and scared as he looked from me to his own arm, where a mouthful of flesh was missing.

"Please no," he said, stumbling away from me. A lump formed in my throat as I looked at him, at his fear. He couldn't have been a day over eighteen. His face was halfway between a child's and a man's, covered in a light and patchy beard, and full of horrible knowledge. Death was coming for him.

"Daniel," Justine yelled in warning, pulling me back to the moment. I lashed out with the hilt of the machete as another survivor-turned-thrall came at my side. Teeth shattered, and the thrall was forced back a step, giving me the room I needed to strike it down. When I turned back to the young man, he was still looking at me but there was something wrong with his eyes. They were rolled back into his head, and his body was shaking, quivering as he swayed gently in place, just barely keeping his feet. When his eyes rolled back down, they were already misting over and shot through with blood. All the fear and uncertainty were gone, replaced with anger and hunger. I took a step closer to the thrall as it raised its arms to reach me and cut it down viciously with my blade, nearly taking its head off.

"Step to your right," I yelled to Justine. A young couple was dodging the groping hands of thralls as they tried to run for the trees. I whipped my machete down at the ground as Justine stepped out of my firing line. It plunged into the dirt and stood upright as I brought the UMP to my shoulder and fired twice, taking down the two thralls farthest from the fleeing survivors. I sighted on the thrall closest to them and stopped. Even if I hit my target, the range was too close; the round might go through the thrall and into whoever was in front of it.

I let go of the UMP and was bending down to grab the hilt of my machete when I caught movement out of the corner of my eye, drawing my head to the right. The gray was already in the air, clawed hands stretching out to reach me as a growl burst from its lips.

I blinked and time slowed. The gray's claws were only inches from my neck.

I started to twist, trying to get the tip of my blade between us, but he was nearly on top of me already; I wasn't going to make it. The gray was so close I could feel the deep bass of his snarl in my chest. I clenched my teeth, steeling myself for the pain. The tips of the gray's fingers were just about to touch my flesh when another sound pierced the night, a primal cry that rose above the gray's hungry roar. I felt a wash of relief as I saw a small dark blur collide with the gray in the air. A single clawed finger touched my throat before the gray was carried away from me in a jumble of arms and legs.

Justine and the gray hit the ground and rolled over each other as they tumbled away. They came to their feet and separated, then joined into a single dark mass as they fought. They were too far from the soft, green light of the glow stick for me to see them. There was the sound of struggling, and then the gray screamed out in pain. I paced forward, searching between the trees for the two runners.

Justine would handle the gray.

"Jack!" a woman screamed from somewhere in front of me. I jammed my machete into its sheath and ran, grabbing a glow stick and snapping it in my fist. The girl screamed again, and I threw the glow stick in the direction of the noise. Green light sailed over the head of a thrall sitting on top of a man's chest as it flailed its arm down on its captive prey.

Behind us, out of sight, there was a high-pitched scream that sent a chill of fear through me. For just a moment, I thought it was Justine's voice, but then I heard her half grunt, half scream, "Die!" and the high-pitched scream was cut short.

The thrall in front of me froze, its head tilted upward as it shook and vibrated. The man beneath it was sobbing, his face battered and bloody. One of his arms was clearly broken below the elbow. He was feebly trying to push the thrall off with his good arm, but he didn't have the strength.

I shouldered the UMP and took a snap shot just as the thrall broke free from its paralysis. The bullet passed through the space the thrall's head had just occupied as it fell on Jack, its mouth closing on the man's flesh. Jack's eyes shot open as teeth bit down on his neck, and then he was screaming as the thrall shook its head violently and pulled back, a chunk of meat and skin held in its mouth. Blood sprayed in rapid jets as Jack's heart pumped his life's blood into the air. The woman screamed again, stepping into the green glow with a tree limb pulled back to strike.

I saw the branch make contact. The first strike caved in the right side of the thrall's head, but the creature was enraged, driven mad by the death of its gray. The thrall ignored the wound, falling back down to put its face in the spraying blood beneath it as the young lady brought the branch around again, knocking the thrall off the young man with a loud crack. The thrall tumbled sideways onto the ground, and the young lady followed it, straddling its body with her feet as she brought her wooden club down again and again, turning the thrall's head into a wet mush shot through with bits of shattered skull. I kept my UMP on Jack as I stepped closer, but every second or so I would look at the woman.

"Step away," I told her as gently as I could. Jack wasn't bleeding anymore. He was still for a moment, a lifeless body on the ground, and then his flesh started to twitch and shiver. A moment later his hands began to move spastically. "Step away," I told the woman more firmly, my UMP aimed at Jack's head. I hated watching them turn.

"No," the woman cried, breathing heavily as she looked at the man on the ground with large, frightened eyes. Justine appeared out of the dark off to my right and approached the girl carefully, leaving me a clear shot.

"Come to me," Justine said gently, as if she were talking to a scared child. She stopped a few steps away and held her hand out for the girl to take.

The girl's head popped up, darting glances from Justine to me nervously. She stepped back slowly into the darkness, shying away from us as her chest heaved, the sound of her hyperventilating loud and ragged in the quiet of the night. Justine took a step closer to the girl, keeping the distance between them the same as it had been a moment before. The young woman raised her club, putting it between her and Justine shakily. "No one else made it?" she said, her voice trembling as her eyes darted about, looking at the bodies lying all around us on the ground.

"No one else made it," Justine said sadly, her voice touched with self-reproach. Then it turned angry. "Somehow the gray was able to bite a few of your friends while they were sleeping."

I put my hand out and motioned for Justine to bring it down a notch. "What's your name?" I asked, trying to pull the girl's attention off of Justine. The girl had no way of knowing Justine was mad at herself and no one else.

"My name is Gabrielle," she said, pausing for a moment. "Jack's dead," she said more quietly, slowly lowering her club. She looked at the blood staining the wood and dropped it, her hand shaking.

"Did any of them bite you?" Justine asked, turning on her flashlight. The tip had a red filter on it, turning the darkness into a sickly shade of deep magenta. The woman didn't seem to be able to answer. "Come here," Justine coaxed the young woman, stretching out her hand again. Gabrielle hesitated, looking at Justine's hand for a long moment before taking it. Justine pulled her away slowly, leading her back into the clearing. "Lift your chin," Justine said. I could see the light of the flashlight moving as it cast strange shadows. I drew my machete and dispatched Jack with a single shot to his neck. "Stay with me," I heard Justine coax the girl as my blade buried itself partially in the dirt, having cut almost through Jack's neck with a sound somewhere between a slap and a thump. I cleaned my machete on Jack's shirt and put it away, walking back to where Justine had led Gabrielle just inside the clearing.

"None of them got teeth on me," Gabrielle said as Justine continued to scan her with the flashlight, sounding almost sad to be the survivor. "Do we have to run again?" She sounded like she'd rather die than be forced to march again.

"Not for the moment," Justine said as I joined them. "I think the gray left his horde behind so he could sneak up on us. Wherever they are, they're tearing each other to pieces at the moment." When a gray died, any thralls linked to it became enraged and would attack anything and everything that moved.

"Gray?" the girl asked, shaking her head, trying to order her thoughts.

"It doesn't matter; he's dead now," I said, trying to sound comforting.

"I want to see you," Gabrielle declared, holding out her hand for the flashlight. Justine handed her the light, and I was immediately forced to put my hand over my eyes as she shone it in my face.

"Below the neck," I grunted, shielding my eyes until she lowered the light to scan the rest of me.

"Sorry," she apologized, her voice numb and far away. She shifted the light to Justine, scanning her more quickly. "I don't know what's going on," she said, stepping away from us. We followed just behind her as she walked among the bodies, shining the light down here or there. "How could this be?" she asked, standing over the body of the gray, shaking her head in disbelief.

"Most people who see a gray don't survive to tell anyone else about it. I doubt most people realize there's anything other than thralls out there," I explained. She turned back to me, her eyebrows in a knot. "It's going to be OK," I said, trying to sound convincing. It wasn't true; she'd just lost everything and everyone she knew, but sometimes you had to lie.

Justine managed to lead Gabrielle back over to the fire ring and ease her down onto one of the improvised benches. The woman turned the flashlight off and handed it back to Justine, her shoulders falling forward as she shrank in on herself. Her eyes were open, but they were unfocused; only her body was in the clearing with us. I gathered some branches, building a fire with a generous squirt of lighter fluid I'd seen in the storage closet while Justine sat with her.

"I'm really hungry," Gabrielle said out of nowhere, her eyes still locked on the ground.

"We'll get you some food," Justine said, lifting herself off the log to go retrieve some of the canned goods. She gave me a worried glance as she passed me. Gabrielle was not handling the situation well. Justine returned and popped the tops off several cans of food before setting them close to the base of the fire to heat up. She had three plastic spoons in her breast pocket.

"That smells good," Gabrielle said, still not looking up as a can of Beans 'n' Weenies bubbled on the side of the can closest to the fire. Justine pulled her sleeve down over her hand and pulled the can away from the flames, setting it on top of the stone ring around the pit. She stirred it with a plastic spoon before testing it to make sure it was not too hot to hold. Gabrielle took the offered food and dug into it, shoveling spoonfuls in with barely a chew between swallows. She darted glances at the two of us as she ate. "You're both too clean," she blurted out between mouthfuls.

"You caught us right after wash day," I said, trying to put her at ease. She didn't seem to notice; she looked at Justine, then me, then back at the flames. There was something about her that was very lost.

"You're safe with us," Justine said, turning the cans of

food still sitting by the fire so they would cook more evenly.

"Nowhere is safe," Gabrielle said just loud enough to be heard over the crackling of the fire. "Jack told me I was safe with him. I believed him when he said it, too."

"How long were you and Jack together?" I asked. Justine glared at me; it was probably the wrong question to ask. Tears slid down Gabrielle's face, and her chest hitched in silent sobs.

"It wasn't that we were together for so long," she said when she got hold of herself. "We'd only found each other a few months ago, but we were both survivors. We actually thought we were safe for a little while.

"We found each other in Smithesville. The town was deserted. There were some roadblocks and some dead National Guardsmen, but there weren't that many walkers. And they mostly didn't come out until night. We raided the local stores for what was left in them and made a cozy place to hide during the night. Jack took down the stairs to the first floor, and we pulled the ladder up at night. We'd both seen some bad things, but after a few weeks of quiet, you start to think that maybe the worst is over."

I was nodding my head, feeling a seed of anxiety growing in my belly. Her story was all too familiar. We'd experienced the same thing living in New Dover. After a few quiet nights, you started to lose the taught wariness that kept you alive during the worst times, and then, after a few quiet weeks, you started to think you might actually be safe. When it finally did come crashing down, the only thing left was a crushing fear and the feeling you wouldn't ever be safe again.

Gabrielle sat on the log, licking her spoon. "What happened?" Justine prodded, handing Gabrielle another can of food. I wondered how long it had been since the girl had eaten.

"We were settling in for the night, talking about nothing. Jack was being silly. Then dumb luck fucked us over. We heard another group of survivors break into the house across the street. They were in a hurry, and it was getting dark; they didn't notice the blood on the windows. It took them a few minutes too long to clean out the walkers in the building. It cost them.

"I don't know where the horde came from, but they spilled around the corner in a huge wave, and the people across the street were still making too much noise. The horde surrounded the house, but they didn't act like any walkers we'd ever seen before. They didn't try to press their way in; they just surrounded the house and stood there. There was something else, something worse," she said, her voice growing very intense. Her eyes were blazing when she looked up from the can of food in her hands. She'd finished off the second can while talking, not even pausing to chew.

"He looked like a man, but he wasn't. The walkers parted for him, and he walked right up onto the front of the porch. He said something to the people in the house. We couldn't hear what he was saying, but whatever it was, it either scared or pissed off someone in there. The front door flew open, and a man came barreling out with a hatchet. One moment he was coming at the man on the porch with the hatchet held over his head, and the next he was flying through the air into the waiting arms of the walkers.

"Me and Jack sat there and watched, too scared to speak. At first I thought the walkers were tearing into the man; he screamed and fought, but they just latched onto him, pulling until his arms were out at his side and he didn't have any energy left. The thing on the porch walked into the house, bringing out the man's friends one at a time. He brought each person out alive, even if some of them were bloodied up a little.

"The thing was just going back into the house when something inside exploded, blowing the windows out all along the first floor. I guess someone figured it was maybe a better way to die than whatever was going to happen on the front lawn." She paused again, scraping the last bits of beans from the bottom of the can with her spoon. She looked at the mostly full can Justine had set aside, her tongue licking her lips. Justine nodded, and Gabrielle exchanged her empty for Justine's leftovers.

"We call them grays," I told her as she devoured what was left of Justine's can of Beans 'n' Weenies.

"Grays," Gabrielle said, swallowing a last mouthful of food. "Yeah, I see how you could call them that. His skin didn't look like any man's I've ever seen, and he definitely wasn't a walker." She sat and shivered for a moment.

"What happened after they were all outside?" Justine prodded. She was never the patient one.

"This gray thing questioned them," Gabrielle said, her voice full of something she wasn't saying. I held up my hand to Justine, telling her to let Gabrielle have a moment. The girl was on the verge of breaking. "He wanted to know if any of them were from New Dover," she said, looking up, her eyes shining as she looked from Justine to me.

"What?" Justine demanded, bolting to her feet.

"The gray asked them each where they came from and then asked if they knew anyone from New Dover. He didn't take 'no' for an answer. By the time the gray was questioning the last person, the man was willing to say just about anything, but his story was changing back and forth every time they took a bit more meat off his bones." Gabrielle paused. "It was the worst thing I've ever seen or heard."

"Did the gray say anything else about New Dover?" Justine asked intensely.

"Do you have any more food?" Gabrielle said, ignoring Justine's question.

"You should slow down, give your body some time to digest it," I suggested.

"I'm so hungry though," she whined. Even as she said it, her stomach made a loud noise, and then she was clutching her midsection with her hands, a look of pain crossing her face. She struggled to turn around and lean over the log before her stomach emptied itself. Everything she'd just wolfed down came back up in a torrent of wet retching. Justine glared at me from across the fire as if it were my fault the woman had eaten two and a half cans of Beans 'n' Weenies.

Gabrielle moaned, wiping her mouth with her arm. "I'm so hungry," she mumbled, lifting her upper body off the log with her arms. A stream of mucusy vomit hung from her mouth as she swayed ever so slightly from side to side. I stood up, not sure if I should grab her and try to steady her or just let her be.

"Uh," I groaned, seeing the mess on the other side of the log. "You OK?" I asked.

"Just feeling a little sick," Gabrielle said, her face hidden from sight by her hair. I was about to offer her some water when my eyes locked on the pool of vomit on the other side of the log. I took a step away from Gabrielle, drawing a pistol. Justine was already at my side, staring at the same thing I was.

One of the weenies Gabrielle had vomited up had a fingernail.

"What happened after you watched the house burn?" Justine asked, her voice suddenly very hard.

Gabrielle whipped her head around, throwing her hair over her shoulder as she looked at us with clouded, bloodshot eyes. "I'm sorry," she said, dropping to her knees. "It's so hard to fight the hunger, especially after I took a little nip from some of those people sleeping back there. I was so afraid when Master caught up with me he'd be mad. But then you killed him. You killed him," she repeated, not sounding like she believed it. "Something broke when he died. I feel strange." Her skin was turning pale as she said it, making the bloody veins shooting across her clouded eyes stand out even more.

"What happened after you watched the house burn?" Justine asked again. Her voice was taking on a deeper, threatening tone.

"We hid in our house for the rest of the day. We thought they'd left. Master woke us up that night sitting on the floor between us. Jack tried to fight him, but that didn't last long." Gabrielle giggled. "I wanted to resist him, I really did. But I couldn't."

"Where did he bite you?" Justine demanded, her fingers splaying out at her side, long claws sliding from her flesh.

"He never bit me," Gabrielle said. Justine growled, shaking her head in disbelief. "He never bit me," Gabrielle spit angrily back, her eyes locked on Justine's.

"How?" Justine said, her voice dropping several octaves.

"I don't know!" Gabrielle screamed. "It was dark, I was hungry, he made me eat and drink, and then all I wanted was to do what he said." She paused, wiping tears from her eyes and smearing vomit across her face in the process.

"Why was he looking for people from New Dover?" Justine asked.

"He was so excited when he found me and Jack. He was sent out to find two people—a man and a woman," Gabrielle said very pointedly. "He wasn't so excited once he realized we weren't them. He was going to kill Jack, but I promised I'd do whatever he wanted if he let him live."

"Why was this gray looking for us?" I asked, restraining Justine with a hand on her chest.

"He was supposed to tell you that you could still save your friend," Gabrielle said, giggling madly. "He just kept shoving the sketch of the dog tags in people's faces, asking them if they were in New Dover. He used me to get into the camps. I asked them soft," she said, laughing. "Then he would ask them hard." Her hands were starting to shake. Gabrielle rose up on her knees and bent over the log, reaching down to pluck a finger from her vomit.

I stepped forward and put the end of my pistol to the back of her head. She froze as she felt the tip of the weapon, talking around a mouthful. "It wasn't supposed to end like this. I don't know what went wrong." Justine's hand reached over mine, locking around the pistol. We pulled the trigger together, ending Gabrielle.

I stood there, looking at Gabrielle's body, a warm flush flooding through me as I raged internally. "Mother fucker," I yelled, kicking the log in anger. "I'm going to kill him!"

"It's not WC's fault," Justine said. "What chance did he have against grays?"

"I'm not talking about WC. I'm talking about Haeslig. I'm going to kill him."

Justine's brow furrowed as she looked at me. "What?"

"When we got out of New Dover, Haeslig said something to me. He told me to keep you safe," I paused to emphasize the last two words, "for him."

"You never said anything," she said, shaking her head and asking me why with a frustrated hand thrown out in front of her face.

"I didn't know what it meant. I thought he was just trying to freak me out. I should have said something. And now he has WC."

"Oh shit, poor WC," Justine said, shaking her head.

We'd hunkered down with a group of other survivors for several months in Delaware and became close friends with a kid. His real name had been Tyler, but he went by WC. The closest I'd ever gotten to understanding how he got to WC was that he'd been in a horrible garage band. I'd never been able to get him to tell me what WC stood for.

"We can't leave him there," Justine said.

"No, and we kill Haeslig this time."

"Oh, yes, he dies this time."

Chapter 6

We found a strange leather pouch and a piece of heavyweight paper on the gray. The inside of the pouch was wet with half-congealed blood and held a single strip of flesh. I held the pouch open just long enough for Justine to peek inside before discarding it. Justine was hanging on my arm as I unfolded the paper. Inside was a simple sketched image of WC's dog tags bearing homage to his girlfriend in the before.

"Do you think they got Dog, too?" I asked.

"I'd punch you, but I was thinking the same thing," Justine said. Neither of us could look away from the piece of paper. We'd rescued the only living dog we'd seen in the after while living in New Dover, and on the last day before we left, we'd asked WC to take care of him if we didn't make it back. "How long do you think WC will last?" Justine asked, turning away from the paper in my hands.

"Depends on what Haeslig is doing to him. He'd know quickly enough that WC didn't know where we were." Haeslig could read your memories in your blood. "So if he doesn't drink directly from the kid and doesn't torture him for fun, he might just be fine."

"We have to go get him," Justine said resolutely.

"I know," I said, slipping the drawing of the dog tags into my pocket before working my map out. "This is where we just were," I said, showing Justine with my finger. "If we follow this back," I continued, pulling my finger across the map, "Smithesville is here." I tapped the map once with my finger as I estimated the distance in my head.

"So we head that way and figure the gray was following the highway?"

"Best guess we have," I said. "We'll know soon enough. There are two towns between here and Smithesville. If they had any people in them, I'm expecting they got the same treatment."

"Let's get our shit together and start walking," Justine said, stepping around bodies to go back to our packs. We got our stuff together in short order, wanting to get on our way as quickly as we could.

We cut cross-country to get back to the highway. Neither of us talked much. Justine was still mad at herself for not realizing that Gabrielle was something we hadn't seen before, and I was full of nagging thoughts that turned my mood sour. Was I ever going to wake up and walk out onto the deck to find Justine staring at the valley ever again? Were we ever going to get to spend a summer day swimming in the lake? It had become so easy to forget about the rest of the world while we hid in the valley. All the sour thoughts slowly turned to anger, and I damned Haeslig a hundred times over for putting grays and whatever Gabrielle was out to hunt us.

Once we made it back onto the highway, the gentle scuffing of our boots was the only sound to be heard. We walked through the morning with barely ten words said between us, not stopping until we reached a long stretch of highway climbing up into the mountains. We ate a quick lunch of protein bars and drank some water from our canteens, then started our climb. My thighs were burning by the time we reached the top of the mountain and started our descent. The downhill section was worse. The farther we traveled, the heavier the traffic became. What had been an occasional car here and there became thick clots we had to work around. Tension and fatigue built up in my shoulders as I constantly shifted the UMP from a low ready to a firing position as we slipped by wreck after wreck. Every car became a potential source of danger.

By late afternoon I felt like I had sand in my eyes, and even with my shades down I was squinting against the sun's brightness. We'd reached the bottom of one downhill and were on our way up the next slope. The road in front of us snaked back and forth, curving around the mountain and out of sight near its peak. "This was so much easier in the Buick," I complained when we reached the first turn in the road.

"Yeah, let's start looking for a place to hole up," Justine said, adjusting her pack straps.

"Yeah, you look beat," I said, trying to rub the grit out of my eyes.

"Sure thing," she said, throwing a leg over the guardrail

to climb up into the trees clinging to the side of the mountain. I followed her, groaning as the steeper slope made my calves burn with effort.

We climbed up into the trees until we found a small shelf behind a fallen oak that left just enough room for both of us to lie down. I sat down and leaned back against the tree, resting my eyes. "Don't fall asleep yet, tough guy," Justine said, sitting next to me.

"Wouldn't dream of it," I replied, cracking my eyes just enough to see her set her pack between her legs and start to dig through it.

"Eat first, then sleep," she said, elbowing me out of a stupor a moment later.

"Sorry," I said. I really had not meant to doze off.

"No worries," she replied, holding an MRE bag of chili between us. We passed the bag and the spoon back and forth until it was gone. "Now you can go to sleep," she said, patting my leg when we were done.

I slept through the night and woke up a little stiff. "You should have woken me for my turn at watch," I said to her as I made my way to a sitting position.

"I couldn't really sleep; I figured at least one of us should get some rest." She gave me a brief smile and waited until I'd relieved myself before telling me to get my butt in gear. We were back on the road for an hour before the sun came up enough for me to put my sunglasses on.

By midmorning we were approaching the first of the two towns between Smithesville and us. We paused at the exit ramp and each took a turn scanning the small community with the binoculars. Neither of us saw anything moving. "I don't think I'll ever get used to this part," Justine said as we walked down the ramp into the deserted town. There was something eerie about walking into a dead town.

We walked onto Main Street and stopped at the first intersection. It was a small town; we could almost see the whole of it from where we were standing. There was the main strip, a few houses on either side of that, and not much else. Off to our right, there was a pickup with its cab buried in the side of a house, and farther down the street at the next intersection, several cars and trucks had been circled in a defensive posture.

"It's the quiet," I said as we started down Main Street. "It makes you feel like you're intruding."

"I think we are," Justine said quietly as we passed by a bakery hiding several thralls. They were standing in the back of the store, facing away from the light.

Three stores away the door to pharmacy was propped open with a wooden wedge. I peeked inside and found a dead thrall lying just off the main path. Its head had been battered in. The stores shelves had been selectively emptied. Food, paper products, and medicine were gone while knickknacks, frames, and greetings cards were sitting where they'd been the day the end started.

The auto-parts store on the next corner was the same. The oil and batteries were gone, but the other items were left untouched. We turned at the end of Main Street, moving over one block to come back through town along a residential street.

"That's interesting," I said after we passed the second house with an X spray-painted next to the front door.

"Yeah, someone definitely picked this place over," she said, pointing to several with their gas caps hanging free. A length of hose had been left in the last car on the block.

"Cleaned out pretty well," I said.

"No sign of people though," Justine said.

"No, not here," I said thinking. "But what if there's another colony of survivors close by? Allowed to survive like at New Dover?" We'd discovered, almost too late, that New Dover wasn't a sanctuary overlooked by the grays; it had been more like a stock pen, full of beasts to be culled when their owners were hungry. Of course, none of the people in New Dover had known the truth—that was the nature of being food.

"You think he'd destroy a whole colony just to find us?"

"Yes, but I don't think he'd have to. If it was his primary food source, I'm guessing he'd know we weren't there already."

"So more questions, but we still don't know where we're going," Justine said with a sigh.

"If there aren't any signs at the next town, we'll rethink

what direction we're heading in," I promised.

When we were back on the highway, I found it hard to keep my eyes off of Justine. A shameful part of me hoped we were walking in the wrong direction, that we weren't going to find where Haeslig had WC and we could go back to the cabin and spend the coming winter safely in each other's arms. It wasn't fear that drove me, at least not of myself. It was the little crack that formed in my heart when I looked at her and thought of any harm coming to her.

She could be fierce and tough, and I knew she could take care of herself, but all I really wanted to do was wrap my arms around her and protect her. She meant everything to me. She made me whole. Even in the Marines, the only other place in my life I'd felt comfortable, I'd been slightly apart, just a bit different. In the Marines I'd been both alone and part of a whole—a special operator who worked with a very small team but supported a much larger one. It was the perfect fit for me. When the Marines had been taken away from me, I'd actually thought about quietly ending it all. Then I'd found Justine.

She was the perfectly fitted gear. She meshed with the oddly shaped bits that made me who I was. She was strong and beautiful, and she made me feel like I could deal with anything, as long as she was part of my life.

She turned and smiled at me as I stared just a moment too long, and the odd smirk on her lips made me feel like she knew exactly what I was thinking. We shared a brief moment of mutual knowledge, a sweet little blossom of happiness as her smirk turned into a smile. In that moment our love was a physical thing, a bridge between us.

Then she turned away, and the moment was gone, disappearing just as rapidly and unexpectedly as it had arrived. It left a vacuum in its place, a void that rapidly filled with anxiety as I thought about Haeslig and the way he'd haunted us in New Jersey and then in Delaware. He'd been stalking us the whole time. Haeslig wanted Justine just as badly as the others of his kind and was perfectly willing to betray his own masters to get to her. He'd already proven that in Dover. And now he'd set a new trap, and we were walking into it without much choice.

I dreamed of ways of hurting him as we walked.

The highway climbed and fell as it twisted around winding mountain turns. What looked like just a few miles on the map turned into several thousand feet of elevation changes. The maps I had of the broader area were all road maps and didn't show the detail a hiking or military map would. The road association assumed you'd be rolling along in a car, not sweating your ass off as you walked. Justine's stoicism kept me motivated. Other than a light sheen of sweat to show she was exerting herself, she just kept putting one foot in front of the other, not even cursing a little bit.

"You're an animal," I said to her as we crested the long rise we'd been working on for half an hour, stopping at its top to take a breather. My shirt was soaked through with sweat, and I was breathing heavily.

"I don't have all that muscle to carry around," Justine said, taking a sip from her canteen as she growled at me playfully. "Come on, soldier boy," she said after we rested a few minutes, starting off down the road. I followed her, telling myself that at least we weren't going uphill anymore, and more importantly, I could see our destination off in the distance. If the last speck on the map had been little more than a street of houses and another of storefronts, this was a decent-sized city in comparison.

We stopped a mile from the outskirts of the city. The highway in front of us was packed with cars, and there was evidence of thralls everywhere. I could see a foot under a car on the other side of the median where a thrall was hiding from the sun.

"Think there's enough time to make it into the city before the sun goes down?" Justine asked quietly.

I looked at the distance in front of us and up at the sky. "Let's be quick and quiet," I said thoughtfully as I gauged how much daylight we had left. If we stuck to the grass between the two sides of the highway and didn't rouse too many thralls, it would be doable, if a little close.

We climbed into the overgrown grass between the two sides of the highway and moved off at a fast walk, hugging the guardrail to stay out of the tallest brush. Cars were pressed from one side of the road to the other, sometimes forcing us deeper into the grass where they'd deformed the guardrail or partially overridden it. The number of thralls we saw went up significantly as we got closer to the city. We saw them lying in the back seats of cars, hidden in the crevices between crushed vehicles, and packed into a rain culvert passing beneath the highway. The smell of rotting meat was heavy in the air.

A mile from the city, we walked by a battered moving truck. The sides of the vehicle were dented and bore the marks of rotten limbs being beaten against the metal siding, leaving behind smears of blood and flesh all around the bottom half of the vehicle. Several two-liter bottles had been cut in half and lined the back of the truck along with what looked like a larger plastic container. We could just see a withered hand lying over the edge of the roof as we passed.

"The thralls probably stood here night and day when they were still moving," Justine said, shivering.

"They didn't have a chance once they were surrounded," I said. We hurried on, neither of us wanting to see what would happen if the thralls stirred while we still had a mile of highway in front of us.

The sun was setting as we reached the edge of the city. We knew the moment the critical hour hit. All around us the air filled with the sound of movement. Thralls dragged themselves out of hiding, knocking things over while they made low and eerie vocalizations as they stirred from their day's rest. The steady beat of fists joined the background noise as thralls struggled to free themselves from vehicles they'd probably been trapped in since the day they turned.

Justine climbed over the guardrail in front of me as we reached the exit ramp and started to jog, then run between the narrow spaces left between the cars. I followed her, feeling the sounds of the thralls around us shift. The general noise of movement had quieted and then redoubled as thralls focused on us, moving with new purpose.

Justine paced me, running just in front of me as I forced my tired and sore legs to push just a little harder. A thrall managed to stumble in front of her, but Justine took it down without slowing, driving its head into the windshield of a van with crushing force. We made it onto the city streets with a growing herd of thralls behind us.

"Fire escape," I barked as Justine slowed half a step. There was no time to be picky; the thralls behind us were being joined by more climbing out of the buildings in front of us. She picked up her speed, stepping up onto a bumper to get through the last knot of traffic before sprinting the final distance. She outdistanced me easily, running directly at the building on the corner.

When she was a step away, she jumped, planting one foot on the side of the building and using it to vault higher as she twisted, turning around in the air. Her hands made a satisfying slap as she caught the bottom rung of the steel ladder and hung there, her body swaying back and forth. She hung for just a moment and then did a pull up, letting her weight fall heavily as she held on tightly with her hands. Metal squealed in protest as the ladder began a slow decent. Justine's butt was in my face when I reached the ladder.

I slapped her on the ass and started climbing as soon as I could get my hands on metal, almost clambering over her as she scurried up in front of me. As soon as we were on the first landing, we pulled the ladder up, just getting it out of the reach as thralls filled the street beneath us. They packed around the base of the building, their hands reaching up as their voices rose in a begging cry of hunger.

"Ladies first," I said, letting Justine get in front of me as we started our way up the metal stairs leading the next level.

"You just want to look at my ass," she said, starting up the stairs. I didn't argue.

"No gym equipment?" Justine asked as we made it to the roof.

"Sorry, short notice," I said as I took in the expanse of black tar around us. Other than an air handler, the roof was empty. "We could try for an apartment," I offered.

"Third floor was a mess," Justine said. I nodded—I'd seen the evidence through the window as well. "I think I'd rather sleep under the stars."

"Stairs it is," I said, heading to the opposite corner of

the building. It put us as far from the fire escape as we could get in the event something did make its way onto the roof.

We took off our packs and settled down in the corner. It was my turn to take first watch. Justine pulled her blanket around her and fell asleep with her head in my lap. I watched her sleep, listening to the sounds of the night as the thralls moved about the streets below us. When it was my turn to sleep, I was out within a minute.

Sometime in the early morning hours, Justine used our packs and her blanket to shield my face from the rising sun, letting me sleep in. "You're the best," I said when I woke up, rubbing the sleep from my eyes.

"I know," she agreed. "Don't go on the far side of the air-conditioner; someone used the restroom over there."

"Thanks for the warning," I said, digging into my pack for an MRE. I used the last of my water, making us some oatmeal, and threw the drink mix into my pocket for later. We were eating our shared breakfast when Justine pulled my binoculars out of my bag and started to lazily scan the interior of the city.

"Found something?" I asked when she stood up and took the binoculars in both hands to steady them.

"Not sure, what does that look like to you?" she asked as she handed me the glasses. "Maybe just the glare off a windshield," she mused.

Something large and reflective was sitting on top of a parking structure roughly ten blocks away. "Too big," I mumbled, not really able to see what was on the roof. Whatever the source of the glare was, it was blotting out everything around it with a bright flare of reflected light. I scanned lower, not able to look at the brightness any longer. "There's a tarp covering the opening of the garage beneath the roof level," I said. Justine took the glasses back from me as I blotted tears from my eyes and pulled my sunglasses down.

"Maybe they put up a greenhouse on the roof," Justine thought out loud.

"Maybe, but the surface almost looks multifaceted," I said.

Justine practically jumped next to me. "Solar panels," she said, handing the glasses back to me with a satisfied smile. I groaned; once she said it, it seemed obvious.

We packed up our gear and went over to the fire escape, looking down. The thralls from the night before had dispersed sometime in the early morning hours, going back to their daytime hiding places. When we made it onto the landing just over the street, Justine looked at me and put a finger to her lips. "Like mice," she said. We couldn't see any thralls, but the reek of their decomposing bodies was heavy in the air. I gave her a thumbs-up, and she climbed over the edge of the fire escape, lowering herself until she could hang from her hands. She fell the last three feet and landed with a quiet rustling of her pack. I followed, trying to be just as quiet and only half succeeding.

I felt like an intruder as we walked down the street toward the parking garage. The city was quiet and smelled of the dead. The third block was lined with storefronts. We moved by like ghosts. Thralls stood in tight ranks inside the stores, their backs to the sun. Two blocks later Justine tapped my arm and pointed to the door to the nearby quickie mart. The front door was held open with a cinder block, and when we came even with it, we could see the shelves inside were empty. It was the first sign we'd seen that anything other than thralls inhabited the city. Someone had survived long enough to go scrounging for supplies.

We found more evidence of survivors halfway down the next block. The dried-out bodies of thralls were scattered along the street, some lying two and three deep in places. As they'd dried their flesh had contracted and darkened, pulling their lips away from their teeth and clenching their fists closed as if they were still suffering. Several cars blocked off the end of the street, their hoods and the ground around them littered with brass casings and shotgun shells.

"I'm thinking at least five or six people," I said, standing behind the row of cars, looking at how the shells and casings had grouped themselves.

"This happened awhile ago," Justine said, biting her lip.

"Daylight's wasting," I said, turning and heading down the street again. We were close enough to see the edge of the parking structure two blocks ahead of us. We took the last block cautiously, scanning the upper levels of the buildings around us as we approached the corner. The parking structure loomed just across the street, occupying our end of the block. Farther down on our right, the garage merged with a multistory mall and a Cineplex.

A florist's delivery van was on the sidewalk just in front of us, its cab wrapped around a telephone pole. We slipped behind the truck and peeked over its hood, looking at the parking structure. The first level was locked down. The rolling security gates over the entrance and the exit had been lowered and an SUV parked just behind each to further block the way. Here and there the fencing sitting atop the first-floor stem wall had been augmented with sections of plywood and lumber. Someone had spent a good amount of time making sure the garage was secure.

"There has to be an entrance from the mall," Justine said.

"Yeah," I said skeptically, looking down the street toward the mall. "But I don't think they would want to risk moving through the mall every time they came or went. Too many places for a thrall to hide," I said, thinking out loud as I looked at the sections of broken plate glass and the bits of department store displays that had been pulled out onto the sidewalk. "Let's work our way around the other side and see if there's another entrance."

"I really didn't want to go to the mall anyway," Justine said, staring at the mannequins lying on the sidewalk outside the shattered windows. I'd seen it, too; there was at least one body lying in the midst of the plaster body parts.

We darted across the street, staying low as we ran, planting our backs to the concrete stem wall around the garage. I lifted my head just enough to look through the fencing and into the first floor. It was dark and packed with cars, but there looked to be some sort of clearing off to our left.

We found another entrance around the corner. "Not a good sign," I said as I dug in my pocket for my flashlight. The steel door that should have secured the service entrance was wide open. I switched my flashlight on and held it against the body of the UMP as I took the lead.

The area just inside the door was surrounded by a hallway made out of portable construction fencing. The gate at the far end was open, leading to a narrow path left through the cars. Justine stalked forward as I scanned the interior of the first floor with my light. The first floor was packed with cars, and broken auto glass glittered everywhere. Only a few of the vehicles didn't have at least one shattered window. Justine was ahead of me, walking along the path that had been left. It led to the second-floor ramp. There was a staircase closer to the middle of the garage, but to get to it we would have to climb over at least thirty cars. I moved along the trail to where Justine was standing, waiting for me.

"She was here; her stench is all over him," Justine said, biting off each word as if the mere thought of Gabrielle enraged her.

"Him who?" I asked a moment too soon. A man's body rested on the bumpers of the two cars he'd slid between. His pants were unbuttoned and pulled halfway down his thighs. I scanned him with my light, making Justine turn away from the brightness. The man's neck was dark and bruised, and his head was rotated too far compared to his shoulders.

"She lures him down here, kills him, and then opens the gate and the door for the gray."

"Sounds about right," I said, turning away from the body to look at the ramp.

I switched off my light and pocketed it as we made our way to the second level. It was mostly empty, and we were high enough that the sun angled in along the edges of the structure. We circled around the second floor, our boots grinding bits of broken auto glass into the concrete as we walked. We stopped roughly halfway around, pausing to look at the mustard-yellow sectional sitting around one corner of a pool table.

"That's a really ugly couch," Justine said, grimacing as she said it.

"They had power," I said, ignoring her fashion commentary. Several lights had been strung around the pool table and the couch. A power cable ran along the ceiling and disappeared to the level above. We left the pool table and couch behind and continued to circle until we reached the ramp up to the third level.

The top of the ramp was walled off by more construction fencing, but the gate at its center was open. We'd clearly reached the primary living space. Several portable toilets were against the exterior wall to our right, and a long, blue building formed out of tarps was directly in front of us, occupying a good section of the interior wall of the garage. We darted to the first concrete upright, each of us peering around one edge. The long, blue building had three doors at uneven intervals. The doors were simple cuts in the tarps reinforced with duct tape.

We played leapfrog along the concrete pillars, advancing on the living quarters carefully. There was no sign anyone was home, but that didn't mean anything. We stopped one pillar away from the closest cut in the blue tarps. "Watch the ramp," I said quietly to Justine before crossing the ground to the tarp building. I pulled the edge of the slit back with one hand, my UMP aimed through the gap. The interior of the building was framed with lumber. The tarps had been stapled in place to close off the exterior and segment the space into rooms. The first compartment was roughly ten by ten and lined with homemade shelving constructed of two-by-fours and cut plywood. The shelves were solidly packed with everything from rice to bottled water.

I slid out and moved to the next compartment. The space was packed with a twin mattress and two cots. The floor of the compartment was covered with multiple sections of mismatched carpeting. I moved to the third and final compartment and slipped inside. It was easily the largest compartment, bigger than the other two combined.

Two king-sized mattresses hugged the rear wall. They were both covered in sleeping bags, blankets, and clothes. The far end of the room was dominated by a large screen TV, an Xbox, and stacks of DVDs and games. I fought the urge to see if the TV would switch on and went back outside. Justine gave me a questioning look, and I shook my head. There was no one home.

We met at the base of the final ramp. The sun spilled in from above, bright and strong. I knocked my sunglasses over my eyes with a nod of my head as we started up the ramp, covering the opening above with my UMP. If anything was still moving in the garage, it had to be on the roof level.

We stopped at the top of the ramp, our eyes scanning the scene in front of us. Justine pulled in a ragged breath. "You OK?" I asked softly, wishing I'd left her to guard the bottom of the ramp. She nodded her head very slightly but didn't speak, her eyes frozen on the slaughter in front of us. I stepped away from her, moving off to the side, covering the bodies as I scanned the rest of the level. Justine had been correct; the glare we'd seen came from multiple solar panels. It looked like local highway department had been successfully raided. Five solar powered road signs were lined up along the edge of the parking garage, their panels angled to catch the sun. A huge bundle of cables snaked around the carts, running to a set of twenty batteries daisy-chained together.

I let the UMP fall against my chest.

Nothing was moving—nothing was left alive. The slaughter had been very organized, its aftermath laid out in an almost artistic manner. At its head was a naked man tied to a wooden chair. Arrayed in front of him were two curving rows of neatly positioned bodies. Each of the bodies lying on the ground had been visited by a slightly different form of hell. One of them had been staked with wooden splinters while another had been disemboweled. Another was in pieces with tourniquets still tied above each cut. The man's legs and arms had been divided into at least six pieces. The only thing all the dead on the ground shared was the same killing blow. Each of their heads had been beaten in. Several of the bodies were so horribly disfigured I wasn't even sure what gender they were. More than one was missing fingers.

The man in the chair had been denied that final, quick death. He had died hard. His feet were crushed and mangled into the concrete of the parking deck, and his knees were twice the size they should have been. It meant he'd been alive for quite some time after they'd worked him over with the hammer. I was guessing he'd died slowly, bleeding out from the soft tissue damage between his legs. Where his groin should have been was nothing but a blackened mess of dried blood that spilled over the edge of his chair.

"They made him watch, didn't they?" Justine asked, swallowing hard.

"It's hard to tell," I said, moving back around the bodies to reach her. I was lying, but sometimes it's OK to lie. The man's wrists were chafed and bloody from where he'd struggled against his bindings.

"This happened because of us," Justine said, her voice thick with emotion.

"We didn't do this; he did," I said, taking her in my arms so I could turn her away from the grisly scene.

"It's hard not to feel like it's my fault," she said.

"I know," I said, holding her tight. "But you can't take ownership for this." I pulled away enough to kiss her on the forehead.

"I wish they would just leave us alone," she said, staring into my eyes.

"We kill Haeslig and then there won't be anyone hunting us," I promised, putting my arm around her shoulder and guiding her down the ramp. I led her over to the outside edge of the garage, pulling out my map, feeling a knot of uncertainty forming in my gut. I knew where we were and what direction we were heading in next, but not exactly where we were going.

"What's the plan?"

"He's got to be somewhere down this highway," I said, tracing the way with my finger. She knew whom I was talking about.

"He'll pay for what he's done to these people."

"We'll make sure he does," I agreed, taking a last look at the map before folding it and putting it back in my pocket.

We raided the storeroom, refilling our canteens with bottled water and eating a meal consisting of canned tuna without any mayo and several mixed-fruit snack cups apiece. The trek out of the city was uneventful and the highway on the far side much less congested with traffic than the inbound journey. We were back on open highway again before the early afternoon.

It was late afternoon when we reached the next off ramp. We'd made it to Smithesville. Halfway through the town, we found a residential neighborhood with a burned-out house on one side of the street and the house Gabrielle had described on the other. The lawn in front of the burned-down house was stained here and there with blood.

"Do you think the gray found Gabrielle after he was on the road for a while? Or pretty much right away?" Justine asked as we walked through Smithesville.

"I guess we'll find out soon enough," I said.

We spent the night in an auto-body shop at the far end of town. When we found it, the bay doors were open, and the rest of the place was intact. We rolled them shut and slept nestled together on an old couch in the back office. We woke early and spent the early morning walking in the relative cool. By midday we were sweating as we followed the highway up another ascent and then around the peak of the mountain. When we rounded the peak, the road stretched out in front of us, sloping gently downward as it sank into a long valley.

We stopped at the top of the descent, and I fished out my binoculars, scanning the land below us. The highway followed the eastern edge of the valley, hugging the mountains. The rest of the valley was covered in large swathes of green bordered on the west by a river and then more mountains. Roughly halfway along the valley, a country road cut it into north and south halves. I followed the country road to a bridge where it crossed over the river and then disappeared into the mountains to the west before steering the glasses back along the highway, stopping when I found the town three-quarters of the way down the valley.

Justine was starting to fidget next to me. "There's a town in the valley," I informed her, scanning the small settlement.

"And?"

"There's smoke coming from several of the buildings," I

said, handing Justine the glasses so she could take a look.

She studied the smoke coming up from several places in the town for a long minute or two and then handed me the glasses back with a nod. I put them away, and we started down the highway into the valley.

Chapter 7

We were almost to the valley floor when the faint odor of decay hit us. Neither of us commented; the smell of rotting meat was one we both knew well. We found the thrall just a short while later. He was strung to a telephone pole with baling wire, hanging limp and unmoving. From the way the wires had worked their way into his flesh, I was fairly certain he'd been moving when he'd been strung up.

"That's a positive sign," I said sarcastically as we stopped in front of the thrall.

"Look up the road," Justine said. A telephone pole farther along the highway had a body wired to it as well, and this was one was craning its head about, trying to bite the crow pecking away at its shoulder.

"Why don't we get off the road?" I suggested. Justine nodded her head, agreeing wholeheartedly.

We moved into the evergreens on the west side of the highway just far enough to shield ourselves from anyone or anything on the road. The going was slower once we were in the trees. The ground was uneven, and the undergrowth ranged from brush to solid walls of thickets. Twice we found ourselves looking at the highway as we worked our way around heavy tangles of thorns.

"You were a scout, right?" Justine joked quietly as we stopped short of the highway for the second time. A heavily decayed thrall twenty feet away thrashed weakly against its bindings as it heard her voice.

"Never got quite so distracted marching with my fellow Marines," I said, putting a finger through one of her belt loops and pulling her back into the woods and away from the highway and the thrall. Some of the grays had strange abilities. You never knew what they might be doing with the strung-up thralls.

We walked another half hour before we heard a whistling call cut through the woods. Justine slipped behind a tree as I dropped to one knee, the UMP lifting to my shoulder as I scanned the trees and undergrowth in front of us. The whistling call cut through the air again. It sounded like it came from just in front of us. Justine looked at me, and I nodded. I wanted to see as well. We crept forward, stepping carefully, trading speed for quiet. We made it through a thicket of undergrowth just in time to see a man dart away in front of us.

"Watch my back," I whispered to Justine as I stalked forward, creeping forward until I was hiding in brush not ten feet from the country road we'd seen from higher up on the mountain. We'd crossed roughly halfway through the valley. The highway was off to my left, and the country road was in front of me, leading off to my right. The other side of the country road was filled with the evenly spaced trees of an apple orchard. A large billboard was tilted to face traffic coming down the country road toward the highway. For just eight dollars, you could pick all the apples you could fit in a basket. I sank lower into the brush as the man I'd seen dart away disappeared behind the sign.

I sat and watched, my finger resting on the trigger guard of the UMP. Justine wasn't good at following directions; she slipped into the brush next to me after waiting less than five minutes. I held my finger to my lips and pointed to the sign across the street. A man's leg was just visible at the rear corner of the billboard. Justine put two fingers to her eyes, and then pointed across the road, then at my chest with a mild look of reproach. I shook my head and pointed up the road. Whoever was behind the sign wasn't trying to hide from us; he was focused on the country road. Justine nodded and hunkered down to wait next to me.

It wasn't long before we saw movement on the road to our right. A man and a teen were walking toward us. The larger of the two fellows was at least six foot two and 230 pounds. He was wearing a blue hoodie that hid his face and swung a sledgehammer at his side as he walked as if it were a cane, gripping the metal head in his hand. The teen had close-cropped hair covering his coffee-colored skin and carried a baseball bat over one shoulder. Both of them wore overstuffed backpacks and walked with the hyperalert head movements of men who'd already run into all kinds of badness.

They were within a hundred feet of the billboard when a man stepped out from behind the sign with his hands in the air, one of them holding a half-eaten apple. "Ho there," he called out, keeping his hands in the air as he walked to the middle of the country road.

The two travelers jumped and took their weapons in their hands, staring at the newcomer, scanning him from head to toe. "We got nothing worth stealing or killing for," the big traveler yelled, stepping in front of his buddy.

"I wouldn't have stepped out and announced myself if I were going to try and rob you," the man said, lowering his apple to take a bite.

"And what about your friends?" the big man asked, pointing at the sign with the end of the sledge with no visible sign of effort.

"We didn't know who you were; we're just playing it safe," Apple Man said, glancing back at the billboard. "Come on," he called out, waving with his free hand until two more men came appeared from behind the sign. They stepped out slowly, trying not to spook the two travelers. One of the men held a crossbow across his chest. It was cocked and loaded. The other fellow had an odd-looking truncheon.

"Who are you?" the big man said loudly before turning and saying something more quietly to his friend.

"My name is Chad," the man with the apple replied. "We make sure everything is safe before it reaches our town," he explained. "And who are you?"

"My name is Felix," the big guy said.

"Why don't you take your hood off so we can see your face?" Chad suggested.

"Huh?" Felix asked, making no move to lower his hood. The three ambushers tensed, and the one with the crossbow looked like he was about to lift it to his shoulder.

"Most bad things don't really like the sun," Chad said,

holding up a hand to keep his two friends still for just a moment longer. Felix laughed and pulled off his hood. The moment he did, the three men from town visibly relaxed. Felix had the same coffee-colored skin as his friend.

"So can me and my brother go now?" he asked, taking another step back.

"You don't have any sunglasses on you, do you?" Chad asked.

"No."

"Then you're free to go. We have a small town up ahead; it's not much, but we have food and there are safe places to sleep. As long as you work, you won't have any problems. Everyone works if they want to eat," Chad said.

"Haven't seen living people since Montrose," Felix mused.

"Food and shelter," Chad said enticingly.

"You going to walk us in?" Felix asked warily.

"No, it's just up the road, past the orchards and then the pumpkin fields."

"OK, are you the ones stringing the walkers to the telephone poles?" There must have been decorations along the country road as well.

"The Farmer runs the town; he's a bit superstitious, but he keeps us safe. He thinks it keeps them away," Chad explained.

"We can leave anytime?"

"Just as long as you only take what you came with," Chad said.

"OK," Felix replied, nodding his head. He took a few tentative steps toward the three men, still watching them warily.

"There's just one thing," Chad said when the distance between them was closed by half. "You don't have any guns, do you?"

"Guns?" Felix asked as if it were a dumb question. The man with the crossbow was easing his weapon up slowly. The big man noticed. "If I had a gun, do you think I'd have been pointing my fucking sledge at you? Lost my pistol back in Scranton."

"You sure? The Farmer runs this town and keeps the

peace; he doesn't need people shooting each other and drawing the biters from everywhere within earshot down on us."

"No guns," Felix confirmed.

"Get going, then," Chad said, nodding to the highway behind him. "You can't miss the town. Look for the big blue barn when you get in. That's where most of the newcomers bed down."

"Thanks," Felix said, watching the three men as they walked back into the orchard.

We waited until the road was clear and slipped back into the trees far enough to talk safely. "No guns, that sound rational to you?" I asked, a touch of excitement in my voice. We were close.

"If you were a gray and you've seen what kind of damage a Marine can do with one, maybe," Justine said. We were both thinking the same thing. This was Haeslig's town.

"Let's backtrack and cut across to the other side of the highway. I want to get around their lookout post without being seen." Justine nodded agreement, and we backtracked through the woods for a good twenty minutes before creeping back out to the highway. We were far enough from where the country road not to be seen, but we had no way of knowing if there were other watchers about. Justine darted across first, and then when no one raised the alarm, I followed.

The cover on the east side of the highway changed from step to step. At times we had thick evergreens and plenty of cover, and at others the mountains pushed down almost to the highway itself, leaving us to scurry across rocky, nearly open ground to get by. We moved cautiously, watching for signs of another sentry post.

After two hours of moving, we came to the end of the woods, or at least the edge of the woods. A firebreak had been cut in the trees. It ran right up the side of the mountain. Out in front of us, in the middle of the clearing, a large steel transmission tower stood. Its base was a mass of writhing, wriggling bodies. Thralls had been wired around each of the electrical tower's struts, and not just singly like the telephone poles. Thralls faced in every direction, and it looked like fresher specimens had been wired right over the expired. In places the bodies were three and four thick.

"Haeslig said he didn't like thralls," Justine said as we watched the base of the tower.

"I think he said he didn't like being linked to them. But maybe it's not him; we already killed one gray who worked for him. Maybe he has more. This has to be some kind of alarm system."

"I figured as much," Justine said, then turned to look up the mountain to our east. "Looks like we hit a dead end," she continued. There was no way we were getting across the firebreak without the thralls seeing us.

"I guess it's time to see what kind of hospitality they have in town," I said, backing away from the firebreak. It didn't take us long to reach the highway. The orchards were directly across from us, and farther south we could see what looked like fields going to seed. Justine crossed first, stopping just inside the orchard to wait for me. When no alarm went up, I followed, and we moved deeper into the rows of apple trees, breathing in the overpowering scent. Justine sneezed once and then stifled a second, cursing under her breath. Her nose was very sensitive.

A few rows in, we found stacks of plastic bushels scattered around the ground under the trees. Some of the plastic containers were half filled with apples, and the ground was littered with fallen fruit. Justine snatched an apple out of a bushel as we walked by, feeling its firmness in her hand before eating it in three large mouthfuls. By the third bite, she could barely keep it all in her mouth, and apple juice mixed with saliva was running down her chin. She smiled at me with a mouth full of half-chewed apple when she saw me staring. She had the strangest way of being lovely.

I picked one for myself and ate it more slowly, savoring the taste as we walked through the orchard. Farther on we found a well-worn dirt road cutting through the trees. We crossed it like we belonged there and kept walking. The orchard ended not too far beyond the dirt road. The trees stopped in a neat line, giving way to rolling farmland. A small hill rose up before us, covered in tall grass, and smoke drifted into the air from the far side.

We were three-quarters of the way to the top of the hill when obnoxious laughter froze us in our tracks. We crouched in the tall, swaying grass and listened as several men shot bravado back and forth. It was hard to hear what they were saying, but it had the feeling of a boisterous game of one-upmanship. We crept up the slope, parting the grass in front of us until we could look down the hill.

Fields stretched out across the gently sloping land in front of us. Several plots were dotted with orange pumpkins; the rest were growing weeds. Off to our left, a shack of a building stood on cinder blocks. The smoke was coming from a chimney in the corner of the building. Almost directly in front of us, two rough-looking fellows with scraggily beards were laughing. One of them was struggling to cock a crossbow. The other fellow was laughing and drinking a beer as his buddy struggled and finally got the thing cocked and loaded with a bolt.

I watched as the man put the crossbow to his shoulder and fired, blinking my eyes several times before I let myself acknowledge what I was seeing. The bolt had flown over a section of pumpkin patch to strike a brute in the back. I had to bite my tongue before I blurted out, "Holy shit," and actually heard Justine mutter it under her breath.

There were two brutes standing in the pumpkin field. They were roughly humanoid but nearly half again as tall as a man. Their heads were large and blocky, sitting almost on top of their shoulders, and their skin was rough and patterned, reminding me of an elephant's hide. The taller of the two brutes might have been the largest of its kind I'd ever seen. His shoulders were broad and wide, and the shirt over his chest didn't hide the massive bands of muscles on his arms. The huge beast turned, his broad face full of rage as he whooped in pain. The crossbow bolt had hit him in the back and dropped to the ground. I watched as the man with the crossbow fumbled for another bolt. They were tipped with a flattened disc of wood.

Chains rattled as the other brute turned around at the noise. I almost cursed in surprise for a second time. The smaller brute had unkempt, black hair framing her square face and what I think were breasts under her crudely made shirt. It was the first time I'd ever seen a female brute. She was shackled to a heavy wooden wagon that was half full of pumpkins.

The two rednecks laughed as the female brute tried to get to the big male, tripping over her chains as she made panicked noises. The two men seemed to think her agitated hooting was the funniest thing they'd ever heard. The male stepped in front of the female as she came to him, putting his body between her and the crossbow. She put a hand on his side from behind him, and I watched as he covered it protectively. It seemed to calm her.

The two men were still laughing when the huge brute raised his head, a look of hatred burning in his large, dark eyes. His blocky head was covered in sparse salt-and-pepper hair, giving him the appearance for just a moment of being old; then my eyes drifted down to his wide shoulders and the bands of muscles that covered his body. If he was old, he still looked capable of benching a school bus. The brute took a half step in the direction of his tormenters, his lip raising to show large, square teeth, and then he stopped with a small jerk as he reached the limit of his chains.

The two rednecks didn't seem impressed. They kept on smiling, and the one not holding the crossbow raised a baton, pointing it at the brute. The big creature looked at the club but didn't react until the man triggered the weapon and I realized it was a shock wand. Electricity arced up and down the length of the wand, crackling all the while. The brute's eyes locked on the little bolts of lightning, and the anger drained out of him, his head slowly falling. The two men laughed as the brute's chin fell to his chest in defeat. "Get back to work," the man with the wand said, poking it in the air at the big creature as it sparked and crackled. The brute turned around sullenly and pushed the female ahead of him, pointing to the pumpkins. The two rednecks were laughing and joking, congratulating each other on a job well done.

"Holy shit," Justine whispered. We'd seen brutes tear through cars, buildings, and men. I nodded my head, just as surprised as she was. I'd seen a brute fight to his last dying breath as his neck was cut open by the slashing claws of a gray, but I'd never seen one cowed before. We backed off the hill slowly and made our way into the cover of the orchard before we stopped.

"That was strange," I said, shaking my head in wonder.

"Yeah, first thralls on telephone poles, and now brutes picking fruit and being watched by a few rednecks."

"I don't think pumpkins are fruit," I said.

"They are," she assured me.

I let it go. "WC better appreciate this."

"I hope he does," Justine said, her voice taking on a thoughtful tone. "We need to get into town and find him."

"I guess I need to lose this," I said, patting the UMP.

"The plan is to walk into town in the broad daylight then?" Justine asked, raising an eyebrow at me as if she didn't completely agree.

"They're letting people come and go. Hopefully two more won't be noticed, and we need to figure out if this is the right place. Some other gray could have put all this together," I reminded her. She hesitated but finally nodded in agreement. "So let's find someplace to stash our gear and get this over with," I said, not overly happy about having to ditch my UMP.

We moved farther into the orchard and crossed back over the dirt road, moving along the neat rows of trees until we found a stump. Not far away tree branches and other debris had been piled in a trash heap. It was a good place to stash our gear. We dug away at the ground under the branches until we had enough room to put our packs in.

"Please be careful," I said, trying to hide my smile as Justine tried twice to put her pistol down her pants unsuccessfully. She stuck her tongue out at me and then sighed, giving in to the inevitable. She just didn't have enough bulk to hide the weapon.

My UMP went into my pack next. "You look like you just lost your puppy dog," Justine said as I stuffed my pack into the ground next to hers. "It's not like you had to give them all up after all," she chided as I pulled on a light jacket to hide my shoulder rig and the pistols under my armpits. We covered the opening with branches and then pulled some of the pile down on top of it.

"One second," Justine said as I started to turn away from her. She grabbed my face with both her hands, smearing dirt across my cheeks. "We're still too clean," she said in explanation.

"Thank you," I said, nodding my head as I reached out to return the favor. She laughed as she twirled away from me, rubbing dirt onto her own face before I had the chance to catch her. It didn't stop me from trying anyway. The only thing I wanted to do in that moment was grab her and carry her to the ground. She saw the look in my eyes and wagged her finger at me. "There will be time for that later, big boy."

"There better be," I grumbled, stopping and looking at her. She smiled enticingly, but she was on the balls of her feet, ready to move if I did. I settled on my heels and started to work dirt into my neck and then across the back of my hands as Justine did the same. I still wanted her, even covered in dirt.

We gave each other a final once-over and decided we looked dirty enough to get by. "You think they'll let us keep these?" Justine asked as we walked back to the highway, patting the combat knife strapped to her waist and looking at my machete.

"If not they're going to find out I still have my Walthers under my armpits," I said. When we reached the highway, we walked out of the orchards and turned south to head in the direction of the town. It felt strange to be standing out in the open after stalking around all day.

"Have you thought about what happens if we walk right into him?" Justine mused.

"I kill him and we rescue WC; then we leave."

"Simple as that?" Justine asked with a smile.

"Simple plans are best. But if everything goes sideways and we get separated, make for the river and head upstream," I said. The town was just coming into sight, the smoke from multiple chimneys drifting into the air.

"Let's just not let things go sideways," Justine said. We kept our eyes on the town as it grew in front of us. It wasn't long before we could hear the general din of the community.

"It looks like a decent number of people live here," I said. "Let's blend in and try to find out where they would be keeping WC, and then get out of here—together."

"Agreed," Justine said, grabbing my hand and holding it in hers. We walked that way until we were almost to the highway exit; then four fellows hanging out around the edge of town saw us and started down the street to meet us. One was carrying an axe, two had shock wands, and one had a crossbow. They met us halfway.

"Hello there," the man with the crossbow said, his eyes squinting up a little as he looked us over.

"We don't want any trouble. Chad said there was food if we worked," I said, letting just a hint of anxiety into my voice as I looked at the four men. I hoped I'd hit the right tone, just enough concern at being outnumbered but not so much that it triggered a response. Predators will attack if you show them fear, and I had no doubt the men in front of me were predators. They were looking at us like we were easy meat.

"Funny how that works sometimes, isn't it? What are you doing on the road?"

"Heading south. We heard there was a shipping depot in Harrisburg full of loaded semis. Food and supplies for the winter."

"Good luck with that. Half of Harrisburg is burned to the ground, and you don't want to walk down the streets that are left," the man said, spitting out of the corner of his mouth halfway through his statement. I nodded, letting the news hit me as it were the blow it should have been. Justine clutched my shoulder as if the news were a punch to the gut.

"You have anything of value?"

"Not much, but I can work."

"Everyone works, or they don't eat," Crossbow said. "You have any guns?"

"No, we had a shotgun, but we ran out of shells and traded it for a box of protein bars back in Hawley."

"Good, there are no guns allowed in town. The big blue

barn is right up the street. They shut their doors at sundown and won't open them until morning. Be inside by then, or you can take your chances in the dark."

"There are thralls around?"

"You mean biters? Yes, there are always some wandering around; just be inside before dark. They come out of the hills in ones and twos mostly, but every now and then we get a good horde." He seemed to enjoy telling me about the horde.

"Got it," I said, fighting back a sudden urge to grab him and ask WTF was really going on in town. I pushed the emotions aside. In all likelihood the man was just as ignorant of the situation as we had been when we first arrived in New Dover. Besides, making a scene would draw unwanted attention.

"Don't cause any trouble, or you'll find yourself in the pit," the man said, motioning for us to get moving. I made a sound that might have been agreement, wondering what the hell the "pit" was.

My first thought as we walked into the community was that it really was more of a shantytown that had sprung up around a farmhouse and its outbuildings than anything else. We spotted the appropriately named big blue barn just ahead of us and went in that direction. My second thought was that Justine and I hadn't rubbed enough dirt into our skin. The people were filthy, and I had to make a conscious effort not to wrinkle my noise and cover my mouth with my shirt.

We stopped in front of the big blue barn. The front doors were open wide, making it easy to see into the interior. A fifty-gallon drum had been converted into a stove and was vented outside with crudely built ductwork. Cots, sleeping bags, and blankets littered the floor and as much of the second-floor loft as we could see.

A sign drawn in black marker listed out the going rates for a night. A stack of firewood, a can of food, and a candle were all equal to a night's rest. The words "Apple" and "Pumpkin" were written at the bottom of the sign with circles around them. A line cut diagonally across each of the circles. Someone else had drawn a remarkably lifelike penis with a hand around it in the corner. It looked like a halfhearted attempt to scrub it away had been made, leaving it smudged but still visible.

"I think you have more experience at that than me," Justine said with a straight face, looking at the crude drawing.

"I have plenty of protein bars in my pockets," I said, shaking off the horrible thought Justine had put in my head. "Let's take a look around before it gets too late." I put my arm out for her to take, and she slipped hers through mine. We walked down the street, looking at the people and the dwellings while trying not to stare. The people watched us back out of the corners of their eyes, looking us over, but whenever I tried to catch one of their gazes they shied away. What I saw in their eyes was a mixture of fear and resentment I'd seen before. It was the glare of people who had very little and were wondering how you were so lucky as to be different. It made me wish we'd rolled in the dirt instead of just smearing it on our skin.

We walked as slowly as we dared without attracting attention. The Farmer's house loomed off to our left above everything else. The town itself had a fairly simple layout. The Farmer's house sat in the middle of the community. There was a respectful distance left around his house, and then an inner street. Alleys cut from the inner street through the back-to-back shanties to the outer street we were walking on. From above it would have looked like two squares, one slightly larger than the other around the central house at the community's core.

We saw every type of construction imaginable. There were garden sheds converted into homes as well as shacks made out of everything from plywood and rough-cut lumber to cinder blocks with corrugated tin roofs. We stopped and stood by an alley that cut across both the streets, giving us a view of the old Victorian house and its wraparound porch in the middle of town. A black wrought-iron fence circled the house, the tips curling outward to ward off anyone who might decide to climb it. Even from a distance, it was clear the fencing was not part of the original property. It looked completely out of place and cut across what had once been the walkway to the side entrance of the house.

We moved on when a kid playing at the front of a shack nearby started to look us over and went inside, calling for his mom. A little farther on, the street changed. Shacks and other living space changed over to tightly packed stalls. Dirty and tired-looking men and women were busy haggling with the owners of the stalls around us, bartering for everything from plastic containers to knives, household supplies, and various other kinds of goods. One of the busier stalls was selling apple mash and other alcohol. The men standing around it were already in their cups, their faces flushed red. Twice we passed solid-looking men standing around looking bored, but they were clearly policing the shopping bazaar. Shock wands hung off their belts.

At the end of the stalls, there was another transition. The outer street turned left, but a smaller path cut straight forward into the fields at the back of the town. There was a wide dirt path lined on either side by tents. Some of them looked like they'd been stolen from a Boy Scout camp while others were simple structures made from tarps and plastic sheeting. A realtor sign had been painted over and modified before it was stuck in the dirt. It said "Closed at Dusk— Open for Everything Else." It took me a moment to realize I was looking at the red-light district. Various ladies, girls, and young men stood in front of the tents, calling out to the light traffic walking down their path, trying to entice them with catcalls and shows of flesh.

"What kind of people would allow that?" Justine said quietly as we turned left and followed the main road. I didn't answer; I didn't have anything I could say. Her faith in humanity was higher than my own.

We were at the far end of town. Shacks and cabins were built up on the left side of the street, but the right opened up on a field of hard-packed dirt. A large multistory barn sat back and off to the left, and a group of men were sitting out in front playing cards at a picnic table.

"What is that?" Justine asked. Directly in front of us, set back a good fifty paces from the street, was what looked like a large oblong ring of timbers sticking up from the ground at about waist height.

"Looks like they started to build a wall," I said, walking toward it. It wasn't until we were closer that we were able to see what the top of the timbers was hiding. A forty-by-twenty-foot pit had been sunk into the ground. The logs sticking up at varying heights were just the ends of the timbers rising up above the grade of the earth. A platform had been built on the far side with a post rising up on either end along the edge of the pit. One of the posts held a cross arm that stretched out over the sunken ground below, and the other had a wrought-iron bell bolted to it. A knotted cord hung from the center of the bell, waiting for someone to pull it.

"Let's get out of here," Justine whispered, sniffing at the air as the smell of wet decay drifted up from the soft earthen bottom of the pit.

"Might be too late for that," I said, looking behind us. Several people were walking our way, and on the other side of the pit a ten-or-eleven-year-old boy was climbing onto the platform wearing dirty jeans and a sweatshirt a few sizes too large for his body. The boy gave us a shy wave as he walked to the bell and grabbed the cord. He rang the bell with hard jerks, using his whole body to pull the rope.

The sounds hit as if they were physical blows, and I felt Justine stiffen at my side. I turned my head, but it was already too late. People were pouring out of the rest of the town and filling the field behind us as the bell continued to ring. Justine tried to pull away, but I wrapped my arm around her and held her close. "I smell thralls," she half said, half grunted into my ear as she touched my side with dagger-tipped fingers for emphasis.

"Shut your eyes and hold still," I commanded, adding between my teeth, "The whole town is coming this way. If we walk now, everyone and their brother will notice." I smiled at the boy on the platform as he stepped away from the bell and put his dirty fingers in his ears, giving me a mischievous grin before disappearing off the back of the platform.

People rushed to get to the best positions around the pit's waist-high wall, pushing us up against the timbers as those behind tried to press forward. For a moment I was afraid we were going to be pinned, and then the press let up as curses and elbows were thrown. The crowd settled further as two men pulled open the doors to the large barn set well behind the pit, and a tight knot of people marched out of its interior.

As they approached I could see that the men on the outside ranks all had shock wands hanging from their belts. The majority of them stopped at the rear of the platform, letting a smaller group climb the stairs. As they arranged themselves on the platform, I could see several men flanking a small figure. Then a tall man stepped to the front of the platform, obscuring those behind him.

I half expected him to recite the Gettysburg Address. The man was dressed in a dark suit and wore a top hat atop his head, partially hiding his stern face. If he'd grown out a beard, he could have made money as a historical actor. People were leaning forward, waiting for him to speak as he looked over the crowd, letting the tension build.

"This is bad," Justine whispered, looking down the edge of the pit at the people staring up at the platform in expectation.

"Yeah" was all I could say as movement in the pit caught my eye. A single large door had been built into the timber walls just below the platform, and something had just pushed against it, opening it just a fraction.

"Justice," the tall man bellowed, breaking the silence. "All is lost without justice." The people around us hung on every word. "Abigail has been caught hording food!" The crowd booed as a small form was roughly pulled to the front of the platform by two men. They held onto her arms from either side, holding her up. Her head hung on her chest, and it was hard to tell if her face was covered in bruises or dirt. She looked to be in her early teens.

"It was one can of stew," she screamed, lifting her head in rage as she yelled at the crowd.

The woman next to us laughed. "Vaughn isn't going to like that," she said to the man next to her. There was pleasure and expectation in her voice, making my skin crawl. No sooner had the woman spoken than the tall man on the stage lashed out, catching Abigail on the back of the head with a blow that would have sent her down into the pit if the men at her sides weren't holding onto her.

"Justice is mandatory," Vaughn continued harshly. He let the crowd cheer and clap before he continued. "And at the same time, justice without mercy has no meaning."

I would have thought the statement would have deflated the crowd, but the word "mercy" only made them twice as eager. "Abigail has been found guilty, but her brother has asked for mercy," he said, taking a long pause for effect, "and so it shall be."

There was a small commotion on the platform as bodies parted to make room for another man to be hauled forward. He was positioned on the lip of the stage just long enough for the crowd to cheer, and then he was hurled over the edge. The crowd roared as he landed in the dirt on all fours and then climbed to his feet slowly, turning around to look up at the platform. I think the man blew a kiss to the girl, then ended the gesture by giving Vaughn the finger. The crowd was going wild.

Vaughn let the sound wash over him, a smile touching the corners of his lips as he looked down at the man in the pit. Then he held out a hand, and everyone fell silent. "For the crime of hoarding food, Abigail's brother has accepted the mercy of the Farmer, taking the place of his sister. If he survives three rounds, he will once again be a member of our community." The crowd cheered and broke out into a hundred conversations as men called out wagers and bets and a folding chair was brought to the front of the platform for Vaughn to sit on.

"I heard Craig fought a horde and killed more than a dozen biters with an axe down in Allentown," the woman next to us said.

"Yeah, let's see if he gets an axe," someone else said sarcastically. Several people around us broke out laughing.

Up on the platform, Vaughn was still standing, staring down at the man he'd just condemned. The crowds around us hushed again as Vaughn held his hands out to his sides, then burst out into a murmur as foremen stepped up with an assortment of weapons and objects. Someone yelled, "Tin can," and everyone laughed. Then the handle of a framing hammer was slapped into one of Vaughn's hands just a fraction of a second before a makeshift club was slapped into the other. Another burst of murmurs broke out behind us as more betting started, and it hit me that this was all a very carefully orchestrated series of events. These people had clearly seen this spectacle before.

"*Panem et circenses*," I mumbled to myself as Vaughn raised both weapons, comparing their weights, raising and lowering them as half the crowd cheered for each choice in turn. Vaughn smiled as he lifted the short section of branch masquerading as a club higher and then tossed it into the dirt at Craig's feet. Sections of the crowd behind us cheered, and others moaned as bets were lost or won.

"Door, door, door," the mass of people around us chanted, at first softly, then growing in intensity as Craig picked up his club and squared off with the large wooden door built into the wall of the pit. The door swung open a moment later to reveal a single thrall.

People booed. The thrall was in bad shape. It moved slowly, shambling out into the daylight and almost falling over as the sun blinded it. Craig felt the weight of his club and moved to the center of the pit, slapping the wood into the palm of one hand, leading the decaying thrall to him with the sound. People continued to boo as the rotten carcass shambled at Craig. As soon as it was within arm's reach, he swung the branch like a baseball bat, crushing in the side of the thrall's head. Half the people booed while the other half disjointedly chanted, "Door."

There wasn't a long wait. Once the thrall was on the ground and not moving, the door opened again, revealing two more thralls. The crowd cheered with approval; the second two were a good deal fresher, and as soon as they saw Craig, they broke into a shambling run. He waited until they'd closed half the distance and then took several steps to his right.

Craig was smart; by changing his position at the last moment, he forced them to come at him single file versus two abreast. The first thrall of the pair went down easy, and Craig was ready for the second a moment later when it stepped into his reach. He swung his club again, making contact with the side of the second thrall's head with a loud crack. The crowd sucked in a breath as the shaft of the club exploded. Craig looked at the bit of wood still in his hand as the thrall crumpled to the ground, the end of the club embedded in its skull.

Abigail started to scream, flailing her arms at Vaughn until he hit her again, driving her to the floor of the platform. She was on her hands and knees, crying, when the door was thrown open again. Craig looked up at Vaughn and shook the bit of wood in his hand as he screamed in anger. They'd given him a branch from a rotted tree.

The crowd was going wild, and several people were screaming about bets to be won or lost as three thralls charged out the open door. The freshest bodies had clearly been saved for last. The three thralls looked like they'd had heartbeats very recently, and they moved with a fluidness and speed the more rotten thralls had lacked.

They were on Craig in an instant.

He used the shaft of his club like a knife as the first thrall charged him, driving it into the thing's neck with enough force to knock the creature a step to the side. But it wasn't a killing blow, and as the thrall stumbled it grabbed onto Craig's shirt with one hand, dragging him with it. He broke its grip with a blow from his forearm, but he'd been carried off balance. The second thrall hit him in the side with an awkward tackle, almost taking them both off their feet.

Craig twisted and drove his elbow into the thrall wrapped about his midsection with enough force to stun it, allowing him to break free. The thrall straightened and stepped forward, its hands reaching out. Craig brushed aside the thrall's groping attack and let loose with a roundhouse, rocking its head to the side. Craig turned, keeping the thrall in front of him as he rocked its head from side to side with well-placed punches. He'd totally lost track of the third thrall until it grabbed his right arm.

I saw the flash of horror on Craig's face as he realized his error. He'd focused too much on the second thrall, trying to finish it off. Craig pulled the third thrall in front of him, punching it in the face with his left hand as he tried to break free. I knew the moment the thrall started to tighten its grip. So did everyone else. The cry that came from Craig's lips was shrill and tainted with surprised agony. He tried to bite off the scream but continued in a high-pitched cry as he punched the thrall in the face. The thrall took no notice, pulling him closer bit by bit. Tears were streaming down Craig's face as he put his hand on the thrall's chest and threw his body backward, trying to break free from the grip of the undead.

"No!" Craig screamed as the second thrall latched onto him. I closed my eyes, not wanting to watch as Craig was carried to the ground. All three of the thralls were on him now, tearing and biting. Craig's screams rose higher for just a moment and then faded to a strangled moan before stopping completely. Abigail sobbed and cried, the sound of her mourning filling the air as her brother's voice faded.

I opened my eyes when I heard the door to the pit thrown open again. A man stepped out, bringing another cheer from the people circling the pit. He was dressed in black body armor and had a riot shield strapped to one arm. His free hand was holding a bulky orange gun. I was trying to figure out what it was as he walked up to the thralls. They were so busy eating they didn't react until he put the end of the odd-looking gun to the closest thrall's head and pulled the trigger.

There was a puff of gas and a pop as the gun went off, and then the thrall was falling to the ground, a nail caving in part of its skull. The man in the riot gear stepped back as the other two thralls surged to their feet. He batted one away with the shield and stepped directly into the path of the next, putting the nail gun to the thrall's forehead before it had a chance to attack. The thrall dropped with a framing nail buried in its head. The surviving thrall grabbed the shield and shook it violently, trying to force it out of the way. The man let the riot shield get carried low and casually put the nail gun over the top. There were two pops. The last thrall went down with a pair of nails in its hairline.

The man hung the nail gun on his belt and pulled off a length of cord. He looped one end around Craig's neck and dragged him to the area in front of the platform, tossing the other end of the rope up over the arm reaching out over the pit. He hauled Craig's body up until it was swinging and tied the cord off to a hitch screwed into one of the timbers. The crowd didn't stop cheering until the man walked back into the tunnels. He never looked up, never acknowledged the crowd in any way. The crowd didn't care—they loved him.

Vaughn dragged Abigail off the stage crying, and then she disappeared into the group of men walking back to the barn in the distance. Justine and I stood there as the crowd slowly broke apart around us. The day was growing short, and the people around us were already talking about going back to their shacks and locking up for the night. We let the tide carry us away from the pit, a little stunned from what we'd just seen.

"It's getting late," Justine said, looking up at the sky. "WC has got to be in the house." She nodded to the center of town with a raised eyebrow.

"Or the barn," I said, my eyes drawn to the structure sitting off in the field with nothing around it except the pit. "We might only have once chance at this. If we screw it up, WC is the one who pays."

"These people are animals," Justine said quietly as she struggled to control her anger.

"We need more information before we move," I said. We'd followed the crowd back to the outside street as we talked.

"Let's go buy our night's lodging then," Justine said resignedly. The streets were already starting to empty. Behind us we heard a generator cough to life, and both of us turned to see several lights around the barn flicker on. "I still think he'll be in the house," Justine said, looking at the ring of light around the building.

"Maybe," I said, distracted by the site of the brutes pulling their wagon in from the pumpkin fields. "I want to see where they go." I grabbed Justine's elbow before she could head off in the direction of the big blue barn. We stepped back off the road to let the brutes pass. The men we'd watched torturing them earlier followed behind the cart, passing a bottle between them. The brutes kept their eyes on the ground in front of their feet as they walked, their shoulders curled forward.

We followed the wagon down to the end of the street and around the corner. By the time we rounded the bend, the brutes were already tilting the wagon up so the pumpkins rolled out in front of a one-story building fronted with three sets of garage doors. When the wagon was empty, they set it down and back away, sitting on their haunches next to each other. The female leaned into the larger male, her head against his shoulder.

Ragged-looking men and woman came out of the building and began to carry the pumpkins inside. One of them rolled a door open wider, and we could see bushels of apples already stacked inside. Across the street, on the opposite corner, was another storage area with stacks of cordwood piled head high. The two foremen guarding the brutes settled themselves on a stack of empty crates and continued to pass their bottle back and forth.

I wandered over to the men sharing their bottle.

"What in the world are those things?" I asked, letting a bit of awe into my voice.

"Ogres," the man carrying the shock wand said. "Be careful, or they'll eat you," he said melodramatically.

"How do you keep them under control?" I asked, not able to hold back. I didn't want to draw any unwanted attention to myself, but I had to know.

"The Farmer trained them. They had all the fight beat out of them."

"The Farmer?"

"You're new." He waited until I nodded. "Whose house do you think sits at the center of town?"

"Was that him at the trial today?" I asked, pretty sure I already knew the answer.

"That's funny. I'll tell Vaughn you said that the next time I see him. He'll piss himself. The Farmer doesn't come out and hobnob with scum like us. Now get lost." It was his turn to take the bottle.

"Any chance of getting on one of your crews?" I asked.

"Tomorrow, meet us here in the morning. You can come pick apples, and you'll get fed some dinner when the work is done," the man said dismissively. It wasn't what I really meant, but I could tell from his demeanor I was pushing it. I thanked him and walked back to where Justine had hung back a little, waiting for me.

We backtracked and headed for the big blue barn, neither of us saying anything until we were a little ways from anyone who might hear us. "How do you train something that can rip a man to pieces with its bare hands?" Justine asked quietly as we walked.

"Maybe it's not so much trained as following orders," I said.

"The plot thickens," Justine said theatrically as we approached the barn.

Chapter 8

The cost of a night in the big blue barn came down to several condiment packets I had in my pocket and two protein bars. In exchange we were given a place on the floor. The large woman running the place was willing to rent us a blanket for the night for the cost of another protein bar, but I turned her down. It seemed like a high price to pay to get fleas and who knew what else. We claimed the barren bit of corner by the wood-burning stove, figuring it would help keep the night chill away.

I sat with my back against the wall of the barn and patted the floor between my legs. Justine settled against me, turning around just long enough to give me a kiss before resting her head on my chest. I let me eyes close to slits, listening as the people around us chatted quietly, settling in for the night.

A middle-aged man next to us was talking to his companion, complaining. "I'm telling you it's not fair; they set up Abigail."

"I heard it was because Craig was talking about taking his sister and making a go of it on their own. They set up his sister knowing he'd take the fall for her."

"Nah," the other man shot back. "I heard it was because Nail Gun Norman thought little old Abbey was a cutie." I felt Justine tense against me.

"You both better keep your mouths shut, or you'll find yourself in trouble, too. The Farmer has a way of finding out when people flap their lips too much," a woman cut in, silencing the two men.

Justine squeezed my thigh a moment after the woman said it, and I tapped my finger on her side, letting her know I'd heard it as well. Some of the grays had special abilities. Haeslig's was the ability to read peoples' memories from their blood. Not conclusive evidence by any means, but it was a hint that we might be in the right place.

I continued to listen, hoping to hear something else of value, but the rest of the conversations were limited to everyday banalities. At some point I zoned out and drifted off. I woke up sometime in the early morning with Justine nudging my leg with the tip of her boot. She was standing over me, her finger to her lips.

My knee popped loudly as I stood up, and I could feel Justine's glare even though I couldn't see it. She held out her hand and guided me toward the dull-red glow coming from the embers sitting in the bottom of the fifty-gallon drum turned into a stove. There was a small gap in the wall where the chimney vent passed through to the outside. She pointed at the line of brighter darkness shining through from the other side.

I leaned forward, trying not to burn my face as I looked through the gap between the chimney and the wall. I stared out into the alley, trying to see something out of the norm. My heart rate jumped as something large moved into view out of the shadows. I held my breath as the shape pounced on something on the ground. There was a brief flurry of movement, and then the shape slowly rose to two legs, taking on the outline of a man. He turned as I watched, giving me just a glimpse of the large rat between his teeth. Then he was staring right at me, or at least at the chimney pipe sticking through the barn wall. I pulled my face away, my hand going for one of my pistols instinctively.

Justine grabbed my hand before I could draw the weapon, looking around us at the other sleeping forms strewn about the floor of the barn. She gently pulled me away and peeked through the gap before nodding her head at me. I shrugged my shoulders, not understanding, so she put one hand out flat and made the motion of walking away with her fingers.

We crept back to our corner and sank to the floor as quietly as we could. "Was it a thrall?" I mouthed in her ear. We switched positions so she could put her mouth to my ear.

"I think it was just man," she said, something in her voice telling me how horrible that was. Justine's ability to sense thralls and grays had saved us more times than I could count. "Gabrielle didn't...wasn't..." Justine said, struggling for the right words. "She didn't feel any different either." She didn't have to say the rest. I knew what she was thinking. Gabrielle had slept right next to us, and she'd been something not human as well—something able to turn others with a bite.

Justine fell quiet, her head resting against me as we both thought about what it meant. Time crawled. Everything in the town felt wrong; and sitting in the near dark waiting for the sun to come up felt like trying to hold still while a dentist went to work with no Novocain—I wanted to get up, I wanted to move, but all I could do was sit there wait.

The barn doors weren't unlocked and opened until the sun was fully up. I had to fight the urge to push my way through the others milling about once the doors were thrown open. I was never so happy to have the sun burn across my eyes. The night had dragged on and on. Justine stretched and moved off around the barn to where we'd seen the rat get snatched up. Then kept walking, moving straight into the brush bordering the town.

"Keep guard, this is really important," she told me as she squatted down in the grass.

"Very important," I said as I turned around so she could finish relieving herself.

"Guys are so lucky; you can pee anywhere," she said as she stood up and buckled her belt.

"Yes, I've always thought of standing to pee as a huge advantage," I said sarcastically. "Now let's go pick some apples and stay out of trouble until tonight."

"Yeah, let's pick some apples, but after that I want to check in on the girl from yesterday."

"We can't save everyone," I said quietly, a lump forming in my throat as I said it. It was a hard lesson I'd learned overseas. There were tons of innocent families and sweet kids walking around Iraq, Mogadishu, and dozens of other hotspots I'd had the pleasure of serving in. There was a limit to what you could do, and if you didn't recognize that, you risked letting it push you over the edge. It was a horrible lesson.

"No, but maybe we can save just one," Justine said, her eyes locking on mine. "If Nail Gun Norman has the pull to get someone thrown into the pit, I bet he knows where WC is," she said pointedly. I hated it when she outthought me.

There was already a mixed group of men and women milling around when we made our way to the storage shed, standing well away from the two brutes chained to the wagon. The foremen with the beard picked four fellows out of the mix as soon as we got there, sending them off to cut wood with two rough-looking men in plaid shirts. The foremen told the four to do whatever the woodcutters told them and moved on to the next order of business, giving the rest of us a short speech about working and not lollygagging that would have done any grade-school teacher proud. Then he got the brutes moving, and we marched out of town.

The foremen led us into the orchards and stopped us a few rows in. He handed out baskets, and we stood there with the others, not sure what was going to happen next. I watched in surprise as the brutes moved to the base of two different trees and grabbed them at neck height in a chokehold. They shook the trees, slowly at first, and then harder until apples started to fall like rain. The female made a harsh grunting noise that I didn't recognize as laughter until she poked her head from around the tree so she could see the other brute. There was a massive smile on her face, and I was surprised by the sheer, simple joy in it.

The brutes shook the trees until the ground was covered in apples, and then they moved down the line to repeat the process. Everyone waited until the brutes were a tree down the line before getting to work. We filled baskets and stacked them in the wagon all morning. As the day wore on, I tried not to look at Justine. Every time I did, the look she gave me was a little harder. We didn't learn anything useful; no one talked more than a few words all morning. Even the foremen were mostly quiet. The only thing I found out was that I hated picking apples off the ground almost as much as watching Justine's butt in front of me and not being able to touch it.

Picking apples did give me the chance to watch the brutes, however. It felt strange to be so close to the creatures. The foreman with the crossbow always kept the two creatures in sight, but he didn't even have his weapon cocked. The people around us clearly felt uneasy around the big creatures, but I never saw the brutes do anything aggressive.

The female in particular seemed almost happy. I saw her eat an apple in a single bite and then call to the other brute in a low, deep grunt as she made a silly face at him. He smiled back cautiously and then pointed at the next tree until she moved on. When the foremen finally called a halt for the day, the female brute hooted and hollered, but she never spoke. It made me wonder if the two brutes the village used for manual labor even had the ability to speak. Maybe they were culled from the fighters because they weren't smart enough to do anything but haul a wagon.

I could almost straighten my spine fully by the time we completed the walk back to the storage shed. If we survived the night, I was going to beg Justine to rub my back. After we helped carry the bushels of apples into the storage barn, we were told to head over to the soup line. We followed the others down the street to where several picnic tables had been pulled end to end. Two older women and a few younger girls were tending to two large pots being heated over open fires. A little ways away, several other girls were washing dishes in plastic tubs full of dirty, soapy water.

We waited our turn, standing behind foremen and other work crews as we shuffled forward. When it was our turn, we were rewarded with a bowl of thin soup that had strips of white mystery meat in it. After we sat down I stirred my soup, staring at bits of meat until Justine nudged my elbow and pointed across the way where a long row of rabbit hutches stood a few feet off the ground.

"You're sure?" I asked, moving my soup around with my spoon.

She slurped down a spoonful of the broth and held a strip of meat between her teeth before pulling it into her mouth. "Definitely rabbit," she said, swallowing.

We finished eating and handed our dirty bowls over to the girls washing dishes before moving off down the street. "We need to find out where Norman lives," Justine said once we were away from the soup line.

"We need to be careful."

Justine ignored me.

We walked around the outer ring, afraid to get too close to the house at the center, and then spent an hour in the stalls of the shopping bazaar, trying to find anyone who was willing to talk. We heard a lot of gossip and a few interesting tidbits about the town. If the man trying to sell me a cast-iron frying pan was to be believed, things had been worse before the Farmer showed up a few months ago. Hardly anyone got bit anymore. No one gave us anything of any real value, though, and we didn't want to draw too much attention to ourselves by pushing the conversation too far in any one direction.

Justine took the lead when we left the bazaar. I followed her, thinking we were just making another pass around the outer street until she darted into an alley and waited for me. "Not a good idea," I said when I reached her, looking behind us to see if anyone was watching.

"We'll stay in the alley," Justine said, slipping forward before I could say anything else. I sighed and followed her through alley until we were looking at the heart of the town. A smaller inner street sat inside the outer one, and beyond that, buffered by an expanse of open ground, was the Farmer's house. I looked over the shacks on the far side of the inner street, looking up at the windows on the second level of the main house, wondering if Haeslig was looking down on us.

"We have to get off this street," I said, putting my arm around Justine and trying to pull her back into the alley. "If the girl is on the inner street, we can't risk it. He might see us." I felt like an ass saying it, but it was what it was. Justine held steady, not letting me move her.

"Three houses up on the left" was the only thing she said. I looked up and there she was. Abigail was sitting on the front porch of a small cottage, looking down into a sewing kit full of multicolored spools of thread. Clearly Norman had some clout; his cottage wasn't some shack made of cinder blocks and plywood. It was a miniature log cabin with windows and a small porch covered by an overhang. Justine started to pull against me.

"Not now, we wait until dark," I whispered, tightening my

grip around Justine as she tried to move forward. Abigail didn't notice. She held a pair of pants up close to her face as she pushed a needle into them from underneath, concentrating on her work. She pricked her finger as we watched, dropping the pants just long enough to show us her face. Her left eye was swollen shut and surrounded by an angry pallet of bruises. Justine was a heavy weight against my arm. "We wait until tonight; then he dies," I said with steel in my voice.

Justine was immediately weightless on my arm, letting me pull her back down the alley and onto the outer street. We slipped out of town by the big blue barn and into the tall grass in the fields beyond until we found a quiet spot to hunker down and wait. We each ate a protein bar and watched the sun move across the sky.

"Do you think he'll ever leave us alone?" Justine thought out loud. She was lying back in the grass, covering her eyes with one arm.

"I plan on making sure he does," I said, listening to the gentle sound of the grass as the wind moved through it.

"I just want this to be over so we can put this place behind us," she said. I knew what she meant. Even when it was at its worst, New Dover had never felt quite as corrupted as what we'd seen in town.

"Me too," I said with a sigh.

Night set slowly. We watched from a distance as the streets emptied and everyone locked up for the night, shutting their doors and pretending that plywood and nails could protect them. "Let's go hunting," Justine said when the sun dipped below the mountains to the west, her voice one octave below its normal range.

I got up and slipped through the grass, leading the way to the rear of the buildings closest to us. We slipped into an alley and made it onto the outer street. Justine stopped at a shack, and I froze, not sure if she'd seen something, but she only stopped long enough to cut free a laundry line with the pressure of one clawed fingertip. She tied a slipknot on one side and wound the rest in a loose coil. I figured it was a good idea. We might have to restrain Norman if we were going to try to get information from him. We got moving again, slipping down the streets as quickly and quietly as we could. If anyone saw us, they did what they always did when things crept by in the dark outside and pretended we weren't there.

"He's mine," Justine whispered hoarsely as got closer. Norman's miniature log cabin was three houses down. It was locked up like all the others, but plenty of light seeped out of the house. I guess he didn't feel the need to board up his windows like everyone else.

"I'll open the front door for you," Justine said, pointing to the window above the porch roof.

"Be careful," I said to the air. She was already moving.

I slipped into the shadows at the corner of a nearby shack as Justine took one long stride and then another before leaping. She landed with one foot on the railing around the porch and vaulted up to grab the overhanging roof before carrying herself up in one smooth motion and immediately moving across the shingles to the window set between the steep A-frame of the house's main roof. The window to the loft wasn't locked. She disappeared inside without a sound, leaving me to wait, holding my breath, expecting to hear a crash or a scream at any moment.

Within three minutes Justine opened the front door, peeking out. I crossed the distance and slipped inside before shutting the door and leaning on it as I looked at Nail Gun Norman. He was hanging with his feet a few inches off the floor, the cord around his neck looped around a roof timber and tied off to the ladder leading to the loft. His face was already turning a deep purple.

"That's going to make him hard to question," I said, a little miffed.

"Sorry, I dropped the noose around his neck, and he grabbed it. It was jump from the loft or risk him raising the alarm."

"What about the girl?" There was no point in being mad. Norman wasn't coming back to life. A faint whimper came from the loft above us after I asked the question. "It's OK; we aren't here to hurt you," I said to the faint cry.

"She's upstairs," Justine said and then grabbed my arm when I went to move toward the ladder. "Let me get some clothes on her first." Then she was up the ladder and out of sight. I heard tape being pulled and the sound of Abigail taking a deep breath. She cried and sobbed, and I heard Justine comforting her, telling her over and over that Norman wouldn't hurt her anymore.

Abigail peeked down from the loft, looking at me from a mask of pain. The bruises I'd seen on her face this morning had blossomed, spreading out to color two-thirds of her face. Her left eye was swollen shut, and fresh insults had been added. Her lips were puffy and split, and dried blood clung to the space under her nose and ran around her right upper lip. She gripped the ladder and threw her legs over the side cautiously, climbing down slowly, grunting as she descended each rung. When she reached the first floor, she turned around and studied me with one eye.

"You're him, aren't you?" she asked out of the right side of her mouth. She reached out a hand and poked me as if she needed to make sure I was real. I raised an eyebrow at Justine as she climbed down the ladder, looking for some support.

"She was tied to the bed upstairs with tape over her mouth," Justine said, shrugging her shoulders. "I didn't say anything to her."

"Who do you think I am?" I asked her. She was totally ignoring the body of Nail Gun Norman hanging next to her, watching me with manic intensity in her one open eye.

"You're him," she said. "Norman made me go with him when he went to the Farmer's house last night. The Farmer said you were dangerous. I think he's scared of you."

It took me a moment to comprehend what she was saying. "You were in the Farmer's house? What does he look like? What did you hear?"

"He's not human," Abigail said, shaking her head for emphasis. Fresh blood ran from her nose and dripped off her lip to splatter on the floor. I don't think she noticed.

"Did you see him?" Justine asked, putting a reassuring hand on Abigail's shoulder.

"Just for a moment. He had a pale face and teeth," she paused, going somewhere else for a moment. "He had fangs," she added quietly, as if she weren't sure she trusted us—or herself—with the truth. "There was a man strapped to a table. I saw his feet moving. Then I sat down on the steps to the second floor and put my head between my knees. I didn't want to see anything else."

"You're not crazy; he's not human," Justine said, slipping her arm around Abigail. "Did you hear him say anything?"

"The Farmer saw you come into town, but he didn't know," Abigail said, laughing softly.

I looked at Justine, afraid we'd rescued the poor girl too late.

"I'm not crazy," Abigail said, putting out a finger to poke my chest again. "The Farmer can see things on the road, I heard him tell Norman that. But he didn't know who you were. He was complaining that there were two new people in town but no sign of the man he was looking for. But you are him, aren't you?"

"Did he say why he was looking for me?" I asked.

"The Farmer told Norman one of his hunting parties hadn't come back."

"Did you hear them say anything else?" I asked, my heart beating faster. We'd found Haeslig.

"The Farmer said their prisoner wasn't doing well, and he was afraid to push him any harder. He told Norman the prisoner kept telling him he didn't know exactly where you were, no matter what he did to him."

Justine swallowed hard, and I knew what she was thinking. WC was being tortured, but he was still alive. "Go get whatever things you have," Justine said to the girl.

"I can't leave. I have an aunt; she's the only family I have left," Abigail said, a touch of fear and panic in her voice.

"It's OK, Justine soothed. "We'll take care of this. Just go get your things." Abigail nodded, going wide around Norman's hanging corpse to get into the small room under the loft. I found a rag in the kitchenette and cleaned the drops of Abigail's blood off the hardwood floor.

"What are doing?" Justine asked.

"Making sure there isn't any blood for Haeslig to read anything from," I told her, scrunching up the rag and putting it in my pocket.

"A little paranoid?" she asked.

"Just a little," I agreed. "Now let's go dump Norman's body in a shallow grave."

"What about WC? He's in the house. That's got to be who she saw," Justine said intensely.

"First we dispose of the body, and then we get Abigail to her aunt. We can't leave her to take the rap for anything we do tonight. Then we go visit Haeslig."

"You're right; I wasn't thinking," Justine said, vibrating with energy. "You do realize he seems a little fixated on you, right?"

"Don't get jealous. He just wants me out of the way so he can concentrate on you again," I said, shrugging my shoulders. It was the only thing that remotely made any sense. Justine didn't comment; she had turned to face Abigail.

"What are you going to do with me?" Abigail asked, doing her best not to let her voice crack.

"We have to take care of this before anyone finds it," Justine said, nodding in Norman's direction. "And then we drop you off with your aunt. If anyone asks, you couldn't stop crying and Norman sent you there for the night. That is all you ever say, no matter what. Will your aunt back you up?" Justine asked.

"Yeah, she's drunk most of the time, but she'll do it."

"Good," Justine said, putting her arm around Abigail's shoulder as she led her to the door.

"It's not safe to be outside after dark," Abigail said. She'd been raped and beaten, but she was still afraid of the dark.

"You're safe with us," Justine assured her, putting a hand on the doorknob and looking back to me. I flicked open my belt knife and cut the cord stringing Norman up so I could take his weight over my shoulder. I grabbed the length of cord hanging off his neck and shoved the rest of it down his shirt so I wouldn't trip on it. Then I hiked his body up as I moved to the door, drawing a Walther from beneath my armpit in the process, wishing I had a silencer for it. Justine gave me a brief glance to make sure I was good to go and then opened the front door, leading us all out into the darkness.

Even in the small amount of time we'd been in Norman's house, the town had quieted. Most of the people probably couldn't afford lanterns or candles on a routine basis. The sound of a generator hummed somewhere in the distance, but the only light we saw came from the house at the center of town. We walked along the darkened streets, the sound of Abigail's scuffing footfalls the loudest thing around us. We were moving as quickly as the girl could walk. She tried to say something once, but Justine whispered urgently in her ear and she shut up.

My back was starting to ache form Norman's weight by the time we slipped through the alley into the open ground just outside of town. I stopped a hundred paces into the field to give Abigail a brief rest and adjust Norman's weight on my shoulder. We walked another few minutes until the town was a good distance off; then I dropped Norman, happy to be rid of him.

"You bring a shovel?" I asked Justine lightly, rotating my left shoulder in its socket.

Justine shook her head. "I knew I forgot something." Abigail looked from me to Justine, not sure what to make of us.

"We get to dig in the dirt, but you have a job, too," I said, motioning for Justine to spin Abigail about. It seemed wrong to let a teenage girl watch as we buried a body.

"Yep," Justine agreed, turning Abigail around to face the town. "You get to sit and watch the field. If you see anything moving, clap your hands together quietly."

I holstered my pistol and dropped to my knees once Abigail was facing the other way and began to pull up clumps of grass, setting them aside so I could use them to cover the burial site once we were done. Justine dropped down beside me and began to pull dirt toward her with her hands, deepening and lengthening our trench.

By the time we had the grave half dug, my shirt was sticking to my back, and I had sweat running down my face into my eyes. I wiped my forehead in the crook of my arm but only managed to make things worse, adding dirt and grime to the stinging salt running into my eyes. I sat back on my heels and wiped my hands down my pants, trying to clean them off as I pinched my eyes closed against the stinging.

The sound of a solid punch landing brought my hand to my armpit, reaching for my pistol as I blinked dirt and grit away from my eyes. Abigail was turning to see what was going on as I surged to my feet, covering the fields around us with my pistol. Abigail gasped and stepped backward, tripping and falling onto her butt as I scared her with the drawn weapon. I scanned the ground around us, my eye drawn to the two bodies at my feet. Nail Gun Norman was lying on his back, and Justine was next to him, her body lying facedown in the dirt.

I watched stunned as Norman's hand shot up into the air, and then fell back to his chest, feeling clumsily for his throat. His fingers found the circle of rope still embedded around his neck and tugged it free. The sound of his breath being sucked down a crushed windpipe sounded savagely loud in the quiet night.

Norman rolled onto his stomach and got his hands under him as my brain tried to process what I was seeing. He was lifting his upper body off the ground when I broke free of my shocked paralysis. I took a half step and planted a savage kick into his flank, throwing him onto his side. I stayed on him, kicking him again and again as he coughed and struggled to breathe. I ended up standing over him, shaking my pistol at him, wanting to put a bullet in his head. Instead I cursed and swapped my pistol into my left hand so I could draw my machete.

The weapon just cleared its sheath when Norman's hand shot out, hitting my leg and throwing me of balance. I fell, the hilt of the machete ramming into my stomach as the blade slid into Norman's chest. I was almost face-to-face with him as he gasped in surprise, the machete spearing him to the ground. I could feel the thrum of his heart against the blade as I let go and rolled off, holding my own gut where the hilt had rammed into me.

"Please tell me you're both all right," Abigail begged, putting her hands out to feel the darkness in front of her.

"I'm OK," I said through the pain. "Just stay there." I crawled over to Justine and put my ear over her mouth. She was breathing. I grabbed her face and stroked it gently until she started to groan.

"I think I got hit by a truck," she said, reaching up to touch my chest.

"Tell me about it," I said, happy to hear her voice. My leg felt like it had taken a blow from a sledge. Norman could really throw a punch.

"Ahhhhh," Abigail intoned, the noise droning on unsteadily as her voice gave out.

"What's wrong?" I asked, looking up.

Norman was on his knees, my machete still spiked through his chest. He took a long, wet breath and opened his mouth wide. The cry that came from his lips was savage and raw, the keening of a wounded animal.

I shot him twice in the head.

It wasn't until the report of the shots was ringing through the valley that I looked at my hand and realized what I'd done. I stared at Norman as he crumpled to the ground, then bolted to my feet as a return cry came from somewhere to the south. "Can you move?" I asked Justine. She'd made it onto her butt and had her head between her knees.

"Yeah, still a little dizzy," she said. Another cry came from much closer to the west.

"We need to move," I said, pulling Justine to her feet as she moaned in protest. "Abigail, help her," I demanded, letting go of Justine to put a foot on Norman's body and pull my machete free. As soon as I had the blade, I pushed Justine and Abigail in front of me, getting them moving. We headed northeast, fleeing whatever had returned Norman's cry.

"He wasn't a thrall or a gray," Justine said after a minute.

"It doesn't matter now," I said, looking behind me. We weren't moving fast enough. We hadn't made it far when a long, howling cry full of pain and anger rolled over us from the south. They'd found Norman's body. Within thirty seconds more cries came from the east and then the west.

There was more than one of them, and they were all around us.

"You can do it," Justine said encouragingly to Abigail as we broke into something just short of an all-out run. Abigail was barely able to keep her feet under her as Justine dragged her along. We made it into the orchards before the cries came again. They were nearly on top of us.

"Keep moving; I'll catch up," I said to Justine, turning to meet the threat. Abigail rammed into Justine as she came to a sudden stop.

"No, we kill them and stick together," Justine said, sniffing at the air.

"Sounds like three of them," I said. I had a pistol in one hand and my machete in the other.

"Four I think, two trying to flank us and two more coming from the south." She let go of Abigail's hand as her claws slid from her fingertips, merging with the black of the night as they lengthened.

I grabbed Abigail and manhandled her behind a tree. "Hide and don't move until one of us comes and gets you." She shook her head in something that might have been agreement, shivering with fear. She was on the verge of breaking. "Stay put," I commanded and went back to stand with Justine.

"They're here," Justine rasped a moment before a figure charged out of the darkness, trying to bowl her over. The man was expecting to plow through her; instead she knocked his hands away from her and hit him square in the chest, sending him staggering back with a loud grunt as all the air left his lungs.

Then my own attacker was on me. I leveled my pistol at his chest and pulled the trigger. I half expected the shadowy form to jump or dodge like a gray as I fired, but he just charged forward, bearing down on me as I fired two rounds, then two more. I heard the bullets hit flesh, but he didn't slow. At the last moment I lowered my aim, firing a burst of rounds into his legs just before he hit me.

His momentum carried me off my feet, and I would have fallen, but his arms were already around me, pinning my limbs to my sides as our faces came within inches of each other. For a split second I thought he was wearing camouflage face paint; then I realized he was covered in dirt. "No guns allowed in town," he growled, his mouth only inches from my face. The smell of wet dirt and rotten meat washed over me as he spoke. I tried to pull away, struggling to get farther from his mouth as he hugged me closer, but his arms were locked around me, beginning to tighten.

I pulled me head back as far as I could and rammed it forward into his nose. Cartilage crunched and blood sprayed as I pulled my head back, but the pressure around my midsection didn't lesson. He lifted me off my feet as he leaned back, his arms tightening, crushing the air out of my lungs. I pulled back to head butt him again but he only squeezed harder, tucking his face down to deny me the softer parts of his anatomy.

A hissing breath left my mouth as his arms continued to tighten, sending a tendril of pain up and down my spine. My arms were locked beneath his, but I still had my pistol in my hand. I tilted it as best I could, trying to angle it away from my junk before pulling the trigger. Burning heat washed down my right thigh, but I continued to fire, sucking in a breath as his arms loosened around me. I emptied the clip into his left leg in a blaze of noise and flashing light. He released one of his arms, trying to bring it around to grab my pistol, but his left leg gave out and I broke away as he stumbled.

I took several deep breaths, holding the machete between us as the man looked at his leg and then back at me, blood streaming from his crushed nose to run into his mouth. Bloody spray sprinkled the ground between us as he snarled and hopped forward. I held my ground as he closed, letting him come to me. I shifted away at the last instant, slashing out with my machete. His hand went flying over my shoulder as I resumed my guard position, the tip of my blade pointed at his chest.

He looked at the stump of his hand, huffing out of his mouth, and something in him broke. He charged, swinging at me with his remaining arm. My blade whipped out, and another hand flew off into the darkness. He didn't hesitate; he continued to hobble forward, swinging at me with what was left of his arms. I hit him two more times, half cutting and half shattering his left arm just below the shoulder. It left him unable to block the final blow that left his head hanging by skin and a few bits of tendon.

I was turning to look for Justine when a shoulder caught me in the gut, carrying me off my feet as I folded in two around my assailant. My machete went flying out of my hand as I sailed back and hit the ground hard. Before I could recover and pull myself to a sitting position, someone dropped painfully onto my midsection. I struck out with the pistol still in my hand, using the butt of the weapon to drive a hammer blow into the person on top of me. They growled and I struck again, only to have my wrist caught in a vice grip, freezing the pistol in place. I tried to punch the figure on top of me with my free hand but was forced to shield my head as blows rained down on me.

"You will pay," a deep male voice said, snatching the pistol from my hand and almost taking my trigger finger with it. I didn't have time to say anything in reply before hands reached down and picked me up by my shirt and a fistful of my pants. "Die," the man grunted, lifting me into the air over his head. I felt him take a single step as I looked up at the stars through the branches above me, and then I was flying through the air.

I kicked and pawed at the air futilely, momentarily weightless. Then my back hit the trunk of an apple tree in a burst of pain. Nausea washed over me as I started to fall headfirst toward the ground. I put my arm out, trying to grab the tree to slow me and turn my body, but I only managed to get partially around before I crashed into the ground. Pain shot through my right shoulder as I landed hard and went ass over teakettle. I ended up on my back, looking up at the dark sky through the tree limbs, trying to suck in air as tears slid from my eyes. My head felt fuzzy and light; it was a struggle to stay conscious. I took long, slow breaths, pushing away the creeping blackness trying to slide over my vision. Justine was snarling somewhere not too far away, and someone else was screaming.

I let my eyes drift shut for just a moment, and the blackness claimed me.

Lightening sparked, turning my vision red through my closed eyelids. I turned my head, trying to get away from the painful light, my memory foggy and disconnected. Another scream cut through the night, bringing me back to the here and now. I lifted my head off the ground and squinted against the flashing light, my eyes trying to focus on a lump in front of me. It took a moment for my eyes to focus and for the lump to turn into the shape of a kneeling man, his hands wrapped around his lower abdomen as greasy snakes spilled over his arms. Seeing his intestines made me feel like I was forgetting something important. I pulled myself to a sitting position, the world swimming around me. The back of my head hurt, and when I tried to move my right arm the pain rose so hard and fast that I had to fight to stay conscious. The lightning flashed again, an angry buzzing filling my ears as the brightness intensified.

"You need to get up," a mousy voice begged as someone grabbed my shirt and tried to lift me. I looked over and saw Abigail, tears streaming down her face as she struggled to help me up. "They're going to kill her," she whined, her voice full of fear. The lightning moved closer, a carousel of buzzing and flashing lights dancing in front of me. As they moved closer, Justine's form appeared in the center of the light show. She was surrounded by a constantly shifting ring of attackers, each of them holding a crackling shock wand. I turned to say something to Abigail only to see her running off into the night.

I couldn't blame her.

Justine was surrounded by attackers, spinning and clawing as they assaulted her from every side. She tried to break free, but they circled her, moving with her, tagging her with painful shocks each time she turned her back. Anger filled me. I surged to my feet, trying to get the pistol from under my left armpit awkwardly with my left hand. I could get my thumb on the snap, but trying to put any pressure on the release pulled the muscles across my upper shoulders, causing a searing-hot pain to stab down my side. I gasped, my hand falling away from the gun. My right arm hung uselessly at my side, the shoulder above it disfigured and oddly shaped.

Justine cursed and raged, daring her attackers to close with her. One of them gave in to her challenge and let himself get just a little too close. Justine grabbed him and yanked his body in front of hers, shielding herself from two shocks as she pulled her hand across his throat. The man staggered as she let go of him, turning to face her as he lifted a hand to his own neck. He pulled it away as his fellows fell onto her from behind, shocking her multiple times.

Something was very wrong.

The man dropped his hand, laughing as he realized he wasn't wounded, and piled onto the attack. Justine fell to her knees beneath the continuous assault. In the flashing brightness I saw her shrink into a ball, holding her hands in front of her face, looking at her stubby, bitten-down nails. Then the men closed around her, cutting off my view as they pressed in, tagging her relentlessly. I took an unsteady step toward them, squinting against the light, anger and rage welling in me as I saw them savagely attacking Justine.

I took another step toward them.

One of the men turned his body and saw me, an evil smile covering his face as he looked me over. The look in his eyes stopped me in my tracks. I was wounded and hurt, and didn't have a weapon. The man turned away from the circle around Justine, and for just a moment I caught a glimpse of her jumping and twitching as they pressed their shock wands into her flesh. Her head lifted, and our eyes met for a split second as crackling light flared around her. She looked at me and then at the man turning away from her to face me.

"No!" Justine roared as she surged to her feet, grabbing a shock wand as it was driven at her chest. Her arms jerked spastically as she ripped the weapon from her attacker's hands. "R…u…n," she stammered, leaping up and bringing the weapon down on the back of the man's head in front of me.

The wand exploded in a burst of sparks, and then Justine was on the man's back, driving the broken bits down into his neck with savage force. She looked up at me again, mouthing the word "Run." My heart broke as I turned my back on her and lurched into the darkness. Behind me I could hear Justine fighting and crying out as they fell on her again.

I stopped a few dozen feet away, looking back at the dazzling brightness that buzzed and crackled as several men stood above Justine's body as it twitched beneath their wands. I put my dislocated shoulder against the closest tree and leaned into it, trying to force the joint back into place, but I just couldn't apply the pressure needed to pop it back into its socket. Tears ran down my face as I slipped away into the night. My arm throbbed with each step, and my head felt as if it might crack open at any moment, but the pain that I could barely withstand was centered in the middle of my chest.

I told myself I'd had no choice, that there was nothing I could have done, but it didn't make the pain go away or stop the voice in the back of my head that kept telling me I should have done something differently. I was so lost in self-recriminations that I almost didn't hear the howl from behind me as something caught my trail.

Chapter 9

I woke up hidden in a pile of rotten pumpkins with a shaft of sunlight burning my eyes. My memories of the night before were a jumble of pain, fear, and exhaustion. I'd tried to get to where we'd stashed our packs at some point, but the things chasing me kept driving me away. I hadn't even gotten close. Whatever they were, they weren't stupid. Once they'd downed Justine, they flanked me and circled ahead, driving me back toward town each time they got the chance.

At one point they drove me close to where they'd ambushed us. I watched from a distance as Justine was bound with duct tape and thrown over a shoulder. I moved back into the darkness, feeling the crushing pain of abandoning Justine for a second time.

Then the slow chase continued. I'd creep through the darkness, trying to slip between my searchers so I could make a run for the woodlands on the far side of the orchards where I would have a better chance of staying hidden. But I was hurt and moving slow, and they always managed to stay one step ahead of me. I'd get close to the old country road that marked the border between the orchards and the woods, and they'd start to call out to each other, tightening their net around me. My only choice was to flee and try to lose them again. Eventually I was forced to flee the orchards all together. Then the sun started to rise, taking away the cover of darkness and the advantage it gave me. Exhausted and tired, I'd crawled into the only cover I could find in the pumpkin fields and passed out.

I squinted my eyes closed against the sun, breathing in the smell of the decaying pumpkins as pain washed over me. My right side had swollen during the night, making my shirt and jacket feel tight and constricted. I moved the fingers on my right hand, balling them into a fist through the fiery pain trying to stop me. My teeth squeaked against each other as I clenched them against the pain. I flexed my bicep and tried to tighten the muscles along my shoulder, hoping beyond hope to feel the joint pop back into its socket. What I got instead was a slowly building pain that pulsed with my heartbeat, rising in intensity until I couldn't take it any longer. I lay there breathing in the smell of rotten pumpkins as I relaxed my fist and let my arm go slack, regretting the attempt as nausea washed over me. I shuddered, and wet seeds fell from a pumpkin above me and slid down my neck as I centered myself, forcing the pain into a little ball, controlling it. When I could focus, I moved very slowly, using my good arm to clear pumpkins off my body. I was struggling to my feet before I even thought about where I was. It was a sign of how hard I was working to control the pain.

"Got one in the field, Ed," someone off to my left yelled.

"Make sure there aren't any others," another man called back.

I was on my feet, leaning to my right because it hurt too much to straighten out. I tried to say something, but all that came out was a garbled noise. My mouth and throat were dry and crusty. A man was standing in the field a stone's throw away, but the sun was behind him, making me squint and hold my left arm up to shield my eyes from the burning sun. The scream of pain that came from my lips when my knee was smashed out from under me didn't sound human to my own ears. I hit the ground, pained noises coming from my lips as I reached down, afraid I was going to find my leg missing at the knee.

I curled up with my left hand feeling its way down my leg. My knee and lower leg were still there, but I had no idea what had hit me. Someone behind me gave a redneck howl and yelled, "Nice shot." I lifted my head to see who was attacking me. There was no one standing there with a baseball bat like I'd expected, but a crossbow bolt tipped with a wooden disc was on the ground next to me.

"My turn, Chuck, don't hog it," someone said. I sat up and used my feet to turn myself around on my butt until I was facing several foremen. I recognized two of them from apple picking, but the third I'd never seen before. I managed to get onto my knees and held up a hand, trying to make them pause, but since I was covered in muck and partially disabled, they still thought I was a thrall. Chuck handed the crossbow off to the other foreman.

As soon as the other man had the weapon, the female brute started to jabber and stamp her feet in agitation. I watched as the foreman aimed and fell to my side just as he pulled the trigger. The bolt flew over me to disappear into the pumpkins. The female brute was howling and jumping up and down, making the heavy chains around her ankles clank and clatter.

"Ha, you missed," Ed said. I heard the crossbow click as the wire was pulled back.

"Just grab a shovel and kill it; you're getting the big girl all worked up," the other foreman said.

I sat up again, groaning in pain as my right arm was jostled. Ed was walking toward me, carrying a shovel over one shoulder. The female brute was stamping her feet and pulling at the chains holding her hands together. The other brute had her by the shoulders, trying to calm her down. She clearly didn't like the crossbow.

I couldn't blame her.

I reached up with my left hand, fumbling at the pistol that was stuck under my armpit, trying to free it. I still couldn't quite get to it. I fell forward onto my left arm, ignoring the pain as my wrist was bent at a funny angle, giving me just the extra bit of reach I needed to unsnap the gun release. Ed watched me as he walked up, trying to figure out what I was doing. I got my left hand down and lifted myself off the ground, wiggling my shoulders until the Walther slid forward and fell into the dirt in front of me.

"Holy shit," Ed yelped, seeing the gun. He raised the shovel as I grabbed the pistol and shot, falling forward onto my stomach in the process. The round hit the head of the shovel with a loud metallic slap and sent it spinning out of the Ed's hands. He screamed in surprise and grabbed something strapped to his thigh as I struggled to lift my arm and fire again. I looked up just in time to see the shock wand press into me.

My teeth slammed shut, and every muscle in my body went rigid as the electrodes touched me. Ed laughed as he kicked the pistol out of my hand, continuing to shock me all the while. I tried to scream through my clenched teeth as the wand was triggered repeatedly, a helpless panic rising in my throat.

"Keep tagging him," Chuck said, pulling his own shock wand free as he headed over, triggering the weapon instinctively in the process. He was standing right next to the female brute when he did it. He never saw the length of chain she whipped at his head. One moment he was standing there, and then there was a wet popping noise, and he was falling to the ground, nothing attached to his neck but a bloody stump.

Everyone froze, stunned by the brute's sudden explosion of violence. She seemed almost as surprised as everyone else. She lifted the chain in her hands, staring at the blood as a low-pitched sound of alarm left her lips.

"No!" Ed screamed as the other foreman fumbled a razor-tipped bolt into the crossbow and jerked it up. "Don't do it," he yelled as the man ignored him and fired. Ed half turned away from me, focused on the female brute, giving me a moment to breathe as the shock wand slipped off my chest.

The sound coming from the female brute never faltered; it just shifted from a sad crooning to a pitiful wailing. She touched her chest where a red stain was blossoming on her shirt and pulled her hand away, looking at her own blood in puzzlement. She coughed, and more blood filled her mouth, spilling over her lower lip. The big male looked at her and pulled his chains off as if they were made from paper. Ed's jaw went slack. The chains had given the foremen a false sense of security. They had no idea what a brute was capable of.

The asshole with the crossbow should have run. Instead he tried to reload. The sound of the wire clicking in its locked position made the female go crazy. She took one step, ripping the chains free of her legs in the process, and then leapt into the air, coming down on top of the foreman as he lifted his weapon and fired another bolt just as she landed on top of him. She was hacking and coughing blood as she stomped the man's body into the ground under her feet. He didn't have time to scream.

Ed dropped his shock wand and scooped up my Walther, pointing it at the female brute as he took a hesitant step backward. The female looked up at him with a snarl and took a step in our direction. Ed looked at her and panicked. Blood ran from her lips with each breath, running freely from her mouth as she snarled. I didn't see the first rounds hit the big girl, but I heard the impacts. When I looked up she was already on her knees, her head turning back to look at the big male as her hand tried to reach out for him. Ed put two more shots into her as she fell heavily and didn't move, a small puff of dust spreading out from her body as she pressed into the earth.

The male brute looked at her and started to shake. Tendons rose along each side of his neck as his eyes locked on Ed. The brute's normally sallow skin was flushed pink, and there was nothing but pure rage on his face as he started to move.

Ed took the Walther in both hands, assuming the Weaver stance. He must have been a cop or a member of the military in the before. His first shot went high and wide. He was trained, but I could see the tip of the pistol shaking as the two-ton brute charged him. His next shot was better aimed; it hit the brute high and to the right along its shoulder.

I don't know why I did it; I don't think I really thought about it. In the simplest sense, an enemy of my enemy is my friend. I twisted in the dirt and kicked Ed in the knee with everything I had. His next shot went wide, and then he was screaming, his knee bent inward from the force of the blow. He crumpled to the ground, screaming all the while as his knee moved in ways it was never intended to. Ed's face was turning red, and the veins on his forehead bulged as he spit unintelligible curses at me. I didn't know what he was saying, but I knew what he was thinking as he pulled his pistol hand through the dirt, bringing it around to finish me off.

I smiled at him, knowing he wasn't going to survive me by long.

Then his body went spinning away as the brute's foot made contact with his chest, punting him across the field. I lay back as the brute's form cast a long shadow over me, shutting my eyes, breathing slowly. There was nothing I could do.

"Sorry about your friend," I mumbled, relaxing into the dirt as I said it. Something in the distance started to howl. Just like the night before, the gunfire had attracted unwanted attention. The cries of hunters cut through the air again as I lay in the shade of the brute. My right shoulder was on fire, and my head was swimming. I was too tired and hurt to do anything but lie there.

"Damn ghouls," a deep voice rumbled above me. Then massive hands scooped me up and I passed out. I dreamed I could feel the rhythmic pulse of the brute's footfalls as he carried me away.

Chapter 10

I woke up the first time for just a moment, brought back to consciousness by a flash of pain. There was a strange mix of fire and relief as my shoulder was positioned back into place with a pop. As I drifted back into unconsciousness, I thought I heard a far-off voice say something about how frail my kind were.

When I woke up the second time, I was sitting with my back against a rock, my left arm resting in my lap. My shoulder still hurt, but it was a dull, aching pain versus the stabbing agony of the day before. I flexed my fingers and bent my arm experimentally before lifting it off my lap. It hurt, but I could do it if I moved slowly.

"Peace, little one," a deep voice rumbled from off to my left. I turned and watched as the massive brute from the pumpkin patch turned sideways to slip between two trees. He approached slowly, his hands open, as if he didn't want to scare a wild animal.

I didn't know what to say. I just watched as he sat down opposite me and settled back against a tree, digging something out of his pocket. The brute's brow was furrowed as he held an acorn between his fingers, rolling it about until he could discard the shell and get to the meat. The look on his face was pained and disgusted as he chewed the first acorn while rolling another between his fingers. He ate two more but stopped as he was about to put the fourth shelled acorn into his mouth, staring at it and sighing.

"Are you hungry?" I asked, very aware I was not going to be outrunning the brute anytime soon, if ever. I'd eaten acorns in survival school and knew that unless you leached the tannins out of them they were horribly bitter. The only reason I knew to eat raw acorns was if you were starving—and maybe trying not to eat something else.

He jumped and looked up at me, startled, as if he'd forgotten I was even there. Then he looked at the acorn between his fingers, and then back at me, a smile touching the corners of his lips as if he knew what I'd been thinking.

"No, not really hungry at all," he said, dropping the acorn and rubbing his fingers clean on his pants with a heavy sigh. "The foremen would drink themselves into a stupor fairly regularly. We liked to come up into the mountains where it was quiet. She always liked to eat the acorns. Never did understand why." He shook his head in thought. I wasn't sure what was more shocking, the clear bass voice that was speaking to me or the sorrow I heard in it as he spoke. The few times I'd heard brutes speak before, they had seemed like very simple creatures.

"I'm sorry," I started, and had to clear my throat, "about her."

The brute paused and rubbed his face with a massive hand. His voice was full of pain when he spoke. "Her name was Solindraye. She was a brilliant youth, a marvel, really." His voice was deep and filled with tones so low I could feel the words in my chest when he spoke, but there was something else there as well. It was something that reminded me of my father. Whenever he spoke I could feel the thought behind each word. It was not something I was expecting to encounter from a brute.

"Did they hurt her?" I asked and stopped, looking for the right words. "She seemed quiet." The brute nodded, knowing what I was trying to say.

"No," he said, shaking his head. "It wasn't them; those men were just spiteful animals. When they were put in charge of us, it made them feel better if we cowered and were afraid. I tried to shield Solindraye from the worst of it, tried to keep her calm and busy so they wouldn't focus on her." He sighed before he spoke again. "But I am the one responsible for the state you saw her in."

I raised an eyebrow, knowing there was more to the story.

"It is mildly involved; do you want the five-word answer or the longer explanation?"

"The longer please," I said thoughtfully, wanting to hear what the brute had to say.

"OK. Your kind have lost so much history, though, I'm not sure where to start. What do you know of the Blutsauger?"

"That's German, isn't it? Blood sucker?" I asked.

"Ha, yes, you would know it as German. But it really translates better to *vampire*." He said the word "vampire" with a strange tone in his voice. It was a mixture of reverence, fear, and disgust.

"Are you Blutsauger?" I asked, wondering if I was partaking in a predinner conversation.

The smile that formed on the brute's face didn't help ease my anxiety. He actually laughed and slapped his thigh before he spoke. "Look," he said, leaning forward as he smiled a toothy grin, showing me his large, square teeth. "These are not the teeth of a blood drinker." He seemed genuinely amused. "Your kind truly has forgotten. But maybe you have not encountered the Blutsauger. They rarely leave your kind in the first life when they let you see them."

The way he said it triggered the realization in me. I felt like an idiot; it was so obvious. "The grays, the Blutsauger are grays," I exclaimed.

"What do you know of them?" the brute asked curiously.

"They're fast and strong. Some of them have abilities. They can control the dead, and I've seen one they called a spider; he didn't move, but he had a huge horde of thralls attached to him." I paused, my mind going back in time to the battle at Mr. Deringer's house. His sister had had an antique bowl, a relic from her religious order, and any water put into it burned the undead like it was acid. "And some very old things seem to have power over them. I think your kind have been here before, and my ancestors made weapons to fight them."

The brute stared at me, his brow furrowing as everything I said sank in. "You know nothing, and yet you understand so much. How is that you know these things?" There was something very formal about the way he asked me, something that put me back on edge, reminding me that he was capable of killing me before I could hope to defend myself.

"I've learned a lot about grays while hunting them," I swallowed, "while killing them." I stared at the brute, not sure how he was going to respond. I figured there was no point in trying to hide the truth; the outcome would be what it would be.

"If I were not looking in your face and could feel the truth of your words as you said them, I'd think you a liar," the brute said, nodding in satisfaction as he spoke. "What is your name?"

"Daniel Ryan," I said, not sure what was going on.

"My name is Tomasa Elingrad Domingradaschick." His voice rumbled as the words rolled off his tongue. "Please feel free to call me Tomasa. It is a pleasure to meet you."

"You're not like any of your kind I've ever met," I blurted out.

Tomasa's smile split across his face as he shook his head in disbelief. "And what do you know of my people?"

"You're tough, tougher than any gray or thrall. You are the shock troops, the heavy infantry and artillery all rolled into one." I'd seen brutes take out military vehicles with spears.

"You've hunted my kind, too, haven't you?" Tomasa asked.

"More like fought them to survive," I acknowledged, staring into Tomasa's eyes. There was no way I could lie to him. There was no way to kill grays without eventually coming face-to-face with brutes. "They were different, though, not like you," I added. Our eyes were locked together, and I could see him thinking. It was not something I'd ever seen a brute do before.

"I have no anger for you, Daniel," Tomasa said, although his voice was sad. "You have taken family and friends from me who were already lost. You may have given them death, but you are not responsible for killing their true selves."

"You are slaves to the grays, the Blutsauger, aren't you?" I asked.

"Yes and no," Tomasa said, rubbing his chin thoughtfully. "My kind are usually too strong willed to be controlled in their first life, and we have no second to give. They can drink from us, and do, but we don't go to the second life like your people. My kind, thankfully, have but one death to give the Blutsauger.

"In my realm the Blutsauger rule; my people are scholars, advisors, and soldiers. We serve the Blutsauger, but we do it with our first lives. Which brings me back to Solindraye." He sighed heavily again. "She was a gifted student. She could have picked any discipline to study. I was an elder, a leader of my people. Her father was my best friend. He came to me before the last choosing, petitioning me to hear his daughter's words.

"She wanted to serve. She wanted to be part of the choosing and cross into this realm to help end the war. I didn't want to let her come. She was too young; she had too much promise. But I had made another decision; I was going to cross over as well. I wanted to see the land my father's father had died in so many years before. I let her come because I thought I could protect her. I had no idea of the nightmare that lay on this side of the gateway."

Large tears fell slowly from his eyes to splatter on the ground.

"You have to understand: for my people, the trip is always one-way. The Blutsauger who control the portals said we were different, that crossing back over to our realm would kill us. My people compete and strive to be chosen, to cross over to serve our masters, knowing they can never return home.

"When I went through the portal, it felt like ten of those shock lances your people have were pressed to my skull. When I woke up, I was lying on the pavement, looking up at a strange sky. Several of the Blutsauger were helping my kind, the Riesig, to their feet, but something was wrong. My best pupils, my elite guard, they were all simpering fools. The Blutsauger were treating them like they were trash. I watched, not realizing what they were doing as they took the ones unable to understand basic instructions off a short distance. The Blutsauger were laughing as they murdered the Riesig who were left too simple to function.

"Up until that point in my life, I had served the Blutsauger without question. Not that day. I killed the three who were leading Solindraye away without warning or mercy. All around me, stunned and stupid Riesig panicked as I raged. I thought I could rouse them; I thought I could bring them back to themselves. I didn't understand the entirety of what had happened yet. I tore the Blutsauger to pieces. Then more came, and I didn't have a choice. I took Solindraye's hand and we ran. We wandered for a while, and then Solindraye wouldn't stop at night. It took me a while to figure out what was going on.

"In my realm we serve the Blutsauger because of duty, but here, the minds of the Riesig are so weak, they can be compelled. Solindraye was so far gone that she was being pulled in by the one your people call the Farmer. I followed her into this valley. When we got to town, the foremen were waiting for her with chains. They weren't expecting me, but I played my part, and they seemed to accept what I showed them. Since then I've been trying to protect her better than I did when I allowed her to come to this realm.

"I failed at that as well."

There was such sadness and self-reproach in his voice that I wanted to reach out and comfort the huge brute but wasn't sure how. I had no idea if putting a hand on his shoulder would have the same meaning to Tomasa as it would to me. "Thank you for saving me," I said after struggling to find the right thing to say.

"You're welcome," Tomas said, bowing his head formally.

"Where are we?" I asked, looking at the darkening skyline.

"Your weapon attracted the ghouls, but I outran them. We are in the mountains to the northeast of Pumpkin Town."

"How far to the northeast?"

"By your legs or mine?" Tomas asked, smiling. It was an oddly comforting expression.

"I think mine would give me a better feel for it."

"For you, maybe two hours, three if your arm slows you down. The ghouls are still in the valley, but what good will revenge do you if the Farmer catches you?"

"It's not revenge I want. Do you remember the girl I was with when we were in the orchard?"

"Vaguely," Tomasa said, scratching his chin. "You are the first of your people I've ever talked to, and you all look so much alike to me."

"The ghouls, as you call them, they took her. I have to go back and free her. I'm afraid the Farmer has plans for her."

"I am sorry, Daniel. If the Farmer has plans for her, you won't be able to save her." Tomasa's face had lost all traces of his smile.

"I've killed grays before, and I'll kill this one, too. It's personal; he's been chasing us for a long time. She's still alive; she's too valuable to the Farmer. I *will* save her," I declared.

Tomas looked me over as the last of the light failed. "You are a strange one, Daniel. I heard some of the foremen talking about the Farmer hunting a man. It made the foremen uneasy to think that the Farmer might have an enemy who made him nervous. They wondered what could be so special about such a man. The Farmer was hunting you, wasn't he?"

I nodded, feeling slightly deceitful for not telling Tomasa the only reason the Farmer wanted me out of the picture was so that I wouldn't try to block whatever plans he had for Justine. I didn't want to take the time to tell him all about the history Haeslig and I had. "I have a bag closer to town. I need to get to it, and then I'm going to go get Justine."

"You think you can walk?" Tomasa asked, standing up and stretching.

"I can," I said, working my way to me feet. He waited until I was standing and then led the way. Tomasa set a slow pace, moving through the trees and over the rocks with barely a sound. I followed him slightly less noiselessly. I had my arm tucked into my partially-zipped-up jacket to support it, which threw my balance off. Even so, Tomasa complemented me on being able to keep up.

"Your people are blind at night and have no ears to hear themselves," he commented at one point. "You, however, seem at home in the darkness."

"It's always been my friend," I said, remembering for just a moment my childhood and the days spent in dark rooms, hiding my eyes from the light that hurt so badly.

"Definitely not like any of your kind I've met before,"

Tomasa said to himself as he continued to lead the way.

We walked for an hour before Tomasa called a break, stopping us by an ice-cold stream. We crouched side-by-side, drinking water from our cupped hands. I'd wanted to ask Tomasa several questions while we walked but was forced to concentrate on just keeping up in the dark. I used the momentary break to ask him about something he'd said earlier.

"What are the ghouls? Are they a type of gray I haven't seen before? Back in Delaware I fought some with eyes they'd cut from my people to give them better sight during the day, but I could have sworn the ghouls were men, at least until I saw how much damage they could take."

"You killed members of the Tagjager?" Tomasa said, looking at me with raised eyebrows. "They are very dangerous. They bind themselves in circles with their clan chief."

"And he gets stronger each time you kill one of them," I added.

"You must have been very good at hunting the Blutsauger; you've survived to learn more than I would have expected, Daniel," Tomasa said. "As for the ghouls, they are not something from my realm. They are something the Farmer made. I don't think he trusts his own kind. He stays hidden in his house and lets his ghouls do his work. There were two other grays with him before, but I have not seen either of them in weeks. The ghouls are your kind, but the Farmer has done something to them, changed them.

"He does something that has not been done before; he holds them in some in-between state. They do his bidding like Nechtruin and have some of the strength of the Blutsauger, but they are not stable. Each night they lose a bit more of themselves. I've seen them go bad, running through the fields on all fours like animals. It is one of the main reasons the townspeople lock up at night. There have been twenty or so ghouls in the last several months. The first three only lived a week or so and then went berserk. This last troop has survived almost a full month, although I have started to see them stalking the town at night. You can always tell when they start to lose control. They can't resist fresh meat when they get hungry."

"We should get moving; I need to get back to Justine." Listening to him talk about what Haeslig was doing wasn't making me feel any better about abandoning her. If he was trying to make ghouls, who knew how he thought Justine's blood could help him?

Tomasa picked an easy path for us to follow when we got going again. An hour and a half later, we slowed, and Tomasa pointed down through the trees. I could see the highway beneath us. "His thralls keep watch. They don't hear so well, but we should still be careful," Tomasa said.

I looked out at the bit of darkened valley visible between the trees as we walked, trying to find a landmark in the starlight. It wasn't until we moved a little farther south that I was able to orient myself. We'd already passed the old country road. The orchards were on the other side of the highway beneath us. "My gear is hidden in a pile of cuttings and garbage in the orchard. There's a tree stump right off the dirt road back to town. My bags are hidden in a debris pile near the stump."

Tomasa picked up his head and sniffed the air. "They haven't given up the search for us. And it looks like the Farmer has strung up some fresh watchers," he said, pointing to a squirming mass wired to a telephone pole below us on the highway.

"I'll be careful."

"You are wounded, and daylight is only a few hours off, Daniel," Tomasa said, looking up at the sky.

"I don't think I can afford to wait another day," I said, shaking my head.

"You're tired and already using up your reserves. Wait here; let me get your bags, and we'll figure out what to do next."

I shook my head in the dark and sighed. The march so far had taken more out of me than I would have liked to admit, but the thought of not doing anything, of sitting still while Justine was in Haeslig's control, put a knot of fear in my gut. "Why are you helping me, Tomasa?"

"My life before last year is a distant dream. I was respected; I knew exactly who I was and served. But for the last year, I have been trying to keep Solindraye safe, to pay a debt of such immense proportions that I can never begin to balance it. And yet a much-larger debt must be laid at the feet of my old masters. Maybe by helping you, I can at least make the Blutsauger pay in some small measure for the horrible evil they have done to my people."

"Be safe, my friend; I'll be right here when you come back."

Tomasa chuckled softly, or at least that's how I interpreted the sound of gravel and sand moving over one another as it left his lips. He moved down the slope without another word. I sat down against a tree, leaning back into it as I watched and listened. The night sounds were muted as if all the little creatures of the woods had decided it was safer to stay quiet and still for the night. I wished I had the same option. I was tired and sore and generally run down. I wanted nothing more than to shut my eyes and fall asleep. Instead I flexed my right hand as I sat there, gradually working the muscles up to my elbow until I was slowly lifting my arm off my thigh, opening and closing my fist and then letting it fall back to my leg. The arm hurt, but it was a pain I could work through. It was a pain I had to work through.

As more time passed, I sat back in the shadow of the tree and willed myself to disappear, listening and watching the slope below me, feeling just a bit helpless. I was weaponless, bruised, and sitting in the dark waiting for a brute to retrieve my gear. If I hadn't been so tired, I would have found it worrisome.

"Daniel, Daniel," Tomasa called gently as he crossed into my view from the right. I could see both packs hanging from one of his fists as he walked.

"Up here," I called out, standing so Tomasa could see me.

I waited on the edge of the slope as he worked his way up to me. "Sorry I took so long; I wasn't sure if the ghouls scented me, so I circled back twice to make sure they weren't on my trail." He looked back the way he'd come. "But we should move in case they get smarter, or luckier, just to be safe." I could see that Tomasa was covered in sweat as he held the packs out in front of him victoriously.

The lump from my UMP was clearly visible at the top of my pack.

"Lead the way," I said, letting my brain answer before the rest of my body could revolt. If the man coming back from the field said you moved, you moved.

We backtracked along the same trail we'd come in on and then cut to the east, moving uphill. I was struggling at the end, moving on all fours while trying not to put too much weight on my right arm. Tomasa pulled me up the last few feet, a massive hand gripping mine carefully. I collapsed to the ground, looking around us as the darkness turned to bruised shadows. We were on a narrow shelf of rock along the tree line. Above us was nothing but gray stone and scrub.

"I need to get my gear ready," I said tiredly, pulling the two packs over to me.

"Are you sure you killed Norman?" Tomasa asked me as I wiped sweat from my brow and fumbled with the clasps on my pack.

"I put two rounds into his head at arm's length. He's dead."

"Good, he was the only one of the ghouls who was still in control enough to be around the others of your kind. Wait until the sun is high in the sky. The Farmer won't risk the other ghouls coming into town while so many people are moving about. You need to figure out where your friend is before committing to the attack."

"I wish you weren't making so much sense," I said, my hand hovering in the air above my UMP.

"You're not going to help her if you get killed because you can't think straight," Tomasa said.

"You're right. I just can't stop worrying about her," I said with a sigh, my hand trembling over the UMP.

"More reason to stop, rest for a few hours. Don't go rushing in," Tomasa said.

"Thank you," I said, moving my hand away from the weapon. I knew he was right; I was tired and worn out, but it didn't take the sting away as I pulled my travel blanket off my pack. I couldn't help but feel guilty, wondering if Justine was shivering somewhere in the valley below me. "I have another blanket in Justine's bag," I said as I wrapped myself up and positioned my pack to use as a pillow.

"When the snows come, maybe I'll accept a blanket, but it had better be a lot bigger than that," Tomasa said, sinking down to lie on his side.

I slept until the sun was well into the sky. When I woke up, Tomasa was gone, but both packs and my UMP were where I'd left them. I rummaged through my pack, pulling out several protein bars and my canteen. I was eating when he climbed back up onto the ridge a few minutes later, whistling a strange, flat tune to let me know he was coming. I guess soldiers in his world got wounded when they surprised their comrades, too.

"Ah, good that you are awake. I was debating on if I should nudge you or make a noise if you were still asleep when I came back," he said.

I stuffed the last bit of a protein bar in my mouth and washed it down with some water before grabbing another and tossing it to the brute. "It's not a lot, but it's better than nothing," I said before throwing him another.

Tomasa ripped the wrapping off and sniffed at the bar before putting it in his mouth whole and chewing. He chewed and swallowed quickly before doing the same with the second. I threw him Justine's canteen as he did his best to smile and thank me. "What is your plan?" Tomasa asked as I buckled Justine's Walther to my hip and threw the UMP's sling over my shoulder.

"I slip into town, find Justine, and slip back out after saving her while the ghouls are all hiding from the sun."

"And if the Farmer or his foremen try to interfere?" Tomasa asked.

"Oh, then I kill them. It's a minor detail," I assured him.

"Give me your blanket," Tomasa said. "You look too much like you," he explained when I hesitated. I handed over the blanket, and he disappeared over the ledge. He came back a few moments later with my blanket noticeably soiled. He rolled it up in a ball to grind the dirt in and then shook it out, easily ripping a hole in its center for my head to fit through. He threw me the homemade poncho, and I caught it reflexively.

"Gross," I groaned, pulling my head back and wrinkling my nose. "Do I want to know what you put on this?"

"I believe it was from a deer. You'll fit in better if you smell like that."

"Good point," I said, rooting through my pack for the olive drab cloth I used to clean the UMP. I tied it around my neck so I could pull it up over my lower face if I needed to.

Our descent down the mountains was quiet. We stopped two-thirds of the way down to take a short rest before we separated. "If I hear shooting, do you want me to head into town?" Tomasa asked easily.

"You would, wouldn't you?" I asked.

"I am not quite ready to be left alone with no one to talk to again," Tomasa said as I worked my right shoulder in its socket. It was sore and it ached, but my range of motion was almost back to normal. "Your shoulder OK?" Tomasa asked.

"It's sore, but it won't slow me down," I said to him before turning away and starting down the final section of slope toward the highway.

I hoped I wasn't lying.

Chapter 11

I'd taken a long and circuitous route to get to within shouting distance of the town. Every pole, post, and road sign close by had been adorned with a thrall, pushing me to the north to get safely across the highway. Haeslig knew I'd come for Justine. Once across I kept moving west, almost to the river. After that, I followed the water south until I passed the town on my left. I'd made a huge circle from where I'd begun, but it let me approach the town from the far side, and I hoped an unexpected angle. And even after all the effort, getting the last hundred feet into town was going to be the hard part.

I was hiding on the edge of the tall grass, looking across the cleared ground between me and the alley that would let me onto the outer street. I stood up from a crouch and pretended to pull my pants up for the benefit of anyone who might be watching and started walking. I kept my hands under my poncho, clutching the UMP to my chest so it didn't bump around, trying to keep a look of nonchalant boredom on my face as my heart raced.

Once inside the alley, I fought down the impulse to put my back to a wall and look around, forcing myself to keep walking. If anyone was watching me, stopping and looking about would only confirm their suspicions. When I reached the main street, I turned to move with the foot traffic, not caring what direction I was heading. I fell in step with the other people and scanned my surroundings, orienting myself.

I was on the south side of town, walking toward the corner that would turn right onto Pit Street. The large barn the foremen lived in was looming in front of me, set two hundred feet back from the closest buildings. I settled into the crowd, following them around the corner and out into the field toward the pit. The bell on the platform started to ring when we were halfway there, but it was clear from the number of people already standing along the timbers that the contest had been preannounced. I was still working my way sideways through the crowd, hoping to escape into the tents along the red-light district, when Vaughn took the stage.

"This is a contest to the death. For the crime of murder, for killing Norman, one of the men who kept this town safe, you will fight until dead. And if not today, then tomorrow," he said. I froze, then let myself be carried forward as those behind me pushed and shoved me along.

Something happened up on the platform, and then the crowd let out a muted cheer and began their chant. "Door, door, door." I tucked one arm over my UMP and used my other to force my way through the crowd, getting elbows and angry curses thrown my way as I pushed my way to the front. A man grabbed my shoulder and started to turn me about, but the look in my eyes warned him off. He let go of me, and I surged ahead, leaving him behind. I reached the edge of the pit and looked down just as they opened the doors to a loud cheer from the crowd.

The small form stood facing away from me, looking small and fragile, dwarfed by the size of the pit. Her head had been crudely shorn, leaving tufts of longer hair here and there amid bald spots. My brain didn't recognize Justine until the two thralls reached her. She moved between them easily, clotheslining one and sending it to the ground as she grabbed the other by its outstretched arm, twisting it around with enough force that everyone above the pit could hear bones breaking. She never stopped moving. One attack flowed into the next as she let go of the thrall's arm and slipped around its side, stepping into the air so she could wrap a thin arm around its neck and snap its spine with a jerk as she landed on her feet.

The crowd booed.

Justine was already stepping toward the thrall she'd knocked to the ground, bringing her leg back to kick it in the face. Then she yelped and stumbled, her back going rigid for just a second. The crowd let out a mixed cry, some yelling foul while others screamed for more. Justine twitched as she shook off the unseen attack to drive her foot into the thrall's chin, knocking it back into the dirt. The crowd united in booing as she fell on the thrall's neck with her knee, killing it.

The crowd bubbled with anger as Justine climbed to her feet and was rewarded with what looked like a seizure. My hand reached out, grabbing the top of the timber wall around the pit as the tendons in her neck bulged and her head lifted to the sky; she let out a squeal of pain she was only half able to hold back. Several people were screaming for more, and I realized they were focused on Vaughn, who stood on the stage, a small black device in his hands. My eyes darted back to Justine, and I realized she had a shock collar fixed to her neck.

"Doesn't seem fair," someone next to me grumbled, shutting up as the people around him turned on him.

I heard a smack, and then someone said, "Wasn't fair when she seduced Norman and then beat up Abigail. There wasn't even anything in the house worth killing for; Norman lived like a monk."

The talking was drowned out by the renewed chant for the doors to be opened. Justine was standing, her shoulders heaving as she panted raggedly. Vaughn stood on the front of the platform, glaring down at her, his thumb lifted over the control on his remote. Justine was staring up at him, but her defiance faded as I watched, her chin falling to her chest as he stood with a victorious grin on his face above her. I took a breath and eased the safety off the UMP beneath my poncho, wondering if the crowd would scatter if Vaughn's life were extinguished with a hail of gunfire.

Vaughn made a motion with his free hand, and the door below him opened once again, letting more thralls spill into the pit. Justine took a step and faltered, limping on one leg as if it had a cramp. She took a clumsy punch as the nearest thrall closed on her and then tried to dance to the side, but she wasn't quick enough, getting wrapped up in its arms just as the two slower thralls caught up to them. I started to lift the UMP as Justine and the three thralls went down in a pile, but something tugged at my elbow. I pushed the hand away, growling, not taking my eyes off the wriggling pile of bodies in the pit.

"They're coming," Abigail said, pulling harder on my elbow. "Put this on," she commanded, shoving a camo John

Deere ball cap into my chest. "We need to get out of here."

I took the ball cap and pulled it on, looking at Abigail in surprise. She hardly looked like the girl I'd seen the day before. She was in the same clothes, but her hair was matted to her head and her clothes were covered in mud.

I looked back into the pit. Justine had made it to the top of the pile and rolled off, taking an arm with her. She threw it down and proceeded to kick another thrall in the face until its neck snapped. All finesse was gone; she was a wild animal, fighting savagely. She dropped onto the last thrall with an elbow, driving its head to the ground with a wet crunch. The crowd went wild, half of them cheering while the other half yelled in protest.

"We have to go; it's only a matter of time before they see you," Abigail said, pulling at my arm will all her weight. I looked around and realized several men were moving through the crowd and that the people gave way to them without comment, leaving a small bubble of clear space around each man. I let Abigail pull me back through the masses and realized there were more foremen atop the storage buildings along the back of Pit Street. At least one of them had a set of binoculars.

I pulled the cap down tighter my head and let Abigail tow me along, taking us to within feet of one of the foremen. If he took note of us, all he saw was a girl leading a john into the red-light district. She led me to a faded-green scouting tent and pulled me inside. The floor was covered in blankets and sleeping bags, and there were two buckets just inside the tent flaps. One was full of dirty, soapy water; the other was full of dirtier, less soapy water. The tent smelled of sweat, body odor, and sex.

She yanked the tent flaps closed and turned on me. "You're an idiot for coming back here," she said, fighting back tears. "I wished you'd never come into town."

"Do you know where they're keeping her?" I asked, my eyes falling from the anger and sadness burning in Abigail's eyes.

"They've got her in the underground attached to the pit. They came and got me at my aunt's the next morning, brought me back to their barn to ask me questions. I told them horrible things about Justine," Abigail said, her voice breaking.

"It's OK; you did what you had to do," I said, reaching out with a hand and then pulling back as she shrank away in fear.

"I saw her for just a moment before they took her down into the tunnels. I was so mad, I screamed and screamed," Abigail said, not able to hold back the sobs. "She told me it was OK; then one of the foremen punched her. I was so mad that she let them catch her. I couldn't step yelling at her. The foremen thought it was funny," she said, wiping tears from her eyes with her forearm.

"Justine would be proud of you."

"Why?" Abigail demanded, actually stamping a food as more tears slid down her cheeks.

"You survived. You told them exactly what you needed to. You did really good," I assured her, trying to calm her with my voice. "Do you know why her head is shaved?" I asked once she'd gotten her crying under control.

"I don't know; she had her hair when I saw her in the barn."

"The shock collar?"

"She was beaten up a little when I saw her, but she didn't have that on either. I heard she killed one of the foremen last night, though. That probably had something to do with it," Abigail said. I opened my mouth to ask another question, but Abigail cut me off. "Look, we're even," she blurted out. "You saved me from Norman, and I saved you today. When the people start leaving the pit, you are walking out of this tent and I never want to see you again."

"I understand. I'm sorry things turned out so badly. We're more than even."

"Good," she said, crossing her arms defiantly as she sniffled.

"How did you get into the tunnels?"

Abigail gave me a hard look and sighed, but she answered. "There's an entrance in the foremen's barn. But there are at least forty people in there."

The show at the pit must have ended, people were starting to move about outside. "Don't come back here,"

Abigail said, slipping out of the tent and holding it open for me before I could ask her any more questions.

I climbed out and let my head hang low, hoping anyone who saw me would assume I was ashamed for being in the red-light district as I made my way back down the row of tents, working my way to the bazaar. Two foremen stood at the entrance to the stalls, talking about whether they should put bets on tomorrow's contest or not. Rumor seemed to have it that they were going to put Justine up against five or six thralls at a time.

I lowered my head and used the bandana around my neck to wipe my mouth as I walked by them, slipping into the stream of people leaving the pit and heading into the bazaar. Three more foremen were walking up from the far end of the stalls, and they weren't chatting or goofing off. They were scanning faces and looking for anything out of the ordinary as they approached.

I stopped at the long stall selling apple cider, putting my back to the rest of the street as I cheered and laughed with the men gathered there. I put my arm around a fellow already in his cups, helping hold him up as he swayed. He gave me an odd look then smiled as I steadied him on his feet, cheering as the bookie called out a winner.

As soon as the foremen passed us by, I headed off in the opposite direction, letting my shoulders slump and doing my best to look mildly tipsy and completely uninteresting. As I made my way along the outer street, I fell in with the normal foot traffic. The townies knew something was up but had no idea what it was. Rumors flew as I walked among them. Justine was being put to death to teach anyone who would kill a foreman a lesson. Justine was an assassin who'd been sent in by another group of survivors to kill the Farmer. Or she was going to take Norman's place as the pit boss if she survived ten days. And those were the rumors with enough logic to them that I could even halfway understand them.

I circled the outside street, making a full circuit of the town until the foremen's barn was in front of me again. I slipped into a small alley just before the end of the street and urinated, taking my time as I waited to see if anyone was following me. When I was reasonably sure I was clear, I moved back to the front of the alley and leaned against the edge of the shack next to me, lingering as I explored one nostril and then the next with my index finger.

I could see the barn and one edge of the pit from where I was, and it wasn't encouraging. The barn had two foremen at each visible corner, and I saw at least two patrols roving around the building as well. A work crew with a ladder was at one corner of the barn, replacing or fixing one of the spotlights. I really wanted to get a closer look at the pit and the door into the underground, but walking out into the open would have been suicide. I pulled my finger out of my nose and flicked an imaginary booger onto the ground before walking away.

I'd made a tactical error thinking that slipping in during the day would give me an advantage. Instead of having to look out for ghouls, I had to be wary of a few dozen foremen on high alert. I didn't blame Tomasa for planting the thought in my head, though; he'd just been trying to give me an excuse to rest for a few hours. I retreated down the street and slipped out of town through the alley I'd come in through, crossing the open ground with even steps. I thought furiously as I walked, formulating a plan. The foremen were clearly on alert, and there was no way I was getting into the barn without being seen, but the pit was out in the open, and there were no lights around it. They'd left a crack in their defenses, and I was going to try to use it against them.

I was following a thin trail through the tall grass when I saw the faint shiver of motion in front of me and off to my left. I'd let myself get distracted by what I was planning to do and had almost walked into an ambush. I cursed at myself internally and forced my pace not to change. The man was crouching in the weeds just off the side of the path. He was wearing camouflaged hunting gear with bits of grass tied artfully here and there. I slipped my folding knife off my belt under the cover of my poncho and used the thumb latch to open it one handed.

I was even with my concealed stalker when he stood up and brought his shock wand around. He thought he was catching me unawares and was trying to tag me in the back of the neck where there was little clothing to blunt the voltage of his attack. I let him have that one brief moment when he thought he was going to catch me by surprise— then I threw my left arm up to catch the wand on the fabric of my poncho. The shock wand went off, sending a jolt down my arm, but it was muted enough that I was able to take the pain with a grunt.

My stalker started to yell, but it turned into an explosion of breath as my right hand hit his chest just below his sternum. I started the strike with my knees slightly bent, driving forward with the strength in my legs just as the tip of the blade broke his flesh. His feet lifted off the ground as I powered him backward, my left hand groping for his face as I landed on top of him. I found his mouth and pushed his head back as I pulled the knife out, punching him again. Teeth closed on my hand as I drove my palm into his mouth, halting his scream as I stabbed him multiple times with sharp jabs. The blade was short, and the man had some meat on his bones; I didn't hit his aorta until the fourth or fifth strike. I knew the moment I cut into it. A geyser of blood plumed from the space right between the man's belly button and breastbone, striking my poncho with enough force to push it against my chest.

I kept my hand pressed into his mouth as I twisted the blade, the plume of blood turning to a weak spray and, a heartbeat later, nothing. I pulled the blade free and stabbed him again, not realizing the biting pressure on my left hand was from me trying to ram my fist down his throat until I looked down and saw the way his body had gone completely limp beneath me. I pulled my knife free and stood on my knees, scanning the tops of the swaying grass around me as my pulse throbbed in my neck. There was no sign of any other ambushers.

I searched the body quickly, but the man had nothing of value on him. His shock wand had broken as I carried him to the ground, and the only other weapon he had was a low-quality chef's knife in a duct-tape sheath. I climbed over his body and crept through the grass, watching and listening for any signs of other ambushers. Once I made it to the river, I turned north and started to retrace my long, circuitous route back to where I'd left Tomasa.

When I made it to the highway, I crept across the drainage ditch and climbed up the berm on my belly so I could look up and down the highway. I was a bit surprised to see the nearest thrall's head was missing; or rather its head from the neck up appeared to have been smashed back into the telephone pole. If Haeslig was hoping to use his network of sentry thralls to catch sight of me, he was going to be disappointed. I darted across the highway and leapt over the guardrail, moving down the berm on the other side before climbing back into the cover of the trees where I stopped to look behind me. Nothing moved for as far as I could see up or down the highway.

Tomasa found me as I was working my way along a game trail. He waved to me from one end of the path, holding a wooden staff as thick around as my bicep in his other hand. "Your work?" I asked, nodding to the highway below us as I reached him.

"I got bored just sitting up here. I started with some closer to town and then moved farther out. I figured any distraction I could give you would be helpful." He smiled. "Plus, it was fun. The Nechtruin, your thralls, they are abominations." He paused before he asked his question. "Your friend is alive?"

"Yes, she's alive. They have her fighting in the pit. They're trying to draw me in."

"No luck with the plan to slip into town, find the girl, and slip back out after killing the Farmer?"

"Not so much," I said. "No sign of the ghouls, but every foreman in town is on high alert."

"One or two less maybe?" Tomasa said, looking at the stain on the front of my poncho.

"Just one," I said, half jogging to keep up with him as he walked. A little farther along the trail, we passed a bundle of saplings as big around as my wrist leaning against a tree. I raised an eyebrow at Tomasa as we passed them.

"They are rough projectiles, and my aim is not so good as when I was younger, but they will do if needed," he said with a nod. There was something about the way he complained about his aim that made me think he was being overly modest. We walked a little farther before he asked me what my plan was.

"They have the barn too well guarded during the day. If I shot my way in to get her, I'd bring everything in town down on my head. But they leave the pit exposed. After dark, I'm going to break into the tunnels and free her. Do you think you could wait for me at the highway?"

Tomasa laughed. "I was thinking I might have other plans for tonight," he said. My heart fell. If things went south, having the big guy there could make all the difference.

"I understand," I said, nodding. It wasn't his fight, and he'd already done more than I had any right to expect from him.

He stopped walking and turned me to him with one massive finger poking into my shoulder. "You didn't really think I was going to let you leave me behind twice, did you?" he asked, raising an eyebrow at me.

"You've already put yourself in danger. If the grays knew you came over intact, I'd imagine they might want to end you."

"Worse than death, they might want to use me for things other than just my brawn," Tomasa said, tapping his temple. "You are an interesting man, Daniel Ryan. I don't think I'm ready to part ways just yet. Besides, you're the first person I've been able to talk to in a long time," he said, smiling just a little.

"Friends are hard to come by," I said.

"Indeed," Tomasa agreed as we moved to higher ground. Tomasa found a stand of young saplings, and we stopped to wait for the coming night. I sat and rested, watching Tomasa use raw strength to turn the young trees into several more spears. I watched him work, not quite able to merge what my eyes were seeing with reality. Sitting so close to a brute still felt unreal.

"What are you thinking?" Tomasa asked as he worked, grinding a tip onto a piece of green wood by forcing it against the rock face behind us.

"You said my kind has lost so much history. You've

been here before, haven't you?"

"Not me, obviously, but yes, the Blutsauger have visited your people in the past. There was a debate in my realm about what triggered the change."

"The change?"

"The awareness in your people that the Blutsauger were among them. For a very long time, your people did not believe, and maybe that led Blutsauger lords to believe you never would. They saw your people as food, as simple. Then one day one of the Blutsauger lords never returned. His second went looking for him and came back with strange tales and horrible wounds."

"We made weapons, didn't we?" I asked, remembering Millie's bowl at Mr. Deringer's house. The memories of Jersey seemed far away.

"Yes, things of power that the lords could barely believe your kind capable of. In the space of one generation your people learned to detect those from my realm and hunt them. It was at the peak of the fighting that your kind found a way to close the gateways. It was the subject of much debate on my realm. Some were convinced that your kind could not have closed the gateways without the help of Blutsauger. Several families lost their bloodlines over allegations that were never proven."

"What do you believe?" I asked.

"I think the Blutsauger were arrogant. They assumed your kind would never realize what walked among them and then their own hubris brought them lower still. In those days your world was a playground for the powerful. The Blutsauger who crossed over kept their gateways small and secret. Those with the knowledge to do more were almost destroyed outright in the initial conflicts.

"Then your ancestors managed to close the gateways, locking our worlds apart just before the lords could mount their counteroffensive. Whatever was done stood strong for several generations. But as the cracks started to form, the Blutsauger started to plan. As soon as they could make a portal just big enough to send a single body through, they began their attack. It started with simple goals. Learn about your world; find out what your people remembered."

"It doesn't sound like a story to you," I said quietly, watching as his head jumped up to look at me.

There was guilt on his face when he spoke. "I was a member of the college of stratagem when the cracks formed. The plan that brought your world low was in part my doing." Tomasa held my eyes after he spoke, licking his lips nervously as he waited for my reaction.

"If only you'd known the reality of what the Blutsauger were doing to both our peoples," I said, rubbing my chin wearily.

"If only I had," Tomasa agreed before continuing with his history lesson. "We started to slowly infiltrate your world, taking advantage of those of your kind we could seduce with promises of power while putting others who were more able to hide among you in positions of leadership. What you saw as an overnight attack was a war we'd been fighting for almost thirty years. It all seems like such a waste now."

"I think that's the nature of war." I pulled the brim of my hat down over my eyes so I could rest. "When this is over, I really want to sit down and have some long discussions with you," I said through a yawn.

"I would like that as well," Tomasa said, the rhythmic sound of his grinding saplings into spears reminding me of the sound of waves as I drifted into a half sleep.

Tomasa woke me from my stupor an hour before dusk. I stood and stretched before checking my gear and peeing down the slope. Tomasa was ready for me when I turned around, his staff in one hand and a bundle of fresh spears under his other arm. We made our way back down the mountain, stopping only to drop his spears off along the trail before continuing down the highway.

We made it safely into the woods on the far side of the highway and headed southwest. I thought we might be slowed by the brute's size as we moved through the thicker brush and trees, but Tomasa never fell behind or raised more than a whisper of noise. We made good time, not seeing or hearing any sign of ghouls as we closed to within striking distance of town. I went wide of the field where I'd killed my stalker earlier in the day, leading Tomasa to the river. We made much better time than I'd thought we would, and we still had a half hour before dusk. I wanted to time our arrival so we moved into town just after dark, while people were still settling in and any noise we might make would be mixed in with the sounds of the town going to sleep.

We moved away from the river just as the shadows were lengthening and merging with the coming dark. The trees around us thinned, giving way to overgrown fields. We stopped just before the cleared section of ground around the town, surveying the open terrain. The circle of light around the barn was in front of us, and hidden somewhere in darkness between us was the pit.

"I smell ghoul," Tomasa said, snorting lightly.

"Close?" I asked.

"Not sure. They've been by here multiple times; it makes it difficult to tell the old from the new," he said, leaning down so he could speak to the back of my head. He was just finished speaking when I felt his hand on my shoulder, pushing me to the ground as he said, "Down," and dropped flat next to me.

I heard it before I saw it. The ghoul wasn't trying to be quiet. It was jogging at a slow pace as it tracked a path on the edge of the clearing. The ghoul looked like it was on the verge of losing control of its limbs. Its arms flopped about as it jogged while its head moved all around, unable to focus, even on the ground in front of it. It almost tripped and fell as we watched.

I reached for my machete only to touch my thigh. I'd lost the blade during the fight in the orchard. A pang of regret went through me; I'd had the weapon since the early days of the apocalypse back in Jersey. I felt naked without it. I crouched, my finger moving from the guard to the trigger of the UMP as the ghoul made its awkward approach. The creature's path was going to carry it to within touching distance of us.

"Quietly," Tomasa breathed out next to me. I kept my eye on the ghoul, willing Tomasa to attack as the distance closed. The brute waited until the last moment, leaping to his feet directly in front of the ghoul as he reached out, palming the creature's head with one massive hand. As quickly as he'd stood, he was falling to his knees, driving the ghoul's head into the ground.

"Time is against us now," Tomasa said as he stood, the remnants of the ghoul's brains dripping from between his fingers. I was running before he finished speaking, sprinting across the open ground in the direction of the tents along the red-light district. I stopped for just a moment when I was between two tents, looking behind me for the brute. He was right on my heels, just two steps behind me. He slowed just enough to get a hand on my shoulder and push me ahead of him, saying, "Go, go, go," as he propelled me forward.

There was open ground in front of us, and then the deeper blackness of the pit. I dug in, sprinting as Tomasa easily pulled even with me. "Two ghouls coming up the street," Tomasa said in a single breath as he overtook me, gaining one and then two huge steps on me. "Jump," he said over his shoulder as he hurdled the low wooden wall before descending into the darkness of the pit.

I was a step from the wall when I heard the gibbering of the ghouls coming up through the bazaar. They were close; they had to be near the corner, and there was no way they weren't going to see me running once they got free of the merchant stalls. I was two long steps away when I dove, the top of the tallest log scraping across my poncho as I flew into darkness.

I was surrounded by complete blackness, falling. Time slowed, stretching out. I heard my heartbeat in my ears as a long, drawn-out thud. Icy fingers of doubt gripped my stomach. In my mind's eye the bottom of the pit stretched down and down, ending in a bed of sharpened stakes. Sudden pressure pushed up into my stomach, and time shifted into fast-forward. My descent slowed suddenly, my head snapping forward as Tomasa's hand slipped up to my chest, catching me. He lowered me to the ground and shushed me like a child as I sighed in relief.

I crouched in the dark, my eyes watching the lighter darkness ringing the pit above me. If the ghouls looked over the edge, I was going to take their heads off. I forced my breathing to slow, counting off in my head as nothing had happened. Tomasa stood behind me, so close I could feel his breath hitting the back of my neck.

By the count of ten, I was fairly certain we hadn't been seen. I blinked my eyes, scanning the darkness around me. Off to my left a faint line of light escaped from the edge of the door leading into the underground. I took slow, careful steps toward the light, my feet sinking into the soft dirt at the bottom of the pit, until I could press my head against the wood and peer through the gap along its closing edge.

The interior of the tunnel looked like an old mine shaft. Wooden timbers held up the roof at regular intervals, and a bare light bulb hung from a wire ten feet farther into the tunnel. As I stared, flashes of light came from farther inside the underground, paired with the unmistakable sound of shock wands discharging.

I pushed my ear to the crack, my heart racing. I heard fists landing on flesh in loud slaps and then a high-pitched scream of pain. "Open this door," I begged Tomasa, slamming a hand into the wood in anger.

Tomasa set his staff against the wall and ran his hands along the edges of the door, looking for a handhold. "This is going to be loud," he warned, giving the door an experimental shove inward.

"Please do it," I begged, stepping back.

Tomasa put his shoulder in the middle of the door and dug in with his feet. The reinforced wood groaned as the brute clawed at the ground, digging a rut under his feet as the timbers popped and crunched. There was a brief moment when I thought the door was going to hold, and then it gave with a sudden explosion of splinters. The sound of the door shattering was still echoing in the pit when we heard the first ghoul cry out, then another.

"Go get her," Tomasa said, picking up his staff before planting himself in front of the riven door.

Chapter 12

I stepped into the tunnel, the UMP on my shoulder as I walked fast into the underground. The air was wet and heavy with the smell of death and rot, which competed with the slightly sharper smell of poorly vented gasoline fumes. The hanging lights cast the path in front of me in a sickly, yellowish light, revealing an intersection off to my left.

I stepped wide of the opening; the light from the main shaft only fell a few feet into the intersection, showing the bottom of what looked like a barred prison door. I flinched when bodies rammed into the bars and rotten hands reached out into the light, trying to reach me. I eased back from the intersection, turning to the main tunnel, my finger resting lightly on the trigger as I heard men yelling ahead of me.

I continued forward, moving along a slight bend in the tunnel until I could see a set of wooden stairs a hundred feet in front of me. Bright light spilled down the stairs from above, accompanied by the sounds of men rushing about. It had to be the entrance from the foremen's barn. Halfway between where I stood and the stairs was another branch in the tunnel. Light and noise poured out into the main shaft from the intersection. I could hear the dull throb of a generator under the sounds of men moving about and talking. I dropped to a crouch as shadows spilled out into the hall a moment before three men came running into view, all of them holding shock wands. They paused for just a moment when they saw me, and I didn't give them time to recover; I opened up with the UMP, firing a burst into each of their chests.

The sound of the weapon in the confines of the tunnel was deafening. I stepped through the haze of smoke, covering the side passage the men had come from as I moved forward. Someone was screaming from out of sight. "Henry, Henry, what's going on out there?"

I glanced down at the three men on the ground as I approached the intersection, looking at their bodies. One of them was still breathing, trying to say something back to the man calling from around the corner as he tried to get a hold of his shock wand. I put two more rounds into him and hugged the wall as I reloaded.

The man around the corner stopped calling for Henry.

A metallic bang echoed through the tunnel as I edged up to the wooden beam forming the corner of the intersection, darting my head around just enough to get a view of what was in front of me. There was a short hallway, and then another set of prison bars set into a concrete sill. Behind that was a large, well-lit room that looked like a combination workshop and torture chamber.

A small gas generator chugged away in the far corner with a section of black PVC piping coming off its exhaust and disappearing into the ceiling. The corner opposite the generator was filled with a cage like the kind used for large dogs. It was attached to the generator with a pair of jumper cables. A stab of pain went through my gut as my eyes stopped on the table set at an almost upright angle in the middle of the room. Justine was strapped to it, her head hanging limply forward. She was stripped to her underpants, her small breasts exposed for all to see. Two men stood on each side of the table, but I hardly noticed them as I pulled my head back, the image of Justine's body covered in bruises and burns etched into my vision.

"You better run, boy!" someone yelled.

Rage filled me. My heart thudded so hard in my chest that my eyes felt like they were being pushed out of my head with each stroke. "You are all going to die," I said, my voice hoarse and croaky, filled with raw emotion.

"This girl's full of piss and vinegar, boy, but she ain't gonna survive me cutting her throat. And I'll do it if you poke your head around that corner again," one of them yelled.

"I'm going, but if you hurt her, I'll hunt you down," I said, waiting a breath after I was done speaking to slide out from behind my cover, the UMP already on my shoulder. The brave bastard with the buck knife to Justine's throat was hiding behind the table, his head next to hers as his arm wrapped around from behind to push the blade into her flesh.

The world slowed as I stepped forward into the short hallway.

I could feel every shiver and pulse of electricity as the overhead lights flickered. My index finger squeezed once, then again, and I watched as the rounds left the muzzle of the weapon just a split second before I felt the weapon kick. My two rounds hit the man holding the buck knife just above his nose, sending him flying backward as his knife fell to the floor.

"H...o...l...y...f...u...c...k!" one of the men screamed in slow motion, trying to scramble for cover as I shifted my aim.

A crossbow bolt went by my head from off to my left as I fired at the screamer, putting rounds into his back as he tried to run for cover. The man with the crossbow reloaded it with expert hands, raising the weapon to his shoulder just as I dropped to a knee. We fired at the same moment, the fletching of his bolt running through my hair as my round punched a hole the size of a quarter through the middle of his face.

Time snapped back to normal as the last foreman hefted his axe like a baseball bat, turning on Justine. He was already twisting, bringing the blade around as I fired. The angle and the bars between us limited my aim so my first round hit him high in the shoulder. I was screaming as he stumbled sideways, his axe blade narrowly missing Justine's side as it sank into the wooden timbers of the table she was strapped to. I stepped closer to the bars and hit him with two more bursts, the first tearing into his chest while the second took off the top of his head.

I stood there screaming, frozen in rage and fear. It had been so close. Just inches more and he would have sunk his blade into her abdomen. I shook the metal bars with one hand as the reality of how badly they'd hurt her set in. Her nearly naked body was covered in bruises and long, angry welts from the shock wands. She was naked except for her panties and the electric dog collar around her neck, and even as I stood there I heard it beep and go off, making her twitch against her restraints. It must have been put on a timer to help control her. I grabbed the bars of the gate and was filled with a momentary sense of futility until I realized the only thing holding it closed was a sliding bolt. The men had been worried about thralls getting loose in the tunnel, not me. I reached through and slid the bolt free, my legs suddenly rubbery as I crossed the open ground to Justine.

I forced back the urge to cry. Justine's small breasts were marred by burns and bruises, and one of her small nipples was tipped with blackened singe. Her eyes fluttered open as I unsnapped the shock collar from around her neck and threw it to the floor as it beeped and went off again.

"I was waiting for you," she whispered as I unbuckled the straps binding her wrists and waist.

"I'm sorry," I said, choking back a sob.

"You came," she said, letting her eyes close again. I found her shirt on one of the workbenches and worked it over her head before pulling her arms through the holes. She groaned and grimaced but helped as much as she could. I would have liked to put pants on her, but they had been cut off and were in strips on the ground around us. I was about to pick her up when I saw something else on the workbench. Scattered among a selection of weapons was my machete. I slipped it into its sheath and patted its hilt, feeling strangely relieved that I'd recovered it.

"This is going to hurt," I said, crouching down and pulling her onto my shoulder. She groaned, but she went limp quickly as she either passed out or gave in to fatigue. I moved back to the main tunnel, stopping at the corner as legs and lower bodies appeared on the stairs at the far end of the underground.

I waited until their bodies were fully in view and took the first two men down with shots to their torsos. I didn't wait to see what happened next; I ran into the main tunnel and hauled ass, spraying a few shots behind me as I heard men yelling and a crossbow bolt sank into a wooden post off to my right. I made it around the gentle bend and could see the broken doorway in the pit calling to me.

Justine was moaning, her hands flopping against my lower back and butt as I ran. I was halfway to the door to the pit when I heard a mechanical scraping noise. I didn't know what it was until the side tunnel in front of me overflowed with thralls. I lifted the UMP with my free hand and gripped Justine's butt over my shoulder hard, charging the horde flooding into the tunnel as I let loose with bursts at head height.

Bodies dropped as rotten flesh exploded. Then I was hugging the far side of the tunnel, fighting to stay moving as they continued to pour out of the holdings cells. I kicked a child thrall out of the way and emptied the last rounds in my clip in a short burst before letting the weapon fall against my chest on its sling. I decked a thrall with everything I could put into it, rocking its head back before grabbing its shirt and using it to pull myself forward at the same time I yanked its body into the hands of the other groping dead.

One moment I was surrounded by thralls, and then I'd broken free, leaving the undead behind me as I ran to the end of the tunnel, climbing through the shattered door back out into the night. The transition from the electric lights of the tunnel to the darkness of the pit left me blinded.

"Move!" Tomasa yelled as a wall hit my side, almost taking me off my feet. I heard a baseball get hit out of the park as I spun about, the night resolving into dark shapes and outlines. Tomasa was next to me, and a ghoul's body was lying on the ground about where I'd been standing before he'd hip checked me out of the way. Two other bodies were not far off. Above us men were starting to yell and holler as the foremen in the barn poured out into the night.

"Can you lift us?" I asked, looking up at the distance between the lip of the pit and me, drawing the pistol on my hip to fire at a shadow darting above us. Tomasa dropped his staff and lifted me like a ballet dancer, his hands on either side of my hips. I continued to rise through the air when he let go, sailing over the stem wall and onto the ground on the other side. I took two rapid steps forward to keep my balance and turned to aim behind me at the entrance to the barn, teaching at least one of the foremen not to stand in the light while he fired a crossbow at me.

Tomasa's staff clattered to the ground next to me a moment before his hands gripped the top of the wall and his head appeared. He levered himself up easily and climbed out, grabbing his staff. The town around us was starting to wake up. The sound of a baby wailing in the distance was interrupted by the twang of crossbow bolts being fired and Tomasa grunting as a shaft sank into his back.

We ran toward the tents of the red-light district as more crossbows twanged in the dark. I emptied my pistol in the general direction of the foremen and kept running, slipping between two tents and into the open ground on the far side. I'm not sure if I hit any of them, but enough of them paused to take cover to lessen the number of bolts flying our way.

I was panting by the time we made it to the tall grass bordering the town. "Give me the girl," Tomasa said, reaching out for her. I hesitated, not wanting to let her go. "If you carry her like that and you get a bolt from behind, all this was for nothing," Tomasa said angrily. I nodded, lifting her off my shoulder so he could take her in one arm, draping her over his forearm like a towel. He pushed me forward, telling me to stay in front of him as more crossbows twanged in the night. I rammed my pistol back into its holster and grabbed my UMP as we ran. My empty clip hit my thigh and spun away into the darkness as I reloaded on the run.

Men were screaming and calling out to each other as lights blossomed in the dark behind us. The town had been roused. A woman started to scream, the sound full of fear. I heard someone screaming, "Biters!" The thralls from the pit must have worked their way back up into the foremen's barn and out into the town. That or some of the ghouls had completely lost control. We escaped into the darkness as the foremen turned to fight the undead.

We kept moving, hugging a thin line of trees and scrub along the edge of the pumpkin fields. Tomasa surprised me when he surged up next to me, holding out Justine, "Take her," he blurted as he slid her off his arm and onto my shoulder. She almost slipped to the ground before I clamped down on her thighs and hiked her back up. Tomasa started to make a strange clucking noise, running in front of me. I wondered if something were wrong with him. There were two crossbow bolts in his back that I could see, and I didn't know if more were hidden by the dark.

He started to cluck louder and faster, and then three forms streaked from the darkness of the pumpkin field and flew through the air at him. Tomasa caught one on his staff, sending it flying back into the night in a mad cartwheel of broken arms and legs. The other two hit him in the torso, swarming up his body, trying to get to his neck. I skidded to a halt, unable to help as Tomasa grabbed one of the ghouls and threw it to the ground with enough force that I heard bones breaking. He stepped on the creature's back for good measure as he reached for the last ghoul scrambling up his body like a spider. He nearly had it as it crawled madly around his side and onto his back.

Tomasa threw his arm over his head, then around his back, trying to reach the ghoul as it scurried about. It would have looked funny if the ghoul hadn't pulled one of the crossbow bolts free so it could sink its teeth into the wound. Tomasa slapped at it, driving it farther down his back only to have the creature tear free the other bolt piercing his back, once again feeding from the wound.

"Abominations," Tomasa grunted as he took his staff in both hands, slamming it back over his head. The ghoul let out an explosive breath as the staff crushed it and then fell to the ground with a shattered spine. Tomasa was shaking with pain and rage as he ground the ghoul's head into the dirt with his foot.

"You OK?" I asked, feeling very small. The air around Tomasa was filled with energy. I'd seen soldiers go berserk in combat before, and sometimes they forgot friend from foe in the process.

"That hurt," Tomasa said with a sigh and a wince, all the energy draining out of him.

"How badly? Can you still run?" I asked, looking around us.

"Ha, these are flea bites." Tomasa laughed, holding out his arm for Justine again. "I am Tomasa Elingrad Domingradaschick," he said, as if his name were also a title. "I can still run." He smiled as he said it and then took off at what was a slow walk for him, letting me catch up before increasing the pace.

The smell of apples filled my nose, telling me we were

close to the orchards before we reached them. As soon as we were moving through the rows of apple trees, Tomasa turned us east toward the highway. Behind us we heard multiple ghouls cry out as they found our trail. "We have to go faster," Tomasa said between breaths, ducking below a branch as he increased his pace. I was running just short of full speed. "Once we make it across the highway, we can lose them in the mountains. We have to get to high ground." I nodded, not caring if he saw it or not. I didn't have breath to waste on words.

We burst out onto the road, and for a moment I thought we'd made it, but my sense of direction had been corrupted in the dark. We were on the country road that bordered the northern edge of the orchards. We'd moved farther north than I thought when we were fleeing. We turned east onto the country road, running for the highway. I heard bodies breaking through the undergrowth around us just as the larger road came into sight.

"Hurry, they're almost on us," Tomasa rasped as he outdistanced me. The sound of bare feet slapping on the pavement was closing on me from behind. I glanced over my shoulder to see a man wearing nothing but cutoff jean shorts closing on me. Bloody froth sprayed from his lips as he groped the air, screaming and panting in one breath as he gave chase.

"Get her to safety!" I yelled.

"They are fresh ghouls; they can barely control themselves," Tomasa warned.

"Go!" I screamed, planting my feet. My boots skidded across the pavement as I shouldered the UMP and fired into the charging ghoul. My first shots hit him in the upper chest, and even in the darkness I could see the bullets passing through his thin torso as he closed the remaining steps between us. His fingertips were reaching for the UMP when I fired into his forehead.

His body hit mine full force, sending us both rolling across the ground until I came up on top, pulling the UMP back to my shoulder as I rammed the tip of the muzzle into the ghoul's face. I jumped to my feet without wasting another round; the ghoul was already dead. I came up facing west, looking down the old country road in the direction I'd just come from. More ghouls burst out of the orchard, one of them doing a face plant as it tripped up onto the road.

I turned and ran.

Tomasa was almost to the highway in front of me, but I had ghouls charging along the orchards off to my right, just ahead of me. If they made it onto the road in front of me, I'd be trapped. I shouldered the UMP at a run, letting loose with three round bursts. Apples exploded, but if I hit any of the ghouls, they didn't slow. I hit the clip release and slammed home a fresh magazine, breathing in ragged gasps as I fought to outrace the ghouls tearing through the orchard.

At least Justine was going to be safe.

I watched as Tomasa made it over the far guardrail with little more than a high step and then disappear into the darkness and tree cover as he scrambled up the hillside at the base of the mountain. I used what energy I had left, pushing myself for just a little more speed. The ghouls in the orchard were veering toward me, still slightly ahead of me as they ran. I could hear more behind me, grunting and breathing hard as they tried to close the distance.

I concentrated on stretching my legs just a little farther, willing the ground to move faster beneath me as I thumbed the selector to full auto. I waited to pull the trigger until they were close, so close I couldn't miss them as I swept automatic fire across their legs in a single, long roar that lit up the night. The three ghouls tumbled over one another as their legs were cut out from under them, going down in a ball of flailing limbs. I let go of the UMP and pumped my arms, looking straight ahead as my feet landed on the highway.

I'd made it.

Just as the thought went through my mind, something caught my ankle, and I went down hard, just catching myself on my hands before my head made contact with the road. I tried to pull my leg away, but the iron grasp around my ankle didn't give. I kicked the ghoul in the face with my other foot, breaking its grip just enough to roll over onto my back. I was kicking and reaching for a clip when another ghoul leapt over the one trying to climb up my legs, forcing me to take the UMP between my hands and use the weapon to hold back its upper body. The ghoul leaned down over the UMP, its teeth snapping shut on the air in front of my face.

My right arm blossomed in pain as the ghoul at my feet let go and piled on top, rearing up and slamming the ghoul sandwiched between us with both its fists. The metal of the UMP bit into my hands as I struggled to hold their combined weight off my chest. The butt of the UMP started to sag on my right as that arm quivered in protest. The ghouls on top of me snapped and snarled at each other as their weight slowly descended on me. They seemed barely in control of themselves, frenzied.

I sucked in a breath as the weight above me suddenly lessened. There was only the one ghoul still straddling me. It looked back, its brow furrowed, then turned to me, its whole body shaking with barely controlled rage. The ghoul lunged, trying to bring its gaping mouth down on my neck and face. I jerked the UMP up just in time, catching the ghoul in the mouth. Broken shards of teeth rained down on me as the creature reared back, snarling and drooling bloody streamers of saliva as it tried to rip the UMP out of my grasp.

I bucked and fought, trying to break free, but it wouldn't let go of the UMP. I could hear more ghouls approaching. I was almost out of time. I let go of the weapon, grabbing my belt knife and opening it with a flick of my wrist. The ghoul pulled the UMP to its chest, surprised to suddenly have control of the weapon. I didn't give the creature time to recover; I reached up with my left hand and grabbed the ghoul by its hair, pulling it down to meet the knife in my other hand. My blade sank into its throat, and I then yanked down on the handle of the blade, opening one side of the ghoul's neck to the bone. The UMP snapped into my chest on its bungee sling as the thrall's hands let go of the weapon.

Blood sprayed across my face as I clamped my mouth shut and pushed the ghoul off. It grabbed at its own throat, blood spraying from between its fingers as it tried to hold onto whatever life it had. Another ghoul tackled the bleeding creature as it desperately tried to hold its neck closed. The new attacker whimpered with joy as it latched onto its brother's neck, blood coursing over its face.

I scrabbled backward and climbed to my feet, never taking my eyes off the feeding ghoul or the other forms stepping up behind him. They froze in a semicircle in front of me, their eyes drawn to the sight of one of their own as it filled its belly in a frenzy of tearing teeth and hungry sounds.

One of the ghouls laughed, stepping around the two bodies in front of it. "You—will—never—make—it," it said, saying each word as if it were a struggle as I looked over my shoulder at the guardrail ten feet behind me.

"You're probably right," I agreed quietly, my hand drifting to the hilt of my machete. My UMP and my pistol were dry, and the ghouls were too close. I'd never be able to reload before they reached me.

"Hungry," a young woman whined off to my left. She was wearing what had been an ankle-length skirt, now torn to bits. My fingers closed on the hilt of my machete.

The feeding ghoul stopped and looked up when it heard us talking. It stood slowly, its chest covered in blood, and stepped up to take its place in the half ring of undead around me. "Fresh meat," it said, growling low and deep in its chest.

"Fu—" I started to say, and then stopped. One moment the bloody ghoul was standing there, and then there was a thump, and the space he was standing in was vacant. The ghouls on either side of the now-empty space darted nervous glances at each other, then at me, crying out in a strange tone. The other ghouls took up the strange vocalization, dropping into a crouch as they peered into the darkness. I slipped my machete free, backing toward the guardrail as they looked to one another, unsure of what to do.

"Meat," the young woman said, taking a step forward. I was looking at her when she folded inward around the long spear that pierced her abdomen and carried her off the highway. I continued to backpedal slowly until I could feel the guardrail on the back of my knees. The ghouls were scanning the darkness, trying to figure out who was attacking them.

I lifted one leg over the guardrail, then the other, still facing the ghouls. Another spear was hurled from somewhere above me, hitting a ghoul in the chest with enough force to take it off its feet as it disappeared over the far guardrail. The other ghouls looked around and broke, running for the trees behind them. I climbed down the berm and jumped over the bottom of the drainage pit before starting up the slope on the other side, panting and breathing heavily as I clawed my way uphill on all fours as fast as I could.

I stopped to take a breath when I was up the first steep section of the slope, looking behind me to make sure nothing was following. I paused just long enough to bring my breathing under control and reload my UMP before starting uphill again. It wasn't long before I heard Tomasa whistle twice from somewhere above me. I headed in that direction and whistled back once to let him know I'd heard him. He waited for me higher up the slope, standing a few feet away from Justine. Tomasa grinned at me as I approached, hefting a wooden spear over his shoulder as he pulled back and launched the weapon with a grunt of effort.

I saw Justine lying on the ground at Tomasa's feet, and I sprinted to her, falling to my knees so I could pull her into my arms. She was so cold. I pulled my poncho over my head, wrapping it around her before hugging her to my chest and rubbing her through the soiled blanket. I closed my eyes as I held onto her, feeling her chest move slowly as she breathed, willing her to be all right.

"I think she's OK, just worn out," Tomasa said, crouching down next to us.

"Why do you say that?" I asked, a lump in my throat.

"Because she was snoring a minute ago."

"Don't let her hear you say that," I warned, a smile touching my face. She didn't snore so much as breathe noisily.

"I was afraid I'd lost you," Tomasa said as he stood up. "The angle was bad. After I took the top ghoul off the pile, I couldn't hit the other for fear I'd spear you together."

It took me a moment to realize what he was saying. "I can't thank you enough for what you've done tonight," I said to him, clutching Justine to me and shivering.

"It was close. If this batch of ghouls weren't so nearly mad, they wouldn't have broken and run like they did," he said.

"We should move deeper into the mountains while we can," I forced myself to say. What I really wanted to do was curl up with Justine and fall asleep.

"We should," Tomasa agreed, bending down. I lifted her into his arms carefully, rearranging my poncho around her to try and keep her warm.

"Can you still run?" he asked as I climbed wearily to my feet.

"No, but I can walk," I said. We both smiled at each other, and then Tomasa moved off, the woman I loved held gently in his arms.

Chapter 13

I lay watching Justine sleep for a long time after I woke. I was hungry, and my body ached all over, but I just couldn't pull myself away from her. Her chest rose and fell in a slow and easy rhythm, her breath forming clouds of soft white in the cold morning air. The thought of getting up, of leaving the shared warmth that bound us together under the blanket, was unbearable. So I lay there, watching her sleep, wishing every moment would last forever.

I'm not sure how long it was before I felt Tomasa's eyes on me. I lifted my head, expecting to see my friend, but the look on Tomasa's face was like a physical blow. He was sitting across the clearing from me, grinding the butt of his staff into the ground, sadness and anger storming across his brow.

I sat up slowly, my eyes squinting against the morning light as I found his gaze and held it. He stood slowly, as if he could barely carry his own weight, a tight-lipped frown on his face. "I'm sorry, my friend," he said, his voice rumbling with emotion as he took a step toward me. I was on my feet and in front of Justine before he could take a second step.

"Don't," I commanded harshly. My little belt knife had appeared in my hand. My other weapons were on the ground next to Justine.

"I am sorry, Daniel. This is no good; we were too late," Tomasa said angrily, his knuckles turning white around his staff.

"What?" I demanded. I had no idea what was going on. I held my little knife between us, wishing I'd picked up the UMP instead of leaping to my feet without thinking.

"She was bit, Daniel. I wasn't sure at first. The smell of the pit was all over her, but she was turned. When she wakes up, she will be hungry. I don't want her to hurt you."

Tomasa's face shifted from sadness to worry as a smile crept across my face. He must have thought I'd gone mad. "She's wasn't bitten, Tomasa; she was always..." And there I struggled. I didn't know what to call her.

"She is Blutsauger?" he said, his thick eyebrows bunching up as he looked at me questioningly.

"No, yes," I stammered. "She can be, but she didn't know." I wasn't making any sense.

Tomasa shifted his eyes, looking at Justine, then back at me before retreating to where he'd been sitting earlier. He set down heavily and rubbed his face with a hand. "You would have tried to stop me with that, wouldn't you?" he asked, looking at the knife still in my hands.

"Yes," I said, nodding my head as I closed the knife and slipped it back onto my belt.

"Bravery and stupidity are often separated only by the outcome," Tomasa said as if he were quoting something from memory. I had to agree with him as I sat down next to Justine, tucking the blanket more closely around her from where I'd slid out from beneath its warmth. "I'm sorry," Tomasa said, his eyes locked on the ground.

"You didn't know," I said, trying to let him off the hook.

"It would have been a bad way to start the day," he lamented, letting his staff lean next to him so he could rub his face with both his hands. "How long have you known her?" he asked after he thought for a moment.

"She moved next to my father's house when she was younger. We didn't find out about her other half until after the grays attacked."

"She didn't know what she was?" Tomasa asked, nodding as if it made sense.

"No, not until they forced her to turn. Since then she can mostly control it." I watched as Tomasa nodded, struck with the feeling he knew exactly what I was talking about. "You know something about her, don't you?" There was an edge to my voice I hadn't intended.

"No, not directly," he said, looking up, realizing I was completely focused on him. "Not about her specifically, but I know what she is. In my realm she would have been called one of the two natured."

"You know why she was sent here?" I asked, the words hanging in the air as I said them.

"What did the first Blutsauger to cross into your realm in several hundred years see?" Tomasa asked, answering my question with a question.

I held up my hands in frustration, but he just stared at me, waiting for me to answer him. "They left a world of horses and swords and came back to automatic weapons and attack helicopters," I said as Tomasa nodded.

"That was thirty years ago in my realm. The war that started last year for you began three decades ago for us. Which brings us back to the two natured; there were two reasons they were sent to your realm. One group was trained since birth to infiltrate your society, to use their strength and their skills to gain power and position."

"That's why the military response was so uncoordinated," I said in a whisper.

Tomasa nodded in agreement. "By the time the first Blutsauger were turning your masses into Nechtruin, your president and all but one of the chiefs of staff were dead. At every level of your military organizations, the two natured waited to strike. Some of them had very simple tasks, to die destroying as much as they could. Those were perhaps the lucky ones.

"The other two natured were watched, kept safe, waiting for the day the portals would open and they would be consumed to hold open the gateways between our realms."

"That's worse than being sent on a suicide mission?" I asked.

"At least the two natured assigned to destruction had a chance, and even in the worst cases, they were likely to die quickly. The portal keepers are well fed, well cared for; it allows them to survive longer even as their lives are burned away to keep the doorways open. It is a long, slow death. And very painful at the end."

I looked at the ground, my memory flashing with images of the four grays with folds of skin hanging off their emaciated bodies we'd seen around the portal in Jersey. "Back in Jersey, they called Justine a key. They needed her to open the portal wider, to hold it open so more grays could come through," I said, remembering the night we'd barely escaped with a chill. It had been a very near thing.

"It is a title of respect in many ways," Tomasa said. "It

takes a lot of energy to punch a hole between our worlds. Once open it is like a tear in your skin; it wants to close, wants to heal. To hold it open, those on each side must put energy into keeping the doorway open. Some energy is worth more than others. You burn green wood, you get smoke and lots of noise, but if you burn dense, dry wood, you can bask in its heat for a long time."

"So they hunt her," I said softly, sadly.

"It makes her very valuable. Any Blutsauger who has her could bargain with a lord for almost anything. Which is why this doesn't make sense," Tomasa said, scratching his head as he thought of how he wanted to word his next statement. "Why did the Farmer try to draw you in? He had the prize already—no offense," the brute added.

I laughed bitterly. "His name is Haeslig, and he's been hunting us, hunting her," I corrected, "since the moment everything started. He wants Justine, but I'm not sure he really knew he had her."

"You think a shaved head would keep him from recognizing her?" Tomasa asked incredulously.

"Not if he actually saw her. But who knows what the foremen told him or if he ever comes out of his house. I think he was spooked, hiding out until his ghouls or his foremen could positively catch us. As for why he's coming after me, he knows that if he doesn't kill me first, I'll never let him just walk away with her."

"It is good that she is safe then. Once she wakes up we should head north. Someplace far away from the Farmer, someplace to sit by a fire for the winter," Tomasa said.

"I can't yet. Everything has gone sideways, but Haeslig may still have a friend of ours. We have to save him if he's alive."

"You would go back?" Tomasa asked.

"If he were your friend, would you?"

"I wouldn't have a choice if my friend were in so much danger," Tomasa agreed. "I guess I will be going back as well."

"Thank you," I said thoughtfully, a lump in my throat. True friends were hard to find.

"Did I get hit on the head?" Justine croaked, pulling the

blanket more tightly around her as she looked at Tomasa and then me. "What's that smell?" she mumbled, scrunching up her nose. The blanket from her pack had been relatively clean, but she was lying on my blanket turned poncho as her ground cloth.

I fell to my knees beside her, hugging her hard as she sat up. "You're safe," I said, repeating it into her neck as her arms tightened around my ribs, hugging me back.

"Who's the big guy?" she whispered into my ear after we'd rocked in each other's arms for a short time.

"My name is Tomasa," the brute said before I could reply.

"No head wound, right?" Justine asked as I let go of her.

"No head wounds, I promise," I said. "Tomasa helped me; he's a friend."

"Then it's truly a pleasure to meet you," she said. "Now will someone tell me where we are and how I got here?"

"Long or short version?" I asked

"Short for now, you can give me the gory details later," she said.

"Haeslig has made something halfway between a gray and a thrall—Tomasa named them ghouls—and they are tough."

She nodded. "Gabrielle and Norman."

"Yep, and apparently they're human enough to fool you." Justine had always had a knack for knowing when the undead were close by. The garrote around Norman's neck didn't kill him. He decked you, I shot him, then every ghoul in the valley came running. They shocked you, and something happened," I said as she nodded again.

"The shock does something to me, keeps me from changing," she confirmed.

"Then I got thrown against a tree, dislocated my shoulder, and ended up hiding under a pile of rotten pumpkins when I got caught out in the fields at sunup. Some badness happened, and Tomasa's friend Solindraye didn't make it. I passed out, and when I woke up, Tomasa had put my arm into its socket and carried me to safety."

"I'm sorry you lost your friend, and I'm in your debt for

helping Daniel," she said solemnly.

"Thank you. I miss Solindraye often," Tomasa said. "Do you remember what happened after you and Daniel were separated?"

"I only remember snippets of the night they took me. I have a hazy memory of being thrown onto the ground in front of the barn next to Norman's body. And being dragged into the barn—I'm not sure if I dreamed Abigail was there; then I was being beaten," she said, trying to think.

"Abigail was there," I told her gently.

She nodded. "Then I woke up in the underground with one of the foremen trying to get my pants off," she said, pausing as the memory choked her up. She felt me bristle and held up a hand to stop me. "He died watching his own blood soak into the dirt. I almost escaped then, but I didn't know where I was. I walked right up the stairs into the barn. There were too many of them with shock wands," she said with a sob. "They were so mad; they kept shocking me, hitting me, yelling at me. They found their friend all cut up and wanted to know where I'd hidden the knife." She held her index finger in front of her face, the nail turning black and lengthening as she looked at it. "They didn't understand.

"They thought I was on something; every time they'd let up, I would fight back," she said, closing her hand into a fist as she buried her head in my shirt. "It just made them angry. That's when one of them put the dog collar on me. They thought the pain was keeping me subdued.

"Then Vaughn came; he told them to have me ready for the pit before the end of the day. The Farmer wanted me to fight. They were going to use me as bait to lure you in.

"A little before the first fight, they gave me a pull-top can of ravioli. I think I may have lost it a little," she said with a grim smile. "I used the lid to cut all my hair off. I was so afraid Haeslig would see me and that he'd take me away before you could find me. I cut all my hair off," she said as if she still couldn't believe it. Tears welled in her eyes as she ran a hand over her head, feeling the stubble where she'd almost scalped herself on the side of her head. I pulled her close and held her as she cried, telling her I loved her and that she was safe over and over again.

"I was so worried about you," I said, kissing the top of her shorn head. Justine lifted her face and kissed me, pulling herself into my lap and falling halfway out of her blanket at the same time.

"Hmm," Tomasa mumbled. "I think I saw a camp not far from here when Solindraye and I would escape for the night." He picked up his staff, blurting, "There were some tents there. I think I'll go do some scouting and look for more supplies."

"Be careful," I said to him around Justine's lips, waving as he moved off into the mountains, giving us some privacy.

I held her and rocked her in my lap, never wanting to let her go. "I bet I look horrible," she said, grimacing. I couldn't help but smile, which only made her eyes harden.

"You are the most beautiful woman I've ever seen," I said, grabbing her face and kissing her until her lips softened, moving against mine again. When I pulled back, I held her eyes, not letting go until I saw the uncertainty fade. "You think a little thing like a shaved head can scare me off?" I said to her softly, jokingly.

She smiled back, resting a hand over my heart. "I'm not having a dream, right?" Justine asked.

"No, this is the real deal," I replied, putting a kiss in the center of her dirty forehead.

"It doesn't matter?" she asked.

"What?" I wasn't sure what she was talking about.

"I heard what Tomasa said. That I really am one of them, a two natured," she said, not able to hide the fear behind her words.

"I knew you were different," I said, rubbing her back through the blanket as I hugged her. "Do you think it's a huge surprise that someone told me you aren't like all the other girls?" I couldn't help but laugh as I said it.

"I love you," she said, melting into me.

"Right back at you," I said as she planted little kisses down my cheek and onto my neck.

"I'm starving," she said throatily, kissing and sucking along my upper shoulder.

"I've got some protein bars," I said.

"No, Daniel, I am really, really hungry," she said, rubbing my chest lightly as her warm mouth sucked at my neck directly over my jugular.

"I'm yours forever," I said to her, pulling her down on top of me as I lie down. I spread my left hand out over the back of her head, cradling her against my neck. Her tongue traced a circle on my flesh, and then she pulled back ever so slightly as she shuddered, her teeth elongating, sharpening. I gasped as two razors sunk into my neck. There was a brief flash of pain, and then pleasant warmth flooded down my spine. The soreness and fatigue of the last few days melted away as I slipped into a narcotic haze. My hand found its way under the blanket and then under her shirt, caressing her side. Each time she'd suck at my neck, she'd move her body down against mine, and my fingertips were positioned just right to caress the side of one small breast. She felt my excitement and moved more purposefully against me, her hips grinding pleasantly into mine.

Justine pulled back just enough to get her hands between us, undoing my belt. She was giggling as she lifted herself on her knees against the force of my hands pulling her down on top of me. I was trying to hold her hips closer to me at the same time she was trying to free me from my pants and pull her panties aside.

"You're the only one," she said into my ear as she lowered herself onto me, her mouth closing in a warm, wet circle on my neck as our bodies moved against each other. My vision blurred and my voice was slurred as I told her I loved her. All I could do was moan as I threw my hips up into her and held onto her waist. I felt the pulses start to build low in my groin and wasn't aware of the cry coming from my lips until I felt Justine's hand over my mouth. She was panting and laughing as she tried to keep my scream from filling the mountain air as she held a ball of my shirt in her other hand, riding me as I bucked beneath her.

The last thing I remembered was Justine crying out as she climaxed, a long, drawn-out sound that I felt as well as heard, her legs quivering around me. Then I lay back, totally spent, tasting the saltiness of blood on her kiss as our lips met. I passed out feeling warm and safe, covered with Justine's body.

I felt hungover and disoriented when I woke up.

I tried to open my eyes, but the world spun around me when I did, so I lay there listening, waiting for the world to stop spinning as I dreamed of coffee and a hot breakfast.

"And you say he's been bitten by others?" I heard Tomasa ask, his voice full of curiosity.

Justine cleared her voice uncomfortably before she spoke. "Umm, yes, he was bitten by two grays that I know of, in combat," she said, stressing the last two words.

"Oh, of course," Tomasa stuttered. "I never meant, hmmm," and he struggled to finish the sentence.

"No worries," Justine said, interrupting him before he could say something embarrassing.

"Does the Farmer know he's immune to Blutsauger bites?" Tomasa asked.

"I think he would; I'm pretty sure he was there when Daniel was bit the second time."

"The ghouls," Tomasa said excitedly.

"What?" Justine asked.

"The ghouls aren't stable; whatever the Farmer is doing to them slowly degrades them until they are little more than thralls."

"And that means?"

"He seems to be very interested in Daniel, and that didn't make sense to me until now. He must think Daniel can help him stabilize the ghouls."

"What?" Justine asked.

"If Daniel is immune to the bite of a Blutsauger, the Farmer might think he can use it to help his ghouls." Tomasa paused, and I heard him swallow before he continued. "At least, it makes some sense, but it is still only a guess."

"In the end it doesn't really matter. We have to know if our friend is still alive, and Haeslig has to pay for what he's done to us."

"This friend of yours, is he two natured as well?" Tomasa asked.

"No, he's just a kid," Justine said. "We met him back in

Delaware; he helped us out when we first got into New Dover. A few hundred survivors walled off several city blocks and made a go of it."

"How did you end up in the mountains?"

"It's a long story, but basically Dover burned, and we were forced to flee north through Pennsylvania." Justine paused, and I heard metal scraping on metal. "You sure you want to go back to Pumpkin Town?" she asked him.

"I have only one friend in this realm, maybe two," he corrected. "I am not yet ready to abandon them, I think."

"It's safe to say two," Justine said reassuringly, adding, "I think Sleeping Beauty is awake." I heard her soft footfalls stop next to me. I smiled but didn't open my eyes as she knelt next to me and rubbed my chest through the blanket.

"Very thirsty," I said. Justine helped lift my head, apparently having anticipated my request because she put the end of a squeeze bottle in my mouth. The orange drink was sweet and tart, and tasted heavenly. I sucked it down as fast as I could, almost choking.

"There's plenty; go easy," Justine said, tilting the bottle so it didn't come out so fast. She leaned down and kissed my forehead, whispering, "Remember to zip your pants," before pulling away and putting the tip of the squeeze bottle back into my mouth.

"I found the camp," Tomasa said from farther away.

"And brought back a shitload of supplies," Justine added as she helped me into a sitting position. I took the bottle of orange drink and chugged it. The sugar was already helping me feel better. I opened my eyes to slits, making sure the world had stopped spinning.

I was surprised to see that what I'd thought was a dream was fairly close to reality. A two-burner camp stove with a small propane tank was sitting a few feet away. One burner had a pot of coffee steaming on it, and the other a pot of soup. Justine moved back to the stove to grab the coffee, filling a blue, enameled cup with steaming, black liquid before handing it over to me. I clutched it in my hands, feeling its warmth as I breathed in the smell. I took a careful sip, enjoying the heat as it spread through me. Justine went back to the burners and stirred something in the pot.

"Very nice," I said, noticing Justine's clothing for the first time. She was wearing jeans that were the right length but were too big around the middle. The fabric was bunched up around her waist where she'd cinched the jeans down with a belt. She'd completed the look with a heavy flannel.

"Say a word about rednecks or hunters, and you will pay," she said, pointing a spoon in my direction.

"Not a word," I promised.

Tomasa watched us closely, his eyes moving between us rapidly as we talked. His face would slip between what I think was amusement and thought as he studied our interaction. Justine brought the pot over, and we took turns eating ramen noodles until they were gone.

After we were done eating, I let Justine help me to my feet, hiding under the blanket as I rearranged my pants and zipped them up. If Tomasa noticed, he pretended not to. I felt like I was a hundred years old as I stretched. "How far from town are we?" I asked. The night before was a haze of memories.

"Three hours, less if we move faster," Tomasa said, looking at me skeptically, then at Justine.

"One more day," she said, putting a finger to my lips to keep me quiet. "I'm still beat, just one more day?" she begged, knowing I couldn't argue when she put it that way. I nodded in agreement, feeling like I was being played just a little. She knew if she'd told me I was the one who needed to rest, I would have fought her. "One night to rest, and tomorrow we find out if WC is alive and pull his ass out of there if he is."

"Tomorrow it ends," I told her.

"Agreed," Justine and Tomasa said together.

Chapter 14

"That's not good," Justine said, looking down on Pumpkin Town from our vantage point on the mountain. We'd left first thing in the morning, moving slowly and carefully along the high tree line until we were even with the town below us.

Smoke was billowing up from various points around the town. We watched for several minutes, but even with my binoculars it was hard to see any real detail. I put them away, and we started our journey down the mountainside. Halfway down we came to a sharp drop-off, a sheer wall that left us stranded on a ledge fifteen feet above a small box canyon.

"I take it this is new territory," Justine said, stepping sideways as far as she could to my right before the ledge became too narrow, the stone beneath her feet melting back into the granite face we were perched on.

"Back up?" I said, looking at the steep descent we'd just made, not really looking forward to the thought of climbing up and finding a new path down.

"Ha," Tomasa said, stepping off the ledge. He landed lightly, bending his knees to absorb the impact. Justine looked at me and grinned before following him over. I winced as she hit and rolled before coming back to her feet, apparently unhurt.

"Don't be scared," Justine said playfully as Tomasa put his hands up to catch me. There was just something very odd about jumping into the brute's arms while we were face-to-face. He tussled my hair as I stepped away from him, and even my best glare couldn't keep Justine from laughing and winking at the big guy.

"This would make a good campsite," I said, looking around us. The small box canyon was roughly twenty by twenty, with a cut at the far end leading back out to the mountain slope.

"Looks like someone else already had the same idea," Justine said, pointing to the far corner. Someone had covered a stack of cut logs in a section of blue tarp and left at least a case of empty beer cans scattered near the woodpile. I could picture hunters standing around a fire drinking after spending a day in the mountains.

We walked across the box canyon to the cut leading back out to the mountain slope. The path out of the canyon was split in two by a massive granite spike that jutted ten feet into the air, a plateau of stone that broke the path into two smaller openings, each only a few feet across. Tomasa's shoulders almost touched as he led the way out the left-hand opening.

The going was much easier once we left the box canyon. The grade was less steep, and there were several game trails to follow. We made it to the valley floor in less than an hour, making our way carefully to the edge of the woods as the air filled with the smell of wood fire. We stopped just inside the trees, looking out across the smoke-shrouded highway as the town came in and out of view in the distance through the haze. The outer street along its northern edge was a mixture of burning and blackened shacks. The big blue barn and all the buildings closest to it were little more than bits of ash and ember. Everything near the barn had burned to the ground.

"It is going to be hard to scent anything in this," Tomasa said.

"That works both ways," I said, trying to be positive.

"Look," Justine said, pointing up the road. A person was stumbling through the haze toward us. We watched as the form walked through the smoke, slowly resolving into detail. I didn't know who she was, not by name, but I'd seen her around the pit during the fights. Half her neck was torn away, and she was dragging one of her feet. It looked like her ankle had been broken.

The thrall staggered by, completely unaware we were watching her. The smoke and haze drifted around her as she followed the road south, dragging her broken foot as she limped along. "Think Haeslig closed up shop after he realized we blew through town already?" I asked.

"Or maybe his half-baked ghouls did it for him," Justine said as one cried out from somewhere within the town.

"We check the house, and if there isn't anything there, we get out," I said, slipping out of my pack and leaving it on the ground. Justine did the same. They would only slow us down, and we were pretty much out of supplies anyway.

We slipped out of cover and moved across the drainage ditch and up onto the highway. Visibility shifted from ten feet to a few dozen as we walked up the road to town, smoke swirling and drifting around us, getting thicker and heavier the closer we came to the source of the fire.

The wind shifted just as we reached the burned-out section of ground where the big blue barn had stood, cutting visibility down to nothing. We stopped, standing almost on Tomasa's feet as he coughed and sputtered, bending partially over us to try to find better air. Justine pulled the bottom of her shirt over her mouth as I pulled my bandana up over my nose. It didn't help.

As quickly as the smoke swirled around us, it drifted away, leaving us with our eyes watering and our throats burning. Tomasa seemed especially sensitive to the irritation. His eyes were red, and he had snot running from his nose. He was wiping his nose when a woman's scream cut through the air. It lasted only a few brief seconds before it was cut off abruptly. I nudged Tomasa, getting him moving again. The smoke drifted around us, obscuring everything outside our small pocket of breathable air as we walked. I kept my UMP on my shoulder, expecting something to stumble into view at any moment.

"I think we passed the barn," Justine, nodding to her right. We were past the burned out ground where big blue barn should have stood, moving back onto a street lined with shacks and hovels.

"I think you're right; let's see if we can get to the inner street," I said, angling us in that direction. More smoke rolled over us, and we paused in front of a shack along the left side of the street, staying close together so we didn't get separated. Somewhere close by we could hear men calling out to each other.

"We're not that far from the main house," I said when the voices moved off.

"If it's not burned down as well," Justine said.

"If it is we're going to get the hell out of here."

"No arguments from me," Justine said, blinking smoke-induced tears out of her eyes.

"There are thralls and other things about," Tomasa said, then sneezed and coughed at the same time, covering his face with an impressive display of mucus and snot.

"Behind us," Justine said. Several ghostly forms were coming up the street, their shadows appearing and disappearing in the smoke. We scrambled forward off the outer street into the closest alley, hunkering down between the shacks on either side as a small horde of thralls passed us by. No sooner had the thralls passed than we heard men coming closer along the inner street.

"Another one!" a man yelled from just of sight. Justine stiffened, but I held her still. They weren't talking about us. I crept forward to the front of the alley and edged my head around the corner just in time to see two men take down a thrall with long-handled axes. They both wore heavy leather gloves, and their faces were covered with what looked like torn-up undershirts. They clanked their axes together in victory just as another voice spun them about.

"Luke, Nolan," a man called out in a booming voice that turned to coughing and hacking. The two woodcutters in front of us called back, guiding the others to them. I watched as a motley crew of townspeople emerged through the haze and gathered in front of me. Vaughn was at the head of the second party. His dark suit was smudged with ash, and his top hat was gone, revealing an almost completely bald head. Vaughn looked much older than last I'd seen him. He carried a baseball bat in one hand, using it like a cane as he walked. The survivors around him had a few crossbows, but mostly they carried a hodgepodge of everyday items. I saw everything from kitchen knives to shovels and hatchets.

"Paul's place is burned to the ground. We saw one body in the ashes; it was too small to be him, but I don't think he'd have left if Helen or his boy were still alive," one of the woodcutters told Vaughn.

"We got turned around trying to get to the Farmer's house. Several of the foremen are putting up one hell of a fight at the south corner. The street for several houses around them is filled with biters."

"We should run, see if we can make it into the mountains," the woodcutter who hadn't spoken yet said.

"I could see his house; the lights were on, and the fence was still up. We have to get to the Farmer's house; we'll be safe there," Vaughn said, his voice full of confidence. I tried to hear what was being said after that, but too many people were yelling and screaming at each other. It sounded like half of the survivors wanted to run for it, while the other half believed Vaughn. Part of me wanted to tell them to run, to get out while they still had a chance, but the cold reality was that I didn't know if they were friends or foes. They'd have to get by on their own.

When the brief argument was over, three men and two women broke away from the main group and headed off on their own. The rest followed Vaughn back into the smoke toward the Farmer's house. "We need to stay on top of them," I whispered back to Justine and Tomasa.

We followed the group of survivors, leapfrogging along the alleys until the lights of the Farmer's house appeared out of the smoke. One moment we could barely see the backs of a few of the survivors, and the next the house was looming up in front of us.

We carefully flanked the party as they reached the Farmer's front gate, giving us a view of the side of the house as well as the front. Vaughn walked right up to the front gate and shook it, screaming for the Farmer to open the gate. The thirty or so other survivors crowded around, thinking they'd made it to safety.

We watched from hiding as the front of the house was cast in flickering orange light from the burning section of town to the south. Survivors milled about in confusion, not sure what was going on. The town had grown eerily silent; the only sound was the crackling of the raging fires. One of the woodcutters pushed Vaughn aside, attacking the gate with a series of strikes that echoed out into the night like a ringing bell.

The crowd of people let out a cheer as the front door to the Farmer's house opened and a man walked out. He was wearing a scarf tied over his face against the smoke, and held up a hand as if to tell the assembled masses to be patient. He walked off the porch as they cheered him, crossing the short distance to the front gate leisurely. I pulled the UMP tight to my shoulder, siting in on the side of Haeslig's head. Justine grabbed me, her fingers squeezing my arm until I had to take my eye off the sight. She was shaking her head at me.

"Kill him now, and all those people are going to turn on us," she said, holding my eyes with hers. "WC first," she said, not letting go of me until I nodded in agreement. I lowered the tip of the UMP and turned back to the front of the house. Haeslig had made it to the gate and was making a show of searching his pockets for the key.

I wanted to hurt him so badly.

"They are coming," Tomasa said, wiping his face with his sleeve. Justine tried to pull me farther back into the alley, but I had to see. Haeslig had found the key. He put it into the gate and opened it inward. Vaughn tried to step forward, but Haeslig stood in his way, blocking the entry. One of the woodcutters pushed Vaughn aside and tried to use the shaft of his axe to check Haeslig out of the way, but the gray's hand shot forward, gripping the wooden shaft between the woodcutter's grasp, immobilizing it. The woodcutter wrenched his upper body, but the axe didn't move.

The second woodcutter pushed his way past Vaughn with his axe held high over his head, trying to help his friend. Haeslig shifted his body, using his strength to half lift and half shove the woodcutter in front of him directly into the other's axe as it fell. Both of the woodcutters screamed—one in pain, and the other in horrified shock—as they stood locked together by the length of an axe.

It took a moment for the mass of people crowded around the gate to realize what was happening. A wave of panic rippled through the crowd. People were screaming, and one edge of the party spun off, running out of sight to the west. The rest milled around front of the gate in stunned confusion.

"I should have killed him when I had the chance," I said

between gritted teeth.

"This doesn't change anything; if you'd shot him, we'd have the survivors coming down on us as well as them," she said, pointing to the billowing smoke to our south.

One of the female survivors near the gate saw the bodies emerge from the smoke at the same time I did. She started to scream, repeating the word "no" over and over. Ranks of bodies were filing into view through the haze and smoke as the crowd at the front of the house watched in shock. Some of the thralls marched in flames, their clothing burning as they plodded mindlessly forward.

Vaughn stepped forward to meet Haeslig, his voice booming through the night. "Do not let the devils take you!" he screamed, swinging his baseball bat. Haeslig took the blow on an upturned arm and then tried to gut the tall man with a swipe of a clawed hand, but Vaughn was surprisingly nimble, pulling back at the last moment. Crossbows hummed as they were fired into the closing ranks of undead, and the outer edge of the survivors bristled as they readied themselves.

"It's time to go," I said, breaking myself away from the battle as Haeslig and Vaughn disappeared out of sight amid the milling survivors. "We need to move while he's distracted." I dragged Justine behind me with one hand. We rushed along the shacks, circling to the back of the house as smoke swirled and drifted all around us. We saw other shapes moving through the smoke as we ran, but none of them seemed interested in us; they were all moving to the front of the house.

The wind picked up just as we were crossing the open ground to the rear of the Farmer's house, obscuring everything in a haze of stinging smoke. Then, as quickly as it had washed over us, it was gone, and we were standing in front of the wrought-iron fencing set around the house.

"You have the key, right?" Justine said to Tomasa, raising her voice just enough to be heard over the dull roar of the burning fires and the fighting at the front of the house.

"Yes," Tomasa said, gripping the fence with one hand while resting his other against the steel post it was welded to. "I..." The muscles on his arms tensed... "...have it..."

...then bulged as he pushed against the post while pulling on the fencing... "...right here," he snarled as the welds gave way with a crackling pop. He leaned back against the metal, bending the fence far enough apart for even his large frame.

Justine was the first through, darting forward as Tomasa flexed his right hand. I followed close behind, catching her as we bolted up the three steps onto the wraparound porch. Justine tried the back door, but it was locked. She smashed one of the windowpanes with an elbow and reached inside to open the door.

"I'll wait for you here," Tomasa said, ducking his head under the overhanging roof to talk to us.

"We won't be long," I said.

"Don't be," he said, his answer fading into the background noise as he put his back to us. The last thing I saw before slipping into the house was a horde of thralls spilling around the corner from the front of the house, following the fence.

The roar from outside muted the moment we stepped into the house, replaced by the faint chugging of a generator. Dust motes danced in the air as we moved through the kitchen, the smell of smoke and fire being replaced with the scents of chemicals and the sickly sweet odor of death. In front of us, a hallway cut through to the front of the house.

I peered down the hall behind my UMP, looking at the bits of aged and discolored wallpaper that hung in little strips off the walls. The hall ran all the way to the front of the house, leading to the foyer. I padded along the uneven hardwood floor, taking point until we reached the section of hallway open to the second floor. I turned as Justine slipped ahead of me, walking backward, my UMP aimed up at the second-floor landing as Justine paced my progress with a hand on my shoulder as we walked to the front of the house. The second-floor landing was empty. The four doors at the top of the staircase were all closed.

I turned to my left as we made it to the front entry, sweeping my UMP into what looked like a sitting room. An empty platter with a slab of bloody red meat sat on an end table in front of one of the chairs, and another table held a chess set and several thick books, but the room was otherwise empty.

"Daniel," Justine whispered. I turned 180 degrees to face the room on the other side of the foyer. I stood shoulder to shoulder with Justine, looking into what must have been a library or study.

Shelves lined the two inside walls from floor to ceiling, but only the higher spaces still held books. All the shelves from arm height down had been cleared of books. In their place the shelves were filled with vials, bowls, and strange apparatus that looked vaguely medical. The windows facing the front of the house had been painted white, and a waist-high worktable had been shoved up against them. The top of the workbench was covered in plastic containers holding bits and pieces of flesh and bloody sections of meat. On the end of the workbench closest to us was a tray filled with surgical tools and household items. Scalpels and steak knives lay side by side with carpet knives and several sets of pliers. Everything was stained with dried, rusty blood.

A half-drawn curtain hung in the doorway. Justine pointed to what was just visible sticking past the end of the curtain. Just inside the library, mostly hidden by the curtain, were the soles of a pair of boots. I slid into the room, covering the inside corner with the UMP. A thin form lay on the gurney, covered from its knees up by a sheet stained through with blood. Thin legs were exposed from the knees down to the black dress socks sticking up above the combat boots. "Please no," I begged, looking at Justine as I reached out with one hand, grabbing the edge of the sheet.

"If it's him we tear this place down and nail Haeslig to a door," Justine said angrily.

I didn't have to answer; she already knew how I felt. I pulled the sheet away, pulling harder when dried blood tried to hold it in place. I stared at the body on the gurney, processing what I was seeing. It took both Justine and me the same moment of pensive recognition to realize the body wasn't WC. Both men had slight, awkward builds, but WC's left arm wasn't covered in a raven tattoo, and even partially mutilated, the broad nose in the center of the man's face was too strong to belong to our friend.

"This guy must have really pissed Haeslig off," I said, scanning the man's wounds. The man on the gurney had been systemically mutilated. Most of his upper body had been skinned, revealing flesh underneath that had been cut away in six-inch strips. One of the man's cheeks had been cut completely away as well, revealing angry holes filled with blood clots where his teeth had been.

Justine stepped close, slipping the machete out of the sheath on my thigh as she leaned closer to the man strapped on the gurney. "Look at that," she said, using the blade to lift the man's fingertips.

"How do you make ghouls?" I asked, looking at the black claws that tipped the man's—or rather, the gray's—fingers.

"Snips and snails and puppy dog tails," Justine murmured, pulling the blade back and letting the fingers fall to the gurney with a click. "And maybe a bit of a gray."

We both jumped when the gray's eyes popped open. Justine cursed as the poor bastard's eyes blinked, angling downward until he saw us. A hoarse sound escaped from the creature's mouth. "Keeeeel…meeee," the gray begged, the words barely understandable as they came out of his ruined face. His eyes were dull and glassy, but even so, they were full of pain.

We turned away from him, ignoring his plea for mercy as we stepped out of the library.

"Go," I said to Justine, motioning for her to head up the stairs as I slipped to the front door and squinted my eye to look through the peephole. The townspeople were surrounded, fighting the ghouls and thralls while Haeslig stood guarding the open gate, apparently content to watch the mayhem. As I watched Vaughn centered himself in front of the gray once again, approaching the gate with slow, measured steps. Blood ran down the left side of his face, and his baseball bat was gone.

Rage flooded through me as I looked at the back of Haeslig's head, thinking how easy it would be to shoot him while he was distracted. All I had to do was open the door and take the shot. Even as the thoughts ran through my head, the gray turned, looking at the front of the house, his head tilting as if surprised. His scarf covered his lower face, obscuring everything except for his eyes, but they locked on me through the door, sending a shiver of cold down my spine. My hand wrapped around the doorknob and froze. I wanted to break away from the peephole and throw open the door; I wanted to see him try and dodge a full magazine of forty-caliber rounds, but I couldn't break away from his gaze.

I lifted the UMP high in my right hand, putting the tip of the weapon against the door. My eye was still pressed to the peephole; I couldn't break away from the gray's hold. Just as my finger was tightening on the trigger, Vaughn screamed, spinning Haeslig's gaze away from me, freeing me. The UMP fell back to my side as I stood there, feeling suddenly relieved that the gray's eyes were no longer on me as Vaughn stormed up to the gate. He had something in his hands, but it was hard to see through the peephole. It wasn't until the rag stuffed into the end of the bottle caught fire that I recognized the Molotov. Vaughn hiked it behind his head to throw and was just bringing it forward when Haeslig moved.

One moment the gray was at the gate, and the next he'd crossed the three steps separating him from Vaughn so quickly I saw it as a blur. Haeslig caught Vaughn just as the tall, gangly man was bringing his arm forward. The bottle flew end over end through the air as Haeslig lifted Vaughn off his feet and carried him to the ground, his mouth latching onto the man's neck as they fell. The Molotov flew through the air and hit the front door, covering my view in a flash of orange flames as the bottle shattered.

"You going to help here?" Justine barked from halfway up the stairs. I turned away from the door and ran to catch up to her. We'd been in the house for less than two minutes, but it felt like much longer.

There were four doors at the top of the stairs: two in front of us and one at either end of the landing. The door to our right side was cracked open just a hair, while the others all had metal clasps and locking bolts on them. I turned and went directly to the partially open door, pushing it with my foot as I burst into the room, sweeping it from one side to the other with the UMP.

The master bedroom was dominated by a large bed covered in rumpled covers. Candles sat here and there, melted into the side tables by the bed. Wax dripped off the windowsill like a frozen waterfall in multiple colors where candle after candle had been burned and the wax left to run where it would.

I cleared the room quickly and went back out to the landing to find Justine with her ear to one of the doors as she knocked on it with her knuckles. She looked up at me, an excited smile on her face just as the front door exploded inward beneath us. There was a whoosh of air and then a roar as the fire clinging to the front of the building flashed through the entry and immediately set the interior of the foyer burning. Bits of flaming wallpaper floated through the air like hellish snowflakes.

The Farmer stepped through the flames, the solid slate in his eyes reflecting the firelight, making his eyes look like two miniature balls of fire as he screamed, "You will pay for invading my house!"

"I'll take Haeslig; you get WC," Justine said, squaring herself at the top of the stairs and twirling my machete once in her hand. Smoke and fire billowed around the Farmer as he crossed the foyer and put his foot on the bottom step. Justine was matching him step for step as I turned my back on them, looking at the door Justine had been listening at.

I pulled at the padlock uselessly and then slammed the door with the flat of my hand. A moment later the door shook as someone pounded on it from the other side in response. I yelled into the wood, but the sound of my voice was washed out by the fire and the chaos raging below me. I pressed my ear hard to the door and thought I heard someone croak Justine's name.

"Back away!" I yelled, and then put one round from the UMP high into the door to give WC some warning.

I pulled the UMP tight to my shoulder and flipped the selector to burst, firing, then correcting for muzzle jump before repeating, squinting my eyes as splinters and chunks of wood flew. The rounds didn't cut a neat semicircle in the wood like they did in the movies, but the wood around the padlock was chewed up enough that I was able throw my shoulder into it and break the door in without too much effort.

The smell of feces and urine swept over me as the door swung open onto a small bedroom. A cot hugged the wall to the right while the left was lined with five-gallon buckets filled with reeking waste. A skeletal figure stood at the back of the room, hiding in the corner with his hands over his ears. The man was wearing dark pants and a button-down dress shirt that was several sizes too big. I could see WC's vertebrae poking through the fabric of the shirt.

"WC?" I asked softly. He looked so fragile. Outside I heard a loud crash and then felt a shudder that ran through the floor and sent cracks up the plaster of the walls.

"I'm sorry; he tortured me. I didn't tell him about the cabin, but I had to tell him something," an ancient-sounding voice said as he turned slowly, painfully. His hands were shaking as he looked at me, fear and apprehension written all over his face.

Chapter 15

The flesh over Haeslig's face was pulled taught over his skull, making his eyes seem overly large and bulbous. His skin was pale and nearly translucent, shot through with blue veins. "Why? How?" I demanded, stepping closer to him, the tip of the UMP locked on his head. A sudden sense of anger and alarm filled me. If Haeslig was in the room, who the hell was the Farmer?

Haeslig cringed away from my weapon as he spoke. "Barrin caught me a few weeks ago. He thinks to elevate himself. He worked for Ravi. He thought he could steal whatever power I had that made Ravi willing to help me."

"I'm going to kill you," I said. Smoke was starting to billow up the stairs and into the room.

"I didn't tell him about the cabin," he begged. Haeslig was pressing himself back against the far wall, putting his hands between us as if that would stop rounds from the UMP. A stab of hesitation shot through me; he looked so old, so frail. What was left of Haeslig couldn't possibly be dangerous. Then his upper lip quivered as he looked at me, and one of his long incisors slid into view.

He wasn't human, wasn't harmless, no matter how much he had been starved and tortured. He was simply being repaid in kind for all the evil he'd done himself. My finger was tightening on the trigger when the floor leapt beneath me. I was able to catch myself, but Haeslig was knocked off his feet. He hit the floor with a weak cry.

"Daniel, we need to go," Tomasa bellowed from the first floor, his voice reverberating through the house just as Justine appeared at the door. Her shirt was torn, and her jeans were cut across her right thigh. Blood was seeping down her leg. "We need to go, the Farmer's..."

"Not Haeslig," we both said at the same time as the gray in question groaned, climbing to a sitting position on his cot. He waved one hand at us feebly.

"Daniel!" Tomasa bellowed again, accenting his cry with a grunt as he threw something through a wall beneath us.

"He's mine; go make sure Tomasa doesn't leave without us," Justine said, her voice growing thick as the nails on her fingers shifted to an ebony black and slid forward to extend an inch from where they'd been a moment before.

I heard Haeslig say Justine's name softly as I walked out of the room, begging for his life. I walked out onto the landing and down three steps, staring at the carnage below me. The front door and a large section of the house around it were gone. Most of it was sitting on the front lawn burning. Tomasa stood in what used to be the foyer, using his staff to brutal effect as thralls and ghouls pressed in from outside. I got a brief glimpse of the Farmer standing in the yard, one hand clutched to his midsection as he screamed unheard words and pointed with his free hand. Off to Tomasa's left, the gray strapped to the gurney was kicking his legs and throwing his body against the straps, ignoring the pain as his bindings cut into his skinned flesh, trying to move himself farther from the wall that was burning only inches away from his head.

I stopped three-quarters of the way down the stairs where they ended in a pile of shattered timbers intermixed with what might have been a ghoul, looking out through the gaping hole in the front of the house. "We need to go; they're coming in from everywhere!" Tomasa yelled over the noise, picking up a stray thrall and using it as a projectile against others trying to come in from the rear hallway.

"Justine's finishing upstairs," I said as I aimed over Tomasa's head, a grim excitement filling me as I found myself looking down my sights at the Farmer. I exhaled and pulled the trigger just as a thrall stepped in front of him, its head exploding as my round hit. When the thrall fell, the Farmer was gone. I cursed, shifting my aim to take my frustration out on the mass of undead crowding in from the front lawn. I'd wasted my chance.

"Good, you found your friend," Tomasa said, driving the thralls back with a swipe of his staff.

I looked behind me to see Justine helping Haeslig down the steps, her arm around his waist. I started to say something, but she shook her head and gave me a look that shut me up. "We need him for now," she said, her voice thick and uncertain as she said it. Haeslig started to say something, but Justine shut him up with a snarl.

Tomasa ignored our bit of drama on the stairs, charging a mass of thralls and two ghouls trying to press inside the building. I jumped down the missing steps and moved to his flank as he pulled back, covering him so he wasn't swarmed from every side. I finished one clip and chewed through another holding off the press just long enough to let Tomasa help Haeslig down the missing steps. "I can't carry him yet; we need to get clear," Tomasa said, waving us to go through the hall to the back of the house.

I took point, leaving Justine and Haeslig sandwiched in the middle as we worked our way to the rear of the house. Plaster and broken lath was exposed everywhere along the destroyed hallway. It hadn't been quite Tomasa sized the first time he'd passed through. We made it to the kitchen where I emptied a magazine clearing the room, then tore through another sweeping the deck outside clean.

Justine and Haeslig followed me out onto the porch as I stood near the back stairs, taking single shots as thralls spilled around the corner of the house. Haeslig was hobbling as fast as he could on his atrophied legs, a hand on Justine's shoulder for balance as they stopped next to me. I could see blood on his lips, and I started to say something; but Justine caught my eye, shaking her head she pulled her sleeve down over her wrist. "He wasn't going to make it far without something," she blurted, her eyes falling away from mine as she spoke.

"Head for the break in the fence," I said, putting my eye back to the UMP as I swallowed the lump in my throat. When they were halfway to the fence, I stepped off the porch, taking a few steps to keep up with them before stopping to clear more thralls. If Haeslig wasn't able to pick up the pace, we were going to be overrun.

A single murderous image leaped into my head as I stepped up behind the gray. Haeslig was only a few feet to the left of where I was shooting. Just a small misstep and he would have a forty-caliber round in the base of his skull.

I only entertained the thought for a moment—a single, very enjoyable moment—before I pushed it aside. The personal satisfaction killing Haeslig would give me wasn't going to matter if none of us made it out of town.

Justine stopped a few feet from the break in the fence, taking down two thralls with my machete as I fired through the fencing at the horde spilling around from the front of the house, following the fence line. I looked back just in time to see Tomasa climbing free of the back door before rolling off the porch, taking a section of handrail out in the process.

"Hold up," I said to Justine loudly, stopping her before she could step into the gap in the fence. "Tomasa!" I yelled, pointing at the horde spilling along the fence.

"Coming," he said, grunting as he twirled his staff, clearing the ground around him of thralls. He charged, flying by us to burst into the gap in the fence, sending bodies tumbling as he threw his arms out, buying him the space to swing his staff. Justine was urging Haeslig through the fence as soon as Tomasa passed, urging the gray into the crushed bodies left in the brute's wake.

Tomasa waited for us to catch up at the edge of the first ring of shacks, his chest heaving as he breathed. "Haeslig, you keep moving no matter what happens," I barked, almost snarling in his face as I spoke. "You baby-sit the gimp," I said to Justine, not letting her get a word in before I turned to Tomasa. "We take turns holding the rear and then playing catch up, got it?"

"Got it," he said, nodding.

"Move!" I screamed at Haeslig, spitting as I yelled into his face. Justine grabbed his arm and pulled him along, her back angry and straight as she brushed by me.

I emptied another clip into the thralls spilling our way from around the house, picking off the ones that seemed to be moving faster than the others as I took my turn holding the rear. Three more clips, and the UMP would be an expensive club. I ran to catch up, taking a position just in front of Justine and Haeslig as Tomasa held back, his staff spinning in a lazy circle as he walked slowly backward.

I was just turning to stop and wait for Tomasa to leapfrog past me when a ghoul leaped from a burning shack onto the brute's head. The ghoul locked its legs around Tomasa's thick neck and started to stab away with steak knives taped in its fists. Tomasa turned his head and sank his teeth into the ghoul's thigh at the same time he reached up and grabbed the creature around its midsection.

The normally-pain-resistant ghoul screamed as Tomasa's teeth sank into its thigh and then its femur, crunching through bone so forcefully the leg kicked up into the air. The ghoul was writhing in pain, but it kept stabbing away at Tomasa's hand and arm as the brute pulled it off like a tick. The screaming didn't stop until Tomasa threw the ghoul to the ground and slammed his staff through its head.

"That hurt," Tomasa said flatly as he caught up to me. I nodded, trying not to grimace at the horrible blemishes dotting the one side of his body. Multiple punctures wept blood in little streaks while one longer cut on his cheek ran steadily down his face to stain his chest.

"Let's stick together; I think we're out of town," I said as the smoke grew thicker around us. The ground beneath our feet was blackened and burned, but I think it had been a field. I started to hack and cough, pushing Tomasa to keep him moving as the smoke swirled.

Something moved off to my left, running through the smoke, leaving eddies behind it. I pulled the UMP up, my eyes watering as I scanned the haze closing in around me. Visibility was dropping from a dozen feet down to three or four.

"Daniel," Justine called out, spinning my head about. The smoke had closed all around me, and I wasn't sure what direction her voice had come from. She called out once more, the sound of her voice turning to coughing as she said my name. I held my breath, trying to figure out what direction her voice was coming from, and sprinted in that direction, my eyes squinted shut against the smoke. I couldn't see anything in front of me; my legs below my waist were lost in billowing clouds. My lungs burned; I couldn't hold my breath any longer. I pulled in a lungful of air and immediately started to hack and cough, acrid smoke burning my airways.

Then I ran into a tree, bouncing off it and falling to the

ground. I was too disoriented to get back to my feet. I put my mouth into the dirt, sucking in a breath through my bandana. Air, slightly less filled with smoke, entered my lungs as tears fell from my eyes. As quickly as the wind had shifted and carried the smoke around me, it shifted again, leaving me lying in a field just outside of town.

The tree I'd hit was Tomasa's back. He was on his knees, his face pale with fear, sucking in air as the panic slowly left his eyes. Justine and Haeslig were lying almost within arm's reach of me. Justine was as fully changed over as I'd ever seen her, her lips pushed out over enlarged, sharpened teeth. Her normally-deep-brown eyes were completely filled with swirling, liquid mercury. Haeslig was lying limply next to her. Justine shook her head and growled, popping off the ground onto all fours, her head lifting suddenly, locking on me.

"Hi, babe," I said hoarsely. She shook her head, her teeth sliding back into her mouth by just a few millimeters. Then she was climbing to her feet, her eyes large pools of slate that were both entrancing and hard to look at all at the same time. There is something about the human condition that finds eyes with no irises disconcerting. She helped to pull me to my feet, handing me my machete before turning to check on Haeslig.

"Get off the ground," Justine roared, picking the gray up by the back of his shirt. Haeslig jolted back to consciousness as she lifted him, clawing at the ground before he realized what was going on. Justine dropped him to land on his hands and knees, the back of his shirt shredded and ripped by her claws.

In the smoke and chaos, we'd made our way into the fields just south of town. Behind us the town smoldered and burned. In front of us the highway beckoned. All around us thralls were starting to appear through the swirling smoke. The closest was only a stone's throw away. "Shhh," I said, trying to help Tomasa to his feet. "Get to the highway." The words burned my throat as I spoke.

Tomasa made it to his feet only to bend over and rest his hands on his knees, retching up mucus and watery vomit as he coughed and struggled for breath. I tugged on

Tomasa's arm, trying to pull him forward. He took a staggering step, then another, slowly starting to move. I pulled him harder; the swirling smoke behind us was filled with bodies. It was only a matter of time before something saw us, and that would bring ghouls and maybe the Farmer down on us.

"OK, OK," Tomasa grumbled hoarsely, pulling his hand away from me once he'd regained enough breath to speak. We caught up with Justine and Haeslig easily enough; the gray was weak and moving slowly after months of confinement. "Once we make it to the road, it will be easier," I said, trying to encourage everyone to keep moving. Justine was gradually reverting back to her softer self, cursing as the strength slipped away from her at the same time.

I edged myself between Justine and Haeslig as I walked, which forced me to help him over the guardrail when he faltered. "I thought your friend was human," Tomasa asked as we made it onto the highway, leaning on his staff as he watched the thralls crossing the field behind us.

"He's not a friend," I said at the same time Justine said, "He's a different friend." My brow furrowed as I looked at her, the pain I felt at her words clearly evident on my face. She looked torn, as if she wanted to say something else, but she just shrugged her shoulders as Tomasa sighed and shook his head.

Off in the distance, ghouls cried out to each other, bringing us all to the here and now. "They're north of us," I said, looking at the swirling smoke that limited the visibility to a half mile or so up the highway.

"They're trying to keep us from leaving the valley," Justine said. More ghoul calls came from the smoke in the fields, and all the thralls in sight froze.

"Keep moving," I said, hurrying to the other side of the highway and dragging Haeslig over the far guardrail. I would have taken us both tumbling down the slope on the other side if Tomasa hadn't been there to stabilize me.

"Should I carry him or let him fall behind?" Tomasa said, ignoring Haeslig as if he weren't right next to me.

Justine shot daggers into the brute with her eyes and started to open her mouth, but I shut her up, telling Tomasa to carry the gray. The brute scooped him up in one arm and leaped across the drainage ditch, scrambling up the other side like a three-legged insect, jamming his staff into the ground before plodding up the slope.

"Daniel," Justine said, her hand trailing across my arm as I moved away from her.

"Later," I said, clipping short whatever else she was going to say.

"It's not..." she said, struggling to finish the sentence.

"Later," I repeated with more urgency, looking over my shoulder to see the thralls moving again. We must have been spotted. Every thrall in sight was moving toward us, and more were spilling out of the smoke every moment. "It's not going to matter if we don't make it out of this valley," I said, holding her eyes as I spoke. Justine huffed once and charged up the slope.

We climbed, zigzagging our way up the side of the mountain, losing sight of the highway as we made our way into the denser band of trees on the lower face. We climbed for a good half hour before Tomasa called a halt, setting the gray down before collapsing on a flat section of stone. He shut his eyes and rested; his face was dotted with stab wounds, and one of his shoulders was wet with blood that ran all the way to his midsection. In the mad race to escape town, I hadn't noticed the extent of his wounds.

"Stop staring at me; I just need to rest for a moment," Tomasa said tiredly, never opening his eyes. I took it as a good sign that he wasn't spent yet, turning my gaze down the slope, searching for some sign of motion through the trees.

"They're coming; don't worry," Haeslig said, stepping next to me with a strange look on his face.

"You're so helpful," I said back to him.

"I'm sorry if I put him on your trail, but Barrin has the ability to read the minds of those around him. I was able to hold him at bay for a little while, but it was too much once he tortured me. He kept asking me what made you so special, why Ravi risked and lost his life to gain influence over you. I just kept thinking of you, over and over, every time he asked any questions."

"Why?" I asked, forcing myself to keep my hands off my UMP.

"The truth, and I am sorry—but I thought it would give Justine a chance to fight back if he targeted you first." Haeslig whispered the last very quietly, shaking his head as if he truly regretted it. "I'm sorry, Daniel."

"Fuck off," I said, my voice shaking with anger. I turned away from him and went over to Tomasa, unable to stand so close to the gray without having violent thoughts racing through my mind. "You sure you're OK?" I asked, dropping to my haunches to touch a stab wound above his left eye.

"I was until you stuck your finger there," he grumbled with his eyes shut.

"I wish we had some bandages," I said, wincing as I looked at the brute's wounds. None of them were life threatening on their own, but the sum of the whole was clearly draining Tomasa's strength.

"My people are not so fragile as yours," he said, opening one eye to look at me.

"Five more and we have to move," I said to the big guy. He gave me a thumbs-up but saved the energy it would have taken to speak. I moved a few feet away, scanning the woods below again, wondering how fast ghouls and thralls could climb. Justine startled me when I turned and she was at my side. I hated it when she did that.

"Why didn't you kill him?" I asked, looking over her shoulder to where Haeslig had settled on a rock across from Tomasa.

"I was about to, and he said, 'I didn't tell him about the cabin.' I froze," she said.

"What?" I said, trying to understand what she was saying.

"He was at our house," she said. The scene from Haeslig's room replayed in my head. He'd said the same thing to me when I'd broken down his door. In the chaos it just hadn't registered.

"He's been hounding us since day one," I said accusingly.

"I was about to do it anyway. Then he said he knew Dietrich Heilbronner, knew about the children."

The slow-burning rage inside me flashed into an inferno. I turned, drawing my machete as I charged the short distance to Haeslig. I had the blade to his throat, the tip of the machete just breaking his skin. "Spill or you die," I demanded as Justine reached out slowly, carefully wrapping a clawed hand around my wrist.

"I'm not your enemy," Haeslig said, swallowing hard, his Adam's apple moving up and down against the edge of my blade.

"Three," I said, starting to count down.

"I didn't tell them where you were."

"Two..."

"They tortured me!" Haeslig roared, pulling his shirt apart in a sudden flash of anger, buttons flying as the machete drew a thin line of blood across his throat. I pulled the blade off his skin as I looked at his chest. His right nipple was gone, a crater of barely healed scars. The wound where his left nipple should have been was much fresher. In its place was blackened and burned skin surrounded by a circle of blisters. "He pressed a red-hot piece of steel to my chest, asking my over and over who you were," he shrieked, vibrating with remembered pain.

"Why?" I asked, still not able to look away from the gray's chest. The missing nipples were bad, but the Farmer hadn't stopped there. Haeslig's flesh was covered in parallel cuts where clawed hands had cut him, and his sides were scarred with pockmarks where shallow divots of flesh had been bitten away.

"Barrin was one of Ravi's lieutenants. When Ravi died in Dover, he struck out on his own with five lesser Blutsauger who followed him. I heard rumors they were looking for the two Ravi had been trying to bring under him before he died. I killed two of them as they searched, but Barrin wasn't as stupid as I gave him credit for.

"When he realized two of his underlings were dead, he set a trap. He put out the word that the search was over, that he'd found what he was looking for. I came right to him, walked right into his hands," Haeslig said bitterly. "I killed his second in command, and almost got Barrin himself; then those abominable creatures he created swarmed me."

"You're not answering my question," I said slowly, pressing the blade back into his neck, a rivulet of blood sliding down the edge toward my hand. "Why are you so worried about what happens to Justine? What do you know about the children?"

"Shared pain," Haeslig said, and then paused as he thought about what he said next. "You weren't the only one who was in that cabin as a child, Justine. I was born two natured like you. I was brought there, given some small taste of what a normal life might have been like, never sure if the things I remembered from the other side were unpleasant dreams or a lost reality. They put me with a family, and then one day it happened. I got really mad, and something in me snapped. I changed, but I wasn't so blessed as you. I am two natured, but once I turned I couldn't change back.

"I was useless to my masters if I couldn't masquerade as a weak, disgusting, human," he said, spitting each word at me like they were daggers. "They were going to…dispose of me. I still remember the hands closing around my neck. I didn't want to die. I fought, biting into my would-be murderer's hand. For a brief moment I thought I was dying, that I was looking at my own body being choked to death. I saw horrible things. I saw the flashes of so many other kids before me. A girl who was tied up and drowned slowly in the bathtub, the water creeping over her face bit by bit; a cord around another's neck, stabbings, throats cut. With just a few drops of blood in my mouth, I saw everything that man had done in the service to his masters. I panicked, screaming at him not to do any of those things to me." Haeslig paused, catching his breath as if the speech had worn him out.

"And they realized you still had value to them," I said, pulling my blade back as I looked down at the gray with something almost approaching sympathy.

"If I didn't have the gift to read other's memories in their blood, they would have disposed of me like trash," Haeslig said, nodding in agreement. "Instead I was sent back to our own realm to drink the blood of traitors and criminals. I spent years wishing they had killed me. Time moves more slowly on the other side. I lived a lifetime telling Han-Su whether those he thought he trusted were worthy of it, and tasted every horrible thing they'd ever done on my lips."

"And Justine?" I asked. "Why have you followed her?"

"I felt sorry for you," he said, looking at Justine. "You had no idea what you were, no idea why they wanted you. It struck a chord, I guess." He swallowed hard. She was staring down at him, her emotions shifting from anger to sadness to uncertainty in a visible rush of confusion.

"And it let you get back at your masters," I prodded, not trusting Haeslig's altruistic version of the truth one bit.

He smiled up at me, his face lighting up with devilish mirth for just a moment. "There is always that, of course."

"So you were at the cabin?" I asked. Haeslig nodded in confirmation. "Was Dietrich dead?"

"Not when I got there," Haeslig said, never breaking eye contact with me. "I didn't know if he was one of them at first. He honestly didn't know what he'd gotten himself involved with. In the end they used him for his wealth and because he was so easily influenced. He honestly thought he was helping to save the children of political refugees. He was shattered when I shared with him the reality of what he'd help accomplish. His end was his choice."

"He was nice," Justine said, her voice trailing off as she said it.

"Ignorance is not the same as innocence," Haeslig said, his tone softening as he looked at Justine with something almost like pity on his face.

"*Ichwusstenicht, aberich bin verantwortlich,*" Justine said in horribly accented German.

"I didn't know, but I am responsible," Haeslig said in translation. "I moved his journal inside after he took his life. I put it on his table. It seemed wrong to let it be destroyed by the elements." A deep silence, full of unspoken sadness, settled over the three of us. Justine started to sniffle, fighting back tears.

"Is WC alive?" I asked, my voice sharp and hard. The only way Haeslig could have known about WC's dog tags was if he'd run into the kid after we fled Dover.

"He was wearing them when I saw him, and he was alive. Would you believe me if I told you I saved his life and he never knew I was there? A dog isn't the best survival companion these days."

"And why should I believe you?" I asked. "Why bring WC into this at all?"

"It was a mistake really. When he tortured me, Barrin caught a glimpse of the necklace around your friend's throat. He didn't really know what he saw, but he thought it would help him find you from what he'd managed to pull from my head. It's a weakness of his ability; he can only read what you're thinking at the moment."

"I believe him," Justine said softly, looking at the gray with eyes clouded over by the change.

"Close your shirt," I spit at Haeslig, wrapping an arm around Justine so I could pull her away.

"Don't trust him," I begged.

"Not far, but he's not lying about this," she said, looking at me as the deep chestnut brown of her eyes returned.

"He's not like you, he's not a good person," I warned her.

"I know," she said, but her voice sounded uncertain and sad. "But if things had been a little different, maybe I'd be just like him." She gave a little shiver.

I wanted to say more, but sometimes knowing when to shut up is important. I turned away from her and went to Tomasa. "We need to get going," I said, nudging his shoulder with the tip of my boot.

"I'm awake," the brute said, opening his eyes and slowly sitting up. "Your friend—not friend—will need to walk for a while." He stood and stretched.

"No worries," Haeslig said, then looked at the brute in genuine surprise. "You are whole, aren't you?"

"I am," Tomasa agreed.

"What a strange band of misfits we are," Haeslig said with a smile before turning and starting to slowly move up the slope.

We climbed for twenty minutes before the first ghoul caught up with us. It flanked us from the north, giving us plenty of time to hear it as it tore down a game trail we'd just crossed moments before. I think it was a scout.

It stopped in his tracks when he saw us, and then turned and ran. "Keep moving," Justine growled, leaping down the slope onto the game trail before tearing off after the creature.

"She can handle herself," Tomasa's voice rumbled from ahead of me. I watched her back disappear and forced myself to keep moving. I barely had time to worry before Justine came racing back up the slope. She was flushed when she reached us.

"More than twenty?" I asked as she panted. She nodded yes, her eyes telling me twenty was wishful thinking.

It took her a good minute before she was able to break the bad news. "They're coming; thralls cover the slopes below us. The north is blocked off by ghouls and the Farmer," she said between breaths.

"We have to make it to the canyon," I said. If they caught us out in the open, we'd have no chance.

"I have always wanted to know how many Nechtruin I could destroy before they overwhelmed me," Tomasa said to no one in particular as he angled slightly farther north, toward the box canyon we'd found on our descent.

"We differ in that," Haeslig said, huffing as he struggled to keep up. "I don't really wish to die in these mountains as Barrin watches."

"I don't intend to die today. We kill Barrin and let his thralls kill each other," I said.

"Great plan, we kill Barrin, and instead of having him watch us die, we get to have his slaves do it when his link collapses."

"Shut up, and keep walking," Justine snapped, leaving us alone on the trail.

"You know your simple plans never seem to work out that well," Tomasa said softly, putting a hand on my shoulder as he moved past me to follow Justine.

Chapter 16

We made it into the box canyon with ghouls snapping at our heels. The first three into the narrow passages died quickly, not realizing we'd turned to stand our ground. The other ghouls held back, giving us time to catch our breath as the Farmer came up the mountain with a horde of thralls at his back. When the horde appeared on the far side of the two narrow allies into the canyon, it looked like every man, woman, and child in Pumpkin Town had been turned.

They shambled toward us, breaking around the massive stone that split the entrance into two narrow alleys. Tomasa stood on one side, his staff ready, while Justine and I took the other. Haeslig was huddled against the sheer wall at our backs, wrapped in a section of the tarp we'd found over the woodpile. The bastard had used up all his strength getting up the slope. He was too weak to fight. It made me mad, and I thought *coward* over and over.

I was standing off to Justine's side with my UMP across my chest, looking over her shoulder. I adjusted my sunglasses and pulled my cap down on my head, trying to protect my face from the bright overhead sun. The UMP felt heavy in my hands.

The thralls pressed forward, stopping just inside the two alleys. They froze in place as a ring of others pushed into them from behind, moving forward through them. Ghouls pushed and shoved, howling and screaming in some barely controlled state as they escorted the Farmer forward to hide behind the granite spike between the two alleys.

"Haeslig, I assume you have corrupted my Riesig," the Farmer called out. "You've served your purpose. Leave with your new pet, and you have my word of free passage."

"It's a little late for that!" Justine yelled back. "Haeslig is barely breathing."

"A pity. I was hoping to cut your strength in half, or maybe more," the Farmer called back tauntingly. "He thinks you're a coward, Haeslig, you can prove him right, and live."

"Fuck off!" Justine screamed back.

"So be it," the Farmer said, just loud enough for us to hear. The horde moved forward in a wave as soon as he was done speaking. Justine flexed her hands, shaking them as her claws elongated. I turned the UMP so I could see the selector switch, making sure it was set to single fire. I had to make every one of my remaining rounds count.

Justine stood her ground as the thralls shambled up our side of the cut, waiting to strike until the undead were almost on top of her. She caught the first thrall to reach her by its hands and drove a kick almost vertically into its jaw in a stunning display of physicality. She let the thrall fall with a broken neck, pivoting on her right foot so she could kick a second thrall in the side of the head, forcing its skull into the stone wall, where it crunched and deformed.

Justine settled on both feet, killing another thrall with her bare hands, her strength a match for the grasp of the undead. I took a step to her right, getting on top of a small rise in the rock so I could aim over her shoulder. My first shot cracked through the morning air, especially loud in the confines of the enclosed walls of the canyon. I tightened my grip on the gun and sited again, looking for another shot around Justine. Next to us Tomasa used his staff to crush anything that came into his reach. I couldn't see him, but I could hear his staff each time it made contact with an enemy.

Tomasa and Justine were equal but opposites. Where Tomasa used main strength to crush everything in his path, Justine killed with equal effect; she was just more elegant. She flowed like liquid between the thralls, striking and grappling in a never-ending ballet that littered the ground with dead. The paths into the canyon rapidly became a jumble of bodies. Blood pooled and ran along the ground, making the footing slick.

I was spacing my shots, trying to make my remaining three magazines last for as long as possible, which left Tomasa and Justine to do all the real work. I was shooting into the horde, but they took little notice of me as I tried to ration my ammunition. The Farmer let the thralls grind away at us, holding back his ghouls as he waited for us to tire.

The thralls took no notice of how quickly we cut them

down. They pressed forward as quickly as those in front were destroyed, climbing over one another to get to the front of the line. Tomasa sang a deep baritone tune in a language full of harsh syllables as he worked, his staff striking in time with the song. The press of thralls doubled, then doubled again. Tomasa was an immovable wall, his staff crushing bodies as fast as they surged forward. Justine, on the other hand, found herself forced back step by step. Blood sprayed against the sheer walls on either side of her as her claws whipped through the air, and thralls fell, but more were right behind, always pushing forward. The sheer weight of numbers was driving her back.

She stopped the surge just even with the mouth of the canyon. Another step back and the thralls would be able to work their way around her; then they would be able to swarm us from every side. I fumbled to get a fresh clip seated, accidentally trying to put the magazine in backward as Justine grunted and snorted in front of me, killing thralls as quickly as she could. I finally got the weapon loaded and let loose from just behind her right shoulder, pulling the trigger as fast as I could on single fire, taking some of the pressure off of her. Sweat poured down her face as she struggled to take back the lost ground, stepping over bodies with slow, deliberate steps, not wanting to lose her footing.

The ghouls timed their strike perfectly. The alley was just wide enough for two thralls to advance shoulder to shoulder. They let Justine take out the thrall on the right, and as she was shifting to her left, the first ghoul sprang forward. Justine tried to react, but the ghoul was already on her, slamming into her body and wrapping its arms around her, pinning her right arm to her side. The second ghoul pushed the thrall in front of it out of the way and hammered her with wild punches. She screamed in anger and pain as she leaned forward, sinking her fangs into the ghoul's neck as it tried to lean back and take her off her feet. The ghoul shook its head, trying to get away from her teeth even as she reached down between them with her left hand, grabbing it by its junk with five clawed fingers.

I leaned forward, hesitating for a moment as I flipped the selector to automatic before pulling the trigger. I held tight to the UMP as my first round went between the second ghoul's legs before the recoil brought the next shot up. The weapon's kick carried my aim from knee height up to the ghoul's shoulders as the bullets chewed through its flesh. The ghoul wrapped around Justine tried to push itself free of her, suddenly feeling the urge to live, but it was too late; she held onto it with her teeth as she heaved upward with her clawed fingers, gutting it from groin to chest.

Justine discarded the ghoul's body, throwing it down with a cry of challenge as she squared her shoulders with the alley, ready for the next attack. A stray thrall stumbled into her grasp and died quickly, but the constant forward pressure from outside the canyon had stopped. We understood why when the Farmer's voice called out to us from the safety of the far side of the cut.

"I can feel you; you really are magnificent, Daniel. There isn't a single part of you that is afraid for yourself. All you think of is your companions," the Farmer said, pausing as if savoring something. "Nothing but pure concentration—oh, I almost can't bear it, to be the focus of so much…lust."

"Grow some balls and come talk to us face-to-face," Justine yelled back to him.

"I promise we'll be face-to-face soon enough," the Farmer said. I cut off the conversation with a burst from the UMP. I couldn't see the Farmer to hit him, but I chewed up several of the thralls off to his left, shutting him up. The horde surged forward again.

I burned a clip very rapidly as I poured fire into the slow rush coming up our side of the split. The undead were crawling over each other to get to the front, turning the path into a squirming wave of bodies. Several ghouls surged forward onto Tomasa at once, sacrificing several of their own so one of them could get in low beneath his guard and sink its teeth into his thigh. Tomasa tore the ghoul away and crushed it against the side of the canyon, but not before it took a huge chunk of meat from his leg.

A wave of thralls rose up right behind the ghoul attack, trying to overwhelm the brute as he staggered. Tomasa swung his staff, half stepping and half hopping on his injured leg as he dove back into the fight. Every time he put weight on his injured leg, a steaming jet of red squirted into the air. The blood enraged the undead. They swarmed onto Tomasa, and he lost his staff as a ghoul took hold of it and wrenched it from his blood-slick hands. The brute was staggering under the weight of bodies on top of him, striking out with wildly swinging fists as he was forced back to the mouth of the alley, almost being pushed into the box canyon itself.

Justine saw Tomasa falter and looked back at me. I nodded, stepping up to take her place as I seated my last clip into the UMP. She darted to Tomasa as I opened up on the thralls at a distance of several feet. It was impossible to miss. Justine dove into the thralls surging onto Tomasa, taking his place on that side of the cut. The brute staggered back, grabbing thralls and ghouls and tearing them free as they pulled chunks of his flesh along as their price.

We were holding, if just barely. Then two ghouls appeared in the press of thralls in front of me. I hesitated for just a moment, then pulled the trigger and held it, guiding the UMP from one side of the alley to the other. The UMP roared as I emptied my final clip in a blaze of fire. The bullets cut the ghouls in half, then tore into the thralls behind, leaving a small bit of clear space between me and the next undead.

I used the brief moment of respite to unclip the UMP from its sling and grip it by the narrow space just in front of the stock. The first thrall to reach the end of the alley fell as I crushed its head with the body of the UMP. I hit the second, but it got an arm up, partially deflecting the blow, forcing me to hit it again to take it down. A ghoul stepped up to take its turn at the front of the line and I pulled back, bringing the UMP down with all the strength I had only to have the weapon caught in midair and ripped out of my hands.

The Farmer smiled a wicked grin as he tossed the UMP into the sea of thralls behind him before he hit me with two open hands, pushing me back a step as he sneered in victory. "I've been waiting for this," he said as I grabbed my belt knife and flipped it open. The Farmer juked forward, and I stabbed at the air as he chuckled. Thralls were already pressing around him, entering the canyon. I stepped close to him and stabbed high, aiming for his throat.

The Farmer raised his arm, catching my wrist on his and sliding the blow aside with ease. "So much confidence for one so weak," he said sweetly to the brim of my cap as he snaked his arm around mine. The knife in my hand was jammed under his armpit, but I couldn't turn it enough to do any damage before he jerked upward and the blade fell from my hand as he brought my elbow to within a hair of inverting.

A loud grunt left my lips as the Farmer pulled me to him, driving his clawed hand into my abdomen at the same time his head battered into mine, forcing my head sideways, my cap flying backward off my skull. My head rolled, staring back at the sky through my dark sunglasses. A cry spilled from my lips as the Farmer closed his fingers in my gut. The scream on my lips turned shrill as his teeth sank into my neck, then faded as he drank a long pull of blood.

My scream faded, blending with Justine's as she turned and saw the Farmer lifting my body off the ground in a deadly embrace.

Chapter 17

The Farmer unlocked his jaw, blood running down his chin as he withdrew his teeth. He set his nose into the crook of my neck, drawing a long breath through his nostrils as he took his blood-covered hand from my stomach and grabbed my face, pulling it down and flicking the sunglasses off so he could look at my eyes.

The Farmer gasped in surprise, looking at the face in front of him as the tip of my machete slid from the front of his shirt. He let go of his grip on Haeslig, a surprised look on his face as he reached for the wide tip of the blade still emerging from his chest. I stepped close behind him, driving the machete into his back until the hilt of the weapon was resting next to his spine. The Farmer's head fell back as he tried to see who or what was behind him. All around me the thralls had frozen.

"You should have held back, let your ghouls and thralls completely overwhelm us," I whispered into the Farmer's ear. "You were so close," I said, lifting the hilt of the machete so the blade cut down through the gray's breastbone.

The Farmer was never going to know just how close it had been. I'd been hiding on the top of the spit of rock splitting the entry into the two allies, waiting for the moment to strike while trying to clear my mind of anything that might give our plan away. I'd given up when Justine was forced to help Tomasa and was climbing off the spit of granite to help my friends as Haeslig burned through his last clip. If the Farmer had waited just another moment before striking, any chance of an ambush on our part would have been ruined.

"So close," I said, pulling the machete from the Farmer's back with a vicious jerk of my arm. I watched the Farmer as he stood for just a moment; then he was falling backward, his face completely void of any expression. It made me mad to see his face so neutral, almost at peace. It seemed so unfair that he should have died quickly after all the pain he'd caused us.

"Daniel, Daniel," Justine yelled, snapping my head in her direction. She had Haeslig under his armpits and was pulling him away. I looked around, realizing I was standing shoulder to shoulder with thralls. They were starting to twitch and shiver. Their link had been severed.

I slipped free of the thralls, trying not to touch them for fear I'd trigger them into motion. I reached Justine and Haeslig and grabbed one of his armpits. We dragged him to the back of the canyon as Tomasa hopped along the wall to our right, dragging his wounded leg. We reached the rear of the canyon at roughly the same time.

"I'm sorry, I don't have anything left," Tomasa said as he collapsed onto his butt, his head swaying as he spoke. He put a hand over the wound at his thigh, but blood still ran over and between his fingers.

"Put pressure on that," I barked, but Tomasa's head was already falling back against the canyon wall, his eyes half lidded as he fell into semiconsciousness. I unbuckled Haeslig's pants, pulling his belt free before jumping over to the brute.

I hugged Tomasa's leg, getting the belt around his thigh just above the wound. "This is going to hurt," I said between my teeth, putting a knee against his thigh as I pulled the belt tight, watching as the blood welling through the brute's fingers slowed. I pulled harder, making Tomasa yelp weekly, but I didn't let up until the blood stopped flowing.

"Lost a lot of blood," Tomasa whispered as I took my hands off the belt, watching to make sure I'd staunched the flow.

"You're going to be OK," I said to the brute, hoping I wasn't lying. "Is he...?" I asked Justine, looking over at Haeslig. There was a horrible wound at the side of his neck, and I could see loops of his intestines prolapsing out of his abdomen.

"He's alive," she said, touching the unwounded side of his neck gently. "But I don't think for long."

"We're going to have some stragglers," I said, stepping away from Tomasa. The thralls had already started to tear into each other in their enraged state, and some of them were spilling into the canyon.

A Lost Friend in Pennsylvania   229

We held back, letting them come to us at the middle of the canyon. The majority of the fighting was going on just outside the canyon entrance, and we wanted it to stay that way. If we moved to hold the entrance portals again, we'd likely just pull the whole angry mass down on ourselves.

"Just like old times, just the two of us," Justine said around her teeth as we waited for the enraged thralls to close on us.

"You are beautiful like this," I said to her, bringing her head around to look at me through eyes filled with swirling mercury.

"I actually believe you," she said around her enlarged teeth, swallowing as the words and their meaning sank in.

Then enraged thralls distracted us from the moment. They came in ones and twos, climbing out of the fight raging just outside the entrance to the canyon and charging across the open ground once they saw us. They died by claw or machete as soon as they reached us.

"Are you OK for a moment? I want to check on Tomasa's leg," I said after the flow of enraged thralls had all but stopped.

"I've got this; go check on him," Justine said thickly, looking at me with mist-shrouded eyes. I nodded and trotted back to Tomasa.

The brute was lying with his hands on his lap, breathing slowly, his eyes half lidded. "I just need to rest," Tomasa said, his lips barely moving. I turned to Haeslig, not sure how the gray was still alive. His chest moved very slightly as he breathed, and he'd moved his hands over his abdomen, trying to hold his bowels in place. His eyes fluttered when I knelt next to him.

"Justine?" Haeslig hissed. I don't think he could see.

"No, it's Daniel. She's OK; she's not far," I said.

"She's can't hear me?"

"No," I said.

"I need to tell you something, but you have to promise not to tell Justine," he said, fighting through the pain of speaking. Each time he pulled in a breath to speak, there was a wet sound as the muscles of his torn abdomen moved.

"You have my word."

"I've been watching her from day one," Haeslig admitted, a smile touching the corners of his lips for just a moment. "That first day, behind your house, I didn't trip; I ran into that gray to save her." Images flashed through my head. It was raining; Justine and I had been turned around by the flooding. We went back to my house to get some gear, and on the way out, we'd been attacked. We didn't even know what a gray was then. Haeslig had slid across the grass, barreling into another gray. It had given me just the moment I needed to get into the car and escape with Justine.

"At Mr. Deringer's house, I knew Billy and Tara were there. I told Sam it was only the two of you because I knew he's already been told two people died at the marina."

"Why?" I asked, grabbing the gray's shoulder.

"In Dover, at the construction site, you didn't find me. I found the Ravens tracking you. I ambushed them before they could do the same to you."

"Why?" I asked again, softer. Haeslig kept talking, ignoring me.

"I orchestrated Han-su's destruction to free her from what Sam had done. I was there so many times you never even knew about. I just wanted her to be safe." He paused, smiling through the pain as he spoke, "I never really liked you, Daniel," Haeslig said with a pained laugh. "Not until today, at least. I told her I knew about the cabin, that I knew about Dietrich. She couldn't let me die without knowing. She let me drink from her so I'd have the strength to get out of town. I felt everything. Her fear, her love, and the guilt she felt at losing him." He paused, having to take another breath and fight off the pain. "For letting something happen to her brother. I saw everything, the way you saved her, the way she saved you. I knew in that moment what love was. You make her whole, Daniel; she needs you." Haeslig's voice was weakening.

"Who are you?" I asked, kneeling down as the gray's lips tried to move. "I can't hear you," I added, getting closer.

"I don't want her to remember me as the monster. My name was Timothy McWatters," Haeslig whispered in my ear, the words barely spoken. "Keep her safe," he said, "for me."

"Oh fuck," I said, looking down at Justine's brother as his mouth slowly opened, his last breath leaving his body in a long exhalation.

Epilogue

We burned Haeslig's body. Some of the smoke got in my eyes as we stood there, causing tears to fall from my eyes each time I blinked. It looked a little like I was crying. Justine put her arm around me, and I leaned against her, not sure how I was going to find the resolve to keep her brother's secret but sure for the moment that I at least had to try. I said a few words of thanks to Timothy McWatters under my breath for everything he'd done, and cursed Haeslig for making me promise not to tell Justine about anything he'd said.

It took us almost five days to get back to our cabin. Tomasa could walk with the help of a freshly cut staff a day after we killed the Farmer, but he moved slowly and needed to rest frequently. We let him set the pace. Taking the first few steps into our own valley was heaven. Neither Justine nor I could keep the stupid grins off our faces. We were finally home again.

The days grew shorter and the nights colder until the first snow fell just after Tomasa finished putting the roof on his own cabin just outside our wall. The three of us sat around the bonfire Tomasa had built and enjoyed the warmth as the snow fell heavily around us. A brute, a two natured, and a man, we sat around the fire and drank and ate, enjoying the night and each other.

For at least a little while, we were at peace.